J. A. TURLEY

BODY SHOTS

Belize Justice—
A Caribbean Mystery

Also by

J.A. Turley

THE ~~W~~HOLE TRUTH
aka *THE HOLE TRUTH*
Fiction (Published 2019)
Winner
Colorado Authors' League
Mystery/Suspense—2018

DEEPWATER HORIZON 2020
Remembering BP's
2010 Disastrous Blowout—
Ten Years later
(Published 2020)

This publication
includes two books:

(1)   THE SIMPLE TRUTH (2012)
(The drilling of the well)
(2)   FROM THE PODIUM (2019)
(The cause of the disaster)

BODY SHOTS

Belize Justice—
A Caribbean Mystery

by
J.A. Turley

Winner
Colorado Gold Rush
Literary Awards
(For opening excerpt)
Mystery

ISBN: 978-0-9858772-8-6 (paperback)
Library of Congress Control Number
LCCN: 2024913889

ISBN: 978-0-9858772-0-0 (ebook)

Copy editor Thomas N. Locke
Cover design and line drawings by J.A. Turley

BODY SHOTS is a work of fiction. Names and characters are products of the author's imagination and are used fictitiously, and any resemblance to actual persons, living or dead, is entirely coincidental. Opinions and errata are the author's.

Published by:
The Brier Patch, LLC
2850 Classic Drive
Highlands Ranch, Colorado 80126

ACKNOWLEDGMENTS

Thanks to Rocky Mountain Fiction Writers and its Southwest Plaza Critique Group—including, among others, Andrea Catalano, Kevin Wolf, Mindy McEntire, Ed Hickok, Z. J. Czupor, and RIP, Mary Ann Kirsten—for years of across-the-table reading, writing, and critiquing.

Kudos and my sincere thanks to copy editor Thomas N. Locke.

My thanks also to those who have significantly touched my life, including family-tree relatives, friends, neighbors, bosses, colleagues, students, professors, and fellow alumni.

And to all military veterans—

Thank you for your service

For Jan

Forever My Love

This book is dedicated to Jan, my forever best friend and CFOOE—and the co-author of all I've ever done well since the early 1960s.

And to JD, Jason, and Cindy—for their incredible efforts to keep us young.

BODY SHOTS

Belize Justice—
A Caribbean Mystery

Prologue

Caribbean Living Magazine, among others, is a credible, informative resource for those who have ever contemplated a clear-water vacation, a two-week timeshare with unlimited fly fishing, or even a paradise-in-the-sun retirement plan.

Of course, drugs, makos, and murder have a way of interfering with moonlight swims and margaritas.

And that takes us to Belize, a small country in Central America, on a quiet sunny morning.

Belize

Central America

Belize earned its independence from the United Kingdom in 1981. The official language is English, yet many residents also speak Spanish, Creole, Garifuna, Mayan, etc. Belize is the least populated country in Central America (about 410,000).

Drawing by J.A. Turley

Belize,
showing Ambergris Caye

Ambergris Caye, the largest Belize island, is twenty-five miles long, a mile wide, and bordered on the east side by the Belize Barrier Reef. San Pedro Town, on the south end, doubles its population of 14,000 during the winter tourist season.

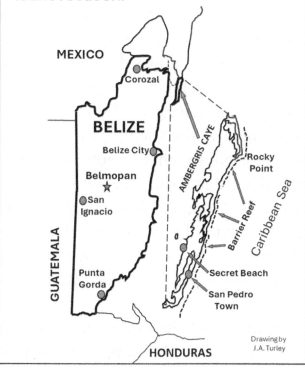

Drawing by
J.A. Turley

1

First, he saw the shadow—then, the shark.

Kennedy Bracken abandoned the ten-pound red snapper he had chased in and out of thirty-foot-deep coral heads and turned upward toward the intruder. The large but common bull shark ignored Kennedy as it cruised in a tightening circle around a feeding frenzy just below the sunlit surface. Kennedy positioned himself to photograph the silhouetted action, aimed his digital camera, and—

Not good, he thought. While the giant carnivore bullied its way into the action, a half dozen of its smaller brethren fed on a body. A dead woman's body—young, nude. No left arm. Ragged tears to flesh, muscle, bone.

Kennedy searched the undulating sunlit surface for the victim's boat. Nothing. His path out of danger—through the coral, back to his kayak, anchored a hundred yards away inside the Belize barrier reef—seemed to beckon him. As did the lifeless body.

The sharks didn't care. Two six-footers—a bull and a mako—competed for the corpse's right calf and yanked and pushed the body into jerky spasms, their actions a tug-of-war battle for flesh.

Unable to abandon the woman, Kennedy sucked a deep breath, swam hard to catch the frenzy, and triggered a burst of pictures toward her twisting, turning, jerking face. A face no person—husband, parent, child—would ever see again.

He looked for a ring, earring, tattoo. Could he get a picture? The adult bull shark waggled its head, the woman's left thigh in its mouth, as if to say no. Kennedy focused on her right hand, triggered another burst of pictures, and caught glimpses of three fingers, two stubs, no rings.

Shoulder-length hair, dark against the bright surface, billowed in silhouette with each twist and turn. He turned on his dive light, adjusted his BCD—buoyancy control device—and swam upward, triggering pictures, ever closer to the mayhem.

The woman had only one ear. No earring.

The Darth Vader rush of air through Kennedy's regulator filled his otherwise-silent world. Silent except for the scream that filled his mask when something big and fast bumped his thigh on its way into the carnage, no longer populated solely by sharks. Other toothy scavengers—attracted by the frenzy—bolted in, grabbed hold, shook hard, and darted away with bits of flesh and muscle. A three-foot-long stubby chunk of barracuda twitched out of the turmoil, mute testament to the need for speed, even among the aggressors.

Kennedy, though aware he could be some carnivore's next meal, twisted, turned, and swam hard to keep up with the fast-moving pack, minutes passing while snapping rapid-fire bursts of pictures hoping to catch a flash of face.

He'd moved in for a close-up, as close as he dared, when the sharks and their fellow feeders scattered en masse, replaced by a leviathan tiger shark that plowed into the scene. Twice the size of the bull shark, the behemoth crashed into the woman's corpse, crushed its jaws around her torso, throat to waist, and shook hard, as if to make sure she wouldn't fight back.

Kennedy could only watch as the one-sided battle unfolded at double-time speed. Concussive shock waves echoed through his chest each time the shark threw its head and chomped its jaws. When the Goliath finally swam off, having consumed the bulk of the woman's remains, the lesser sharks and scavengers returned and slashed their way through the trailing cloud of blood and gore.

Palsy-like shakes wracked Kennedy's tired body—engulfed in vulnerability, minuscule in a large ocean, trivial in the food chain, fortunate to be alive with death so close.

He drifted, detached, stomach churning, and then checked his single-tank air supply—borderline empty, the pressure near zero. But it didn't matter—

he was going home.

He broke the surface, searched for his kayak, and saw . . . nothing, nothing but trouble, trouble in the form of big seas. He looked down to get his bearings and again . . . nothing, nothing but deep, blackish-blue water, which suddenly felt cold, its icy fingers creeping beneath the warmth of his wet suit. He cursed himself for being outside the reef, way outside where the big boys lived, the big boys with insatiable appetites.

Ebb tide, he thought. Not good. Experience told him the woman's body, the sharks, and the self-proclaimed photographer himself had drifted with the falling tide, through the Basil Jones Cut—a natural deep opening through the barrier reef—into deep water and off the edge of the continental shelf where the current sets north.

From the top of a swell, he looked for landmarks nested in coconut palms and glimpsed a faraway speck of a tile roofline, possibly Bacalar Vista, his island home. He judged his position a mile north of the cut, an impossible swim against heavy seas and the northward current. That left two choices: west, a several-hundred-yard shortcut over the coral and toward the beach, or north, toward Mexico, and walk back.

He looked landward toward the maelstrom of seas pounding the reef wall, its surface lined with razor-sharp coral, and shook his head, his minutes-old memories of torn flesh and shattered bones all too vivid. Take the shortcut? No. Not a good choice, he told himself. Not good at all.

Swimming north by default, Kennedy secured his camera and dropped his weight belt. His BCD provided buoyancy. He considered dropping his empty tank but reckoned he might need it later. He cleared his emergency snorkel, swam with the current, parallel to the beach, and worked his way as close as he dared to the reef wall and breaking waves.

Mexico? he wondered. No. Too far north, too long in the water. Rather, he targeted a spit of land called Rocky Point, a mere three miles farther up the north end of Ambergris Caye's twenty-five-mile-long coastline. Rocky Point—where the cliffs, the coral, and the deep converged—was a good place to fish but a terrible place to land a boat or swim ashore.

He flushed away visions of jagged rocks and decided he'd worry about them later—if his fifty-one-year-old lungs held on that long. In the meantime, he kicked northward, his every thought on survival, his body mimicking exhausted bait.

The quarter-moon night sky dimly lit Kennedy's path as he worked his way south, one careful step at a time, along the rocky portions of the beach, trying not to break an ankle or slice a foot in the process.

A half-mile south, during a black-night driving rain, he sat for an hour on broken coral and conch shells. Hugging his knees, he queried the dead woman's life, its meaning, her likely fears, the why of it all. Thoughts of her family, never to see her again, knotted his guts.

Then, long-ago memories of his own absent father pushed the young woman aside and forced Kennedy to get off his ass, get on his feet, and get the hell home.

The distant lights of Bacalar Vista—home to Kennedy in every way—twinkled through coconut palms and welcomed him as he trudged through sand and neared the beachfront complex. The last quarter mile of his three-mile trek seemed an impossible task.

Most residents of Bacalar Vista owned their high-end condominiums for one or more weeks a year, the resort their annual vacation destination. Not Kennedy—he owned and lived in his two-bedroom unit year-round, and he relished the king-size bed that occupied the master suite and awaited his return.

He stepped onto a lighted path and checked his watch—8:35. He bent over, hands on his knees, and hoped he could make the last two hundred feet. One step, and then another.

Someone yelled and pointed, and a gaggle of staff, guests, and fellow residents, as if paparazzi, poured from Bacalar Vista's open-air restaurant and bar and surrounded him.

Kennedy, thankful to be among living people, drained a proffered mug of Belikin beer—Belize's national beer, aka, to some, Belize's *only* beer—and felt it all the way down to his navel.

Among the excited voices, somebody announced into a squeaking radio: "He's here. Mr. Bracken's here. Call off the search."

"Was that the police?" Kennedy asked, his voice husky, his throat parched.

No, somebody said. Not the police. Words, questions, and answers seemed garbled and far away. He learned nobody had missed him until sundown, about six thirty, when his dog, Krash, had barked and howled. Alerted by his absence, staff members had manned a powerboat and found his kayak anchored near the Basil Jones Cut. Somebody had said he was probably night diving. Nobody had called the police. And yes, he'd been the only person missing.

He'd hoped otherwise, had wanted the woman to be the subject of a search, a woman with a name, with somebody looking for her. He didn't mention the woman, the sharks, the photos, or even the camera, still strapped to his wrist.

He told the crowd the tide had swept him out the cut, and he'd walked back from Rocky Point. He'd hid his mask, fins, air tank, and BCD in the jungle for later recovery.

"Rocky Point?" somebody asked, his eyes bugged. "How in hell did you get to the beach?"

"All I remember is a big swell, swimming with all I had . . . then a long nap on hard rocks."

He didn't tell them he had chosen to challenge

fifty feet of ancient coral rocks and thrashing seas only because exhaustion threatened to pull him under. With his BCD providing buoyancy, he'd removed his empty air tank, wrapped his hands in the straps, and pulled the tank to his chest as a makeshift skid plate between his body and the coral rocks. The tank clunked and screeched on coral rocks as he battered his way to shore, where his crash landing on the beach had been anything but graceful.

Laughter, beer, and more stories followed, one resident to another, each macho diving story more exciting than the last, each story less related to Kennedy's ordeal. He found himself detached from the crowd, devoid of feelings, and no longer the catalyst for the evening's merriment.

He pushed back from the table, mentally exhausted and too tired to eat. "Thanks, everybody, but I'm fading fast. See you in the morning."

His words prompted handshakes with staff, bear hugs from buddies, and air kisses from women in the crowd. Alone once again, he lumbered on sore feet down the lighted path to his graveyard-dark condo.

Not good, he thought. Dead girl. Open ocean. Nobody looking for her. No remains to be recovered. His gut rumbled as he fisted his camera and dug out his key. He looked over his shoulder. Outside the door—the black of night. Inside—his sanctuary, his escape from memories of the tragic event.

Hah, he thought, unable to fool himself. The shitstorm's just beginning.

2

Kennedy watched snippets of no-name television channels, glanced without enthusiasm at his Maya vampire manuscript, and then admitted he couldn't ignore the inevitable. It took him only ten minutes to download the pictures from his camera to his computer. A quick glance at more than a hundred shots allowed him to eliminate those that showed nothing but fins and flotsam. Sixty-two pictures of the woman and parts thereof made the cut. He closed his eyes at times to get from one screen to the next.

Throughout his two-decade career as a construction-site accident investigator, Kennedy had snooped his way through broken buildings, collapsed walls, and overturned cranes. Too many sites were bloodied by injuries and deaths, stark justification for asking the logical questions: What happened? Who did what? What failed? Each accident site became his world. He interviewed the injured and represented the dead. Evidence—procedural, mechanical, biological—had become pieces of puzzles.

But this case, he reckoned, was different on three counts. The site encompassed miles of open ocean, the dead had been consumed on the spot, and he had the only evidence—a few photographs. His career obsession—bringing closure to the families of the dead—seemed a remote possibility.

Wanting neither food nor drink, he thought of his soulmate, his long-distance love, Sarah McGarrity—a marketing executive in Denver. Missing Sarah, he opened his email. An icon indicated she was online. That, or she'd left her computer turned on and gone to bed. He opened a one-on-one chat and typed: "You there?"

Sarah: "You're up late. How's Belize?"

Kennedy: "Missing you."

Sarah: "Counting the days. Get my itinerary?"

Kennedy: "Got it. I need a few kind words if you have a minute."

Sarah: "All night if you need me. But call me on Skype, I need to see your face and hear your voice."

Maybe not, he thought as he dialed the number.

3

Sarah marked the page she had been reading—contract compliance for a marketing project—an easy decision now that she had a good excuse to put it off. Two minutes later, her computer monitor showed Kennedy's warped face in a small square box to one side of the screen.

"I'm here," she said, "but I can't see you—yes, now I can." She paused. "Holy wow. Looks like you've been on a two-day binge."

"And you're beautiful too, as usual. But I need your help."

"Sounds serious," she said as she tilted the laptop screen to focus on her face.

"Somebody I don't know had a very bad last day," Kennedy said. He took his time as he described what he'd seen and the pictures he'd taken.

Sarah watched his face but forced herself to continue even when her eyes teared. Hands to her face, she fought raw emotion, wanting only to listen to his words.

When he finished his story, he stared at Sarah.

She stared back, afraid to blink. "I'm sorry; give me a minute." She went to the kitchen and gulped a small glass of tap water. Two trains of thought battled for brain time. She wiped her eyes on a paper towel, and then blew her nose.

She said nothing until she was square in front of the computer screen, the camera, his face. "Before I say anything about the pictures, about that poor girl, I have to get something off my chest."

She got Kennedy's shoulder nudge and a slight nod, his typical I'm-listening-go-ahead response.

"You, going out there alone," she said, "was the absolute dumbest, most asinine, idiotic stunt that anybody has ever had the right to survive."

His face registered nothing, as if his brain were on mute.

"How stupid can you be?" she continued. "Alone. Out in the ocean. Sharks. And what were you doing? Taking pictures. Crap, Kenn, ships sink, planes fall out of the sky, and bodies disappear in tsunamis, yet there's nobody there to take a single damn picture of the underwater carnage. What the hell were you thinking?" She stopped, but only to catch her breath.

"No excuses for being alone," he said, "but I'd do it again if I had to." Fatigue defined his face, his voice, his words. "You said you had some thoughts on the pictures."

She hadn't expected a definitive answer and wasn't surprised when she didn't get one. She logged her diatribe into deep memory—that place where she kept such topics for later recall.

Resolved to be fully engaged in the more important issue, she said, "I can't imagine her husband or parents, or maybe her roommate, sorting through pictures, looking for a face they don't want to find."

"They shouldn't see all the pictures," he said, shaking his head. "Most are gross, beyond horrible."

"Have you spoken to the police?" she asked.

"Tomorrow morning, first boat. I'll give them the entire photo file."

"Go through them," she said, "and crop what they don't need to see."

"I can pick a few pictures that best show her face, what there is of it, but I've got no clue how to crop away the gore."

"Send me copies of everything," she said, "and I'll do it."

"Email will work only if I'm lucky enough to get a connection—and the photos are nothing you can imagine."

"Kenn, those are excuses, and I'm not a kid. You need it done by morning so send the pictures in small batches. I'll fix them and return a file."

"Give me a few minutes," he said, "but don't say I didn't warn you."

He disappeared from her screen. She stayed online and opened a second screen so she could watch her email account. One minute. Two. Ten.

When he reopened his Skype connection, she was waiting.

"The pictures are on the way. I sent a dozen groups, in separate emails, for a total of sixty-two frames. They're in Web-quality low-resolution, easier to send."

Sixty-two pictures, she thought, and checked the time. "I can't talk and work, so get yourself some coffee and I'll call you back when I'm done."

"I've got a fresh pot," he said. "It'd be nice if you were here to share it with me."

"Sixteen days and I'll be there. Then you can make coffee, breakfast, lunch . . . and . . ."

Kennedy said, "And, what?"

"And . . . I just got your first email, with attachment."

"Then I'll let you get to work. Thanks for your help. I'll make this up to you when you get here."

"Then be ready," she said. "I'm there for only a week, not a month. I'll call you as soon as I can."

Kennedy's face disappeared as soon as she opened and viewed the new photo file on full screen.

Horrified by the photos, she went back, found, and attacked an OK face photo with editing tools. She tried to center the parts she wanted and trim the excess . . . which didn't work. Which would never work, she reminded herself, on low-resolution pictures.

She wrote down the number and continued through the file, looking for the woman's face. Lots of candidates, except for shadows, silhouettes, hair, fish, gashes, torn skin, missing flesh.

She found a second picture with a fractional face peeking through the carnage. And a third. She pressed her hands to her face and took a deep breath. Tears came hard when she found a promising frontal shot of the battered face of the very dead young woman who could have been her daughter. Or her sister.

Or me, Sarah thought, her guts in a rumble, the dam finally broken, her anger focused on Kennedy for the stupidity of his act, her compassion for the woman reduced to pixels on a screen.

4

Kennedy noted the hands on the wall clock crept slowly, as if disabled, and he stared at a late-night gecko perched below a wall sconce, perhaps waiting for dinner. He thought about Sarah working on pictures, pictures he should have picked through and selectively chosen or deleted before sending. She'd retch, though driven by the fire of resolve to finish what she started, a resolve he'd seen before.

During what she would later call a moment of weakness, she'd confided to him that despite having excelled in graduate school, she'd had to fight her way through internships, menial jobs, entry-level busy work. But she had done well during her years in Denver, where her career had—

Sarah's face popped onto his screen. "There're seven pictures I need you to resend in high resolution so I can blow them up as much as possible." She listed the numbers of the photos.

She's on a roll, he thought. "Three minutes," he said.

It took two. As soon as he sent the file, Sarah's face again disappeared.

The gecko raised its right front leg.

Kennedy checked the time—1:34, same as in Denver. He pictured himself, standing behind her chair, hands on her shoulders, massaging lightly.

Sarah was back onscreen at 1:48. Before her picture settled in, she said, "I'm finished, but this is horrible. It's hard to believe you took the pictures while it happened."

"Believe it." In the quiet that followed, he added, "How're you doing?"

"Not good, but I just sent you a short email, with the file attached. Seven morbid pictures. I rearranged the order. The first one, even though the woman's dead and underwater, is all you'll need for identification. It's the only one her family should see, though a couple of the profiles might also be OK."

"I'll take everything to the police tomorrow and let you know what I find out."

"Promise me nobody except the cops will see your originals. If you're not careful, they'll be on the internet, gore and all."

"I promise. Now get some sleep."

"Her right breast," Sarah said, almost to herself. "That's what first confirmed to me she was female. And that was only in the first few pictures."

"Forget what you've seen. We both need sleep. Dream about sunshine, sand, and R and R."

"Send me a note, an update," she said. "I'm on the

road the next few days."

Kennedy blew her a kiss. "Thanks for all your help. Travel safe." Sarah's forced-smile image was nodding when the screen went blank.

Kennedy studied her work, which told a sad story but hid the worst of the terrible truth. Death defined the woman, her face consumed, a chunk at a time, picture-by-picture, before the camera. Four front-on shots, a right profile, a quarter-right profile, and a quarter-left shot—these were the best pictures, the only pictures, of the young woman's face. The only pictures her husband or friends or parents would see, the last memories of someone's special somebody, someone's wife or child.

Child? Adult child, for sure. Twenty? Twenty-five? Younger? Older? Petite, he recalled, all too graphically. Her body full, mature, when he first saw her. Later pictures, in better light, near the surface, showed her coloring was a Mississippi River brown. Perhaps a tourist, but a soft brown that matched many Belizean women who ran shops, strolled with children, held hands with husbands and lovers, and rode bikes and golf carts down San Pedro's cobblestone streets.

Not her, he thought. Never again.

The gecko moved two legs—left front and right rear—perhaps readying itself to pounce on some unseen no-see-um.

Kennedy pulled himself from his trance and saved Sarah's work. He burned the two sets of pictures, his complete set and Sarah's edited set, onto two 4GB flash drives, turned off his computer, and went to bed, eyes wide open.

Retired from the business world, he'd had no morning pressure to get up early, though he often did to check the weather. Cloudless mornings with a mild sea breeze often enticed him into the challenging world of sunrise fly-fishing for bonefish. Too much breeze, though, as evidenced by the early-morning eager dance of coconut palms, and he'd spend the day in a cozy computer world of make-believe lies and deceit—writing fiction.

Struggling to sleep, his thoughts were nowhere near books or bonefishing, but on bodies and blood. Then, somewhere above him, up close to the ceiling, a massive shark circled the room—hunting, closing in, chasing Krash.

"Krash!" Kennedy's cold-sweat scream yanked him from his nightmare. He reminded himself of his neighbors' words during the welcoming party—they had Krash, Kennedy's muscular chocolate lab, settled-in for the night with their two boys. They would care for Krash and return her to Kennedy in the morning.

Kennedy's digital clock flicked forward another minute, another after that, another . . .

5

Soon after sunrise, Kennedy got Krash from his helpful neighbor and answered a few respectful questions while enduring Krash's slobber-face, I-love-you ritual.

The duo then ran on the beach, but weariness kept Kennedy from playing her games.

Back at his unit, he fed Krash and ate a big bowl of oatmeal—his first food in twenty hours—and planned his trip to town.

Most important, he loaded two thumb drives with his original and edited photos and then made sure his backpack contained sunscreen and bug spray. In minutes, he boarded the eight-o'clock boat to San Pedro Town—aka San Pedro—Ambergris Caye's only town.

He picked a portside seat, facing the beach, for the half-hour thirteen-mile trip, his backpack in his lap. The skipper and a dozen other passengers got Kennedy's cordial treatment, but he avoided conversation.

From the starboard side, he would have faced and seen the Caribbean stretch eastward to the horizon, interrupted a quarter- to a half-mile away by waves breaking over the reef. His preference, though, as always, was the westerly view, which included coconut jungles, mangroves, beachfront homes, and crystal-clear water that ranged from pastel blue over sand to a darker blue-green over turtle grass. Turtle grass, in which he stalked bonefish with passion, made him think about afternoon fishing. Probably not, he reckoned, because after his dead-body business with the police, he'd need a comatose nap.

Kennedy made his way down Middle Street—Pescador Drive on local maps—to the San Pedro Police Station, across the street from Harmouch's Hardware. A temporarily recovering alcoholic, working as a mate for one of Kennedy's fishing guides, had told Kennedy the year before that the police station's cells could accommodate overnight and weekend stays, but those incarcerated for longer periods of time were invited to Hattieville, Belize's only prison, just west of Belize City. Kennedy had no desire to spend the night in either place, but he was glad to be able to turn over to local police the pictures he'd taken and tell them everything he knew about the incident, which wasn't much.

Sergeant Ernesto Gutierrez of the Belize Police Department, a big man dressed in a clean and pressed uniform—khaki-colored shirt and dark pants—listened to Kennedy's story and then loaded the first of Kennedy's two flash drives.

"My God, man," Gutierrez said. "That's horrible." He scrunched his rotund face and leaned back in his chair. "What a terrible thing to happen."

"There are sixty-two pictures," Kennedy said.

The sergeant studied each of the first ten frames and then clicked through additional shots as fast as they popped onto the screen.

Kennedy had stared at the photos, unmoved, but not because he didn't care. The pictures, bad for sure, offered little comparison to his living memories. But his lack of feeling was more related to his years as an accident investigator, where the sights and smells from multiple accident scenes had merged over time into a single ugly memory—which now included the dead girl's images.

Sergeant Gutierrez showed heightened interest, less discomfort, when Kennedy gave him the second flash drive, which included Sarah's seven carefully edited selections—more face, less carnage.

"Conclusions?" Kennedy asked.

"Good photos," Gutierrez said. "Her puffy skin tells me she was in the water for many hours. And the lack of blood means she was probably dead before the sharks got to her."

Kennedy focused on *many hours . . .*

"Gather your stuff," Gutierrez said. "We need to go down the hall."

During the next three hours, Kennedy showed both sets of pictures to increasingly senior officers, culminating with a show and tell in the office of the Eastern Division commander.

The commander thundered his words. "We will issue a bulletin to Belize authorities countrywide." He pointed to "the best picture" of the seven on the screen. "This photo, *only* this photo, will be posted in the news, on television, and in our missing-persons site on the internet. And when we find the young woman's next of kin, we will confirm identification with this picture." He turned to Kennedy. "And to you, sir, my personal thanks. Your name, as you have requested, will not be found in the news."

Kennedy left the seven-picture flash drive with the commander, as requested, slipped the sixty-two-picture flash drive into his pocket, and returned to Sergeant Gutierrez's office to retrieve his backpack.

The sergeant cleared a spot on his desk and folded his hands. "Mr. Bracken, I have two goals: identify the woman and determine the cause of her death. So, I must ask you to remain on Ambergris Caye, as I will need you again, and please do not discuss the case with anyone outside this office, including the news."

That suited Kennedy just fine. He thanked his host, left the building, and walked into the street, where sunshine and a cooling sea breeze engulfed him in a beautiful Belize afternoon. He bought a bottle of Belikin beer in Blue Water Grill—a seaside restaurant and bar with an associated dock that serviced Bacalar Vista's vessels—and went straight to the boat. Seated in the sun, eleven minutes before the scheduled two o'clock departure, he mused about the good things that awaited him at home—a stiff rum and lime, an online chat with Sarah, and a much-needed nap, Krash at his side.

Krash met Kennedy at the door and ran circles around his legs, her tail racing just in front of her head. Kennedy knelt and traded loving hugs and words of comfort in exchange for her typical tongue-lashing of whatever she could reach—ears, neck, and grocery sack if he'd had one.

After feeding Krash, he jiggled rum-and-lime-soaked ice cubes in a cut-glass tumbler. Unable to think otherwise, he focused on the dead woman. Though no alarm had been raised at Bacalar Vista, was anybody looking for her? Maybe in San Pedro? Or on the mainland? Had she left behind an empty apartment? He thought of multiple scenarios, with no evidence toward or away from any possible choice— but always with the same questions. How the hell had she ended up in the water? Where was her boat? How could such an accident—

Accident? Maybe it wasn't. And if it wasn't, what? Suicide? Murder?

The thought of murder, which he'd never been exposed to in all his years of investigating deaths, drove him back to reality.

With Krash at his feet, he raised his glass to sip his favorite Belize rum—Travellers 5 Barrel—only to find the tumbler empty. He recalled nothing of how it had tasted or of munching the ice. Easy solution— pour another slug, squeeze another lime, add rocks.

Back at his desk, fresh drink in hand, he emailed Sarah's office address and told her about his meeting with the police.

Sarah's return email: "This is an Auto Response. I am out of the office Wednesday Aug 20 through Monday Aug 25. If you need assistance, please call Tess Krandle, extension 2502."

Sarah had mentioned travel, which meant she'd answer when she could, and he had no need to talk to Tess. But he damned sure needed a nap.

He drained his refilled glass—slow and easy— just before his head hit his king-size pillow.

Wide-awake, he wondered what he could do to make Sarah's upcoming vacation perfect. And, perhaps, what he could do to entice her to quit her job and move to Belize. He reckoned his pictures of the shark-feeding frenzy and the woman's disappearing body were not high on Sarah's list of positive attributes for moving to Belize. But he looked forward to telling her the police were carrying the ball, he was out of the picture, and she would have nothing to do but read books, drink piña coladas, and enjoy time at the pool.

Hah. His gut told him to enjoy the dream while he could.

6

While in San Pedro to shop on Thursday morning, KENNEDY stopped for coffee at the Lavish Habit Café on Front Street. He took a seat facing the beach and placed his order—large coffee with cream. While he waited, a newsprint headline caught his attention: "Swimmer drowns, sharks feast."

He snagged the paper and confirmed the banner date—Thursday August 21—and then opened it on his table. There she was, seven face shots, front page. His pictures, Sarah's pictures. In no more than a minute, he read the pertinent parts of the article and then folded the paper and snapped it under his arm.

When his coffee arrived, he added cream, and then added more, and even more.

The weekly Ambergris Caye newspaper had informed readers that Tuesday's carnage had a witness and photographer—Kennedy Bracken, formally of Evergreen, Colorado, USA—who resided at Bacalar Vista on Ambergris Caye. The article asked readers who knew the victim to call the police.

The police want help? Hah. He'd given them help. The commandant had promised a quiet nationwide sweep. They would release only one picture. They'd keep Kennedy out of the limelight, away from the press. But he knew the predictable not-to-worry Belizean answer he'd get if he asked the cops about the pictures—"Probably something happened." Yeah, right.

The seven morbid pictures were likely already on their way to the internet, accessible around the world. He wondered to what extreme a reporter—or any perverted lover of gore—might go to obtain the other flash drive, the one with five-dozen digital photos of unadulterated carnage. Kennedy, far from mollified by what he saw, noted with some degree of comfort that the gross wounds shown in the slightly blurry newsprint copies were less explicit than those in his original high-resolution pictures.

And what about his promise to Sarah? Protect the pictures, which he'd already screwed up. He snapped the paper against the table and then reread a critical line, the one that told any number of dark-shadow sons of bitches his name and where he lived.

On the good-news side, he hoped the victim would be identified from the pictures. But the last swig of coffee in his cup, normally as good as the best on the island, went down cold as he thought about potential problems from those chasing the scent of gore.

7

Friday night, no word from Sarah.

Kennedy: "Are you OK?"

Sarah: "Yes. Sending contracts to my office. Two minutes. I'll call."

Kennedy knew her well—constantly on the road, meeting clients, writing new marketing contracts, busy enough to ignore him like a potted petunia. Then, a day or a week later, here she'd come, missing him, loving him, wanting him to move back to Denver, to her.

The connection went through, and Sarah's image appeared. "Has the woman been identified?"

Typical, Kennedy thought. No hello. Down to business. "Not yet," he said. "Been traveling?"

"Yes, sorry. Saw your note. I flew to New York Wednesday, meetings that afternoon. Thursday morning to Chicago, same deal. Thursday night to LA, and this afternoon to Houston, where I just closed two deals. How's mistress number two?"

"That's too much traveling for me. And mistress

Krash will be thrilled to see you."

"Good, because I moved my vacation forward a couple of weeks, to Saturday, and that's tomorrow. I'll be on United 1627 out of Houston, nine in the morning, nonstop to Belize City. I get in at 11:28. Open return. I called Bacalar Vista's office again. The woman who answered was very nice and spoke English. She changed my reservation and got me on the first available Tropic Air flight to San Pedro, to arrive about two, maybe earlier. I'll send you an email with all the details. How's that grab you?"

Kennedy's persona shifted into oh-shit mode. While his right-brain and mouth said, "Wow. I love you, can't wait, made my day, everybody here speaks English, fly safe, I'll be at the airport," his left-brain scanned the comfort, so to speak, of his well-lived-in bachelor pad. He moved closer to the camera to block the view behind him.

"I'll see you about two," Sarah said. "I hope you're ready."

Seconds later, his computer screen blank, he scanned the room, the disarray, and analyzed what he wanted and needed to do to create the pristine palace he'd planned for Sarah's perfect vacation.

Then he focused on the wall clock. Not two weeks. Not even one week. Midday tomorrow.

Krash, always intuitive, laid her head in his lap.

He scratched her ears. "Get ready, ol' girl. We've got a bit of work to do."

8

Kennedy got up early Saturday morning and ran with Krash along the beach. Sending sand and water flying, she chased a Frisbee, and, sure enough, her hind legs passed her forelegs and, sure enough, Krash crashed. Kennedy laughed but allowed one thought to prevail—Sarah, today.

Back at his condo, he brushed sand off his feet and used a clean towel from a basket by the front door to dry Krash's short coat before letting her in.

Now, Sarah time. He scrutinized the disorder, got busy, and in ten minutes had the place picked up enough for the Bacalar Vista housekeeping staff. He showered and shaved and then donned pressed shorts and a button-up shirt—formal attire compared to his normal three-day-softened, lap-wrinkled shorts and tee.

He walked barefoot fifty yards to the palapa—Bacalar Vista's open-air restaurant—and ordered a full Belize breakfast: bacon, eggs, fry jacks, stewed beans, and the resort's made-to-order, dark-roast coffee from the Caye Coffee Roasting Company in San Pedro. He stayed around after the waitstaff cleared his empty plate, sipped refills of the steamy brew, and watched for the concierge.

As soon as he saw her, he gave her the news about Sarah. "She's coming earlier than planned. Like today."

The concierge, ever the optimist, clapped her hands. "That's wonderful. Shall we get housekeeping to give your place a good going over?"

Kennedy rubbed his hands. "Great idea. Please have them work this morning and make sure they bill me for the extra day." He had no doubt Sarah would be impressed to see his condo clean, especially with her early arrival.

With the pressure off, he refilled his cup and watched a fellow resident, ten yards off the beach, fishing in a foot of water. The young man, with the sun behind him, stalked tailing bonefish, their triangular tails glistening in the morning sun as, heads down, they rooted for crabs in the turtle grass. From Kennedy's perspective, the fisherman's concentration never wavered as he cast a great turning loop in his fly line before laying his too-far-away-to-be-seen fly in front of the schooling pod of bonefish. Then he did it again. And again. Fifth cast, strip set, fish on. The early morning scene played out as if choreographed, and Kennedy's adrenaline surged as if he, himself, held the rod, fought the fish. Three pounds? Five? A rocket up its ass? The morning silhouette and the soft rumble of distant waves breaking over the reef masked what Kennedy knew to be the physical details—bent rod, the scream of line flying off the reel, the fish's fast-moving wake.

But the reef, the waves—the thought of the woman's body as well as his own who-the-hell-is-she questions—quashed the serenity of the moment, released him from the scene, and returned him to his coffee.

Back at his unit, Kennedy worked around the housekeeper, careful to give her room while he reloaded the refrigerator with beer, bottled water, Coca-Cola Light, and three bottles of chardonnay, Sarah's favorite.

A ripe pineapple on the counter spurred him to empty the fruit drawer in the fridge and pull out a cutting board and carving knife. Minutes later, he reopened the fridge and slid in a large bowl, filled to the brim with chunks of pineapple, papaya, orange, and apple, all soaked in splashes of fresh-squeezed lime. He'd add the bananas later.

Bored and anxious, he checked his watch and booted his computer. He revisited the *Ambergris Today* website for new developments, new surprises. Only one, a headline: "Sharks on rampage, second woman dies in Caribbean."

The article had a paragraph that reminded readers about Tuesday's Belize Barrier Reef shark death, followed by a blurb about a second woman who had fallen overboard Wednesday night north of

Cozumel while she and her American family fed sharks for fun. The Mexican Navy joined in the search. As of Thursday night, the woman had not been found.

Kennedy felt a chill. Nobody deserved such a death, but he couldn't avoid the comparison. Sharks consumed a young Belize woman's body, her name unknown. And then another woman, in the presence of her family, including two grown kids, falls overboard while feeding sharks. She's presumed dead. Hah. More like *presumed consumed*. And now the family is sad.

Tough shit, he thought. Play stupid, die stupid. Kind of like diving alone. He wondered if the husband of the dead woman had any idea what his wife's body went through before it ceased to exist. And the kids, adult kids, watching their mother die? No, don't go there.

He checked the time, turned off his computer, and gave the housekeeper a generous tip, her work well worth the price.

Krash had to settle for a goodbye pat, but she nested herself back into Kennedy's favorite rattan chair and settled in before he could open the door to leave.

Thoughts of Krash and Sarah made Kennedy smile. He'd often accused Sarah of sharing Krash's gene pool, her shoulder-length hair a beautiful chocolate-lab brown, their eyes the same deep color. Sarah would beam when he teased her about their similarities.

But it wasn't Sarah on his mind while he walked the hundred-yard-long Bacalar Vista pier to the boat slip. Rather, his thoughts were on a reported accident—the woman in Mexico and her stupid shark trick. A guy, maybe, a macho guy with a bunch of other guys, a bunch of drunk guys—him, maybe.

But a woman chumming sharks for fun? Her kids at her side? Feeding the toothy bastards at their feet?

No woman he knew of.

Damn sure not Sarah.

9

Kennedy's portside boat ride proved uneventful, just another blue-sky, swaying-palms, eighty-degree, crystal-clear-water day. Having been cordial to his fellow travelers when they boarded, he'd then leaned back and closed his eyes, not to sleep, but to think. To think about Sarah.

He knew her too well to plan each day or to set a schedule. When it came to reading, lounging by the pool, sipping cool drinks, and late-night passion, they were perfectly compatible. And he'd done his part— no plan, no schedule, just ready for her, for whatever he could do to make her time so perfect she'd never want to leave.

A half hour later, he walked from the Blue Water Grill dock to the police station to get an update. He talked to a uniformed officer, who escorted him to Sergeant Gutierrez's office.

Gutierrez waved him to a seat. "Good timing, Mr. Bracken. I took a call last night from San Ignacio, maybe the victim's parents, named Castillo. They drove to Belize City and are on the way here, on the water taxi." He looked at his watch. "I will see them at eleven, and I expect you will join us."

It wasn't a request.

Kennedy returned to the police station after an early lunch. Sergeant Gutierrez gave him a note with the Castillos' names and explained the need for good manners during the difficult identification process. Kennedy sat next to one of two empty chairs set up for the interview yet to come. He appreciated the sergeant's preparations. The same kind of post-death preparations Kennedy had managed too many times for meetings with relatives during his accident-investigation career. Each meeting was unique; each, demanding; each, just one of many.

A young policewoman escorted Terryl and Rosella Castillo into Sergeant Gutierrez's office and made the introductions. Kennedy guessed their ages to be near forty. The heavy-set couple looked deflated, their faces drooping, their eyes swollen from crying. Terryl Castillo, a big man with laborer's hands, held his wife's arm as if it were a butterfly wing and helped her to her seat.

Sergeant Gutierrez spoke to the couple with a tender softness. "Mr. and Mrs. Castillo ... Mr. Bracken took the pictures you saw in the paper."

Both looked into Kennedy's eyes, said nothing, and crossed themselves.

Sergeant Gutierrez spoke through their grieving. "Please tell me about your daughter."

Terryl Castillo spoke with a deep bass voice, though barely louder than a grumble. "Our Azalee is all we have. Her life is to sing, and she is such a good girl. In church. In school. To her grandparents and her godparents." He hugged his wife. "She is twenty-two."

Kennedy found himself uncomfortable with their use of the present tense—*is* versus *was*—his memory too vivid of a life now gone.

Rosella Castillo finally spoke, half English, half sniffle. "Azalee has a good job at Punta Gorda."

Kennedy pictured the small town on the mainland Belize coast. Pristine waters. Great fishing.

"The resort, Coral House Inn," Terryl Castillo continued, as if he shared his wife's brain, "is magnificent. Azalee works two weeks, and then she comes home for the weekend."

Rosella Castillo clasped her hands, struggled to talk. "Last weekend, it was her time, the end of the second week."

Her husband took over. "I called Coral House Inn and spoke to her boss. He told me she left with friends Friday afternoon. That was a week ago."

Mrs. Castillo: "But she didn't come home. Not Friday, or the weekend, or now for more than a week."

Kennedy said nothing, as he knew where she'd been, at least on Tuesday.

Sergeant Gutierrez nodded and frowned

throughout the Castillos' impassioned story.

Azalee's father continued. "We saw the pictures. Yesterday. A neighbor, she was crying, brought the newspaper to us. It was terrible news. We cried all day."

Sergeant Gutierrez: "I would like you to look at a picture and tell me if the person you see is your daughter. Can you do that for me?"

Rosella Castillo leaned forward in her chair, head down. "It is not her." She rocked forward, and then back, without looking up. "It cannot be her. My Azalee is still alive." Eyes closed, she rocked even harder.

Kennedy gnashed his teeth, fully aware of the couple's pain, denial, fear of the truth. A fear Kennedy had seen in his mother and experienced as a twelve-year-old kid, when she'd told him his father had died.

Sergeant Gutierrez got the Castillos—and Kennedy—back on track. "Mrs. Castillo, if you would rather not look at the picture, perhaps Mr. Castillo can—"

"No. It is OK. I can look because it is not my Azalee. A young woman, perhaps, but not my Azalee."

Sergeant Gutierrez clicked the mouse on his desk and turned the large flat screen monitor toward his small audience.

The screen portrayed the best face shot Sarah had cropped—the commander's "best picture."

Rosella Castillo screamed, "My Azaleeeee." Tears flowed as she kept both hands on the screen, touching her daughter's face, even as she scrunched her eyes clothespin tight.

Terryl Castillo's muscular arms enveloped his wife's shoulders, hugged her gently, and pulled her back to her seat. He, too, sobbed hard and blinked fast, able to manage little more than a quick glance at the dead face on the screen.

Kennedy reckoned the "best" picture taken of the Castillo's beloved daughter, the daughter who would never deliver to them a grandchild, had just confirmed her death. He watched raw emotions unfurl, their lives likely devastated by mourning and grief that would never end. Even with all his years of practice, he had no words to lessen their grief.

The meeting ended no better than it started, Kennedy uncomfortable with the circumstances. No closure during his career had ever been joyous, but each had included circumstances of the accident, the cause of death, the release of the remains for interment. Not so for the Castillos, and Kennedy could offer nothing more. Except to promise himself no picture from his original file would ever see daylight in the presence of Azalee's parents.

Kennedy made his way to San Pedro's airport, a ten-minute walk, and found a seat on a bench in the shade, his thoughts on Sarah.

They'd talked for months—online and in Denver—about her vacation in Belize, time away from the office, time to relax, time to enjoy one another. She'd not been happy to learn Ambergris Caye is an island, and that San Pedro—the only town—is accessible only by boat or plane. Nor was she excited to learn that Bacalar Vista is a thirty-minute boat ride north of San Pedro, up the beach, and butted up against the jungle. She'd balked at boats and beaches and jungles and small planes—like there'd been a choice.

Get over it, he'd said. Raw fear never hurt anybody.

Bullshit, she'd said. It boiled down to work versus play, the value of her time, the importance of her role toward the health of her company.

Self-aggrandizement, he'd argued, which also hadn't gone over so well. He spent hours backpedaling and coercing until she had acquiesced, picked dates, booked tickets.

And now . . . arriving early.

Clear blue skies. Only minutes before she would land. It'd taken him days to realize she'd had multiple reasons for not wanting to make the trip—everything she'd listed plus something she hadn't—a bullheaded reluctance to yield to what he'd wanted. He considered it payback. Payback for his year-old decision. His decision to throw it all in, to move to Belize. To write fiction. Maya vampire fiction.

Wounded to the core by his decision, she'd found no room for compromise.

His move south hadn't just happened. It had evolved from a demanding career fighting winless battles, always another accident, a bone-deep exhaustion both physical and mental, cognizance of his own mortality, wanting to leave footprints. He'd pursued the one-eighty change in lifestyle so hard he'd forgone Sarah's oft-repeated invitation to settle in Denver, to marry her, to play stay-at-home hubby, the perfect corporate spouse. He'd stood his ground, retired early, sold his consulting company, purchased a one-way ticket to Belize, and left Sarah behind. He estimated he'd need three years. Three years, maximum, to regain his sanity.

The soft drone of Sarah's approaching plane, likely loaded with other tourists who would fall in love with the place he'd called home for more than a year, made him wish he'd said three years, *minimum*.

And with Sarah at his side? Belize forever.

He reckoned he would know in the next few hours.

10

Safely on the ground in Belize City, Sarah cleared customs and hired a porter to haul her luggage out one door and into another to the Tropic Air check-in counter, where Bacalar Vista staff had booked her a ticket to San Pedro and charged it to Kennedy.

She'd added a note in her day planner to track down the cost and reimburse him since he would never mention it unless she insisted.

Inside the combination departure lounge and duty-free arena, she wandered shop to shop to keep her mind off the prop-job puddle-jumper flight that awaited her. It didn't work.

Ten minutes before departure, she booted her laptop and sent Tess Krandle an update: "Arrived OK. Will advise when I know return date. Please look for a bigger plane."

How nice, she thought, a short line. Short because the plane carried only twelve passengers. Two of her fellow waiting travelers wore Levi's, and one of the women wore lightweight slacks. The others had dressed for the occasion: sandals, tennis shoes, shorts, T-shirts, short-sleeved blouses. Because the small plane had no overhead storage space—she'd been advised—carry-on luggage could include nothing bigger than purses, broken-down fishing rods, and perhaps shopping bags. Sarah wished her laptop case contained a defibrillator to go along with her pulse of one fifty.

The small group followed a uniformed agent single file across tarmac to a waiting plane. He directed passengers, weight-related, to specific seats. To better balance the plane, he told them.

Sarah climbed four steps, and the attendant directed her to a single seat near the rear of the plane. She ducked as she inched her way through the doorway and into her seat. Claustrophobia sent chills up her back and around her neck and numbed her fingers as she placed her laptop case behind her feet and worked to fasten her seatbelt.

The attendant directed one lucky man to the copilot's seat and instructed him to touch nothing.

Sarah shuddered, glad she wasn't the one riding shotgun, puking on the controls with a full-blown anxiety attack, her spastic gyrations taking over the cockpit.

During takeoff she closed her eyes and imagined her chariot to be a Boeing 757. It didn't work—the comparison was more like a go-cart versus a

Hummer limousine. She realized that voices of passengers talking among themselves, pointing out Belize City sites and the beauty of the Caribbean, had replaced the rumble of the wheels.

Belize City? The Caribbean? What the hell had she been thinking? Life had been good when she and Kennedy played together in Denver. Then in her young forties, with a prick for an ex from a marriage she wanted to forget, she'd avoided the cute word *fiancée*, though that's what she'd been, about to marry Kennedy. That is, before he got the wild hair, packed up, and moved to Belize—for his new mistress, a draft manuscript. A lifelong dream, he'd said, for only a couple of years, or maybe three. Three years? Bullshit. Give her a week, and she'd have him packing to come home. Home to Denver—

Something jolted the plane, and she almost peed in her pants. She opened her eyes, saw no blood on fellow passengers, and chanced a glance out her window. Low elevation, clear water, sandy bottom. Small islands. Pleasure boats.

No, she thought. No boat's a pleasure boat. Cars, good. Small planes, bad. Boats, never.

She saw occasional small dwellings, welcome signs of life, on the bigger barrier islands, and more homes with each passing minute. The area wasn't utopia, yet she found no way to compare its blue-water beauty to Cherry Creek and Chatfield Reservoirs in Denver.

One of the women passengers, her voice door-hinge squeaky, pointed out the southern end of Ambergris Caye.

Sarah saw a swamp, with grasses, lagoons, small huts, and the skeletal hulls of long-abandoned fishing boats. She wasn't impressed. Flying above the island, she saw small homes and a couple of larger, well-manicured places, but nothing looked like the pictures Kennedy had sent of Bacalar Vista.

Bacalar Vista, the place she would call home for maybe a week, if she lasted that long. She needed the vacation, but why such a horrible location, such horrible timing? Two days? She could hold her breath that long. Four days might push it. A week? Bullshit. She had things to do, contracts to chase, clients to keep happy. But, no, she had to visit poor lonely Kennedy, reciprocity for his last visit to Denver. And now, with the trauma of what he'd witnessed, she'd given her mouth way too much freedom and suddenly here she was, flying over third-world jungle in the form of Belize, spiced with bugs, open ocean, iguanas, and God only knows what else. And with what justification? What goal? She knew only one. Convince Kennedy to return home to Denver.

To Sarah's joy, the plane touched down—no fire, no explosion—taxied briefly, made a U-turn, and rolled to a stop. She looked toward a crowd bunched up near a small three-story building, perhaps the terminal, but couldn't tell which individuals waited for arrivals or prepared to depart. She looked for tall, blond, dark eyebrows, luscious lashes.

And there he was—tall.

Kennedy leaned against a small fence, fifty feet from the plane. Taller than all those around him, he wore a casual white shirt and cargo shorts. A deep tan went well with the shock of graying, blond, sun-bleached hair that protruded from a bright-orange baseball cap. His head faced her way, his face stoic. Behind his dark glasses, she imagined, his always-darting eyes scanned each window.

Then the hat poked forward, and his head tilted ever so slightly, just before a giant smile fractured his face. He waved.

Sarah waved back. Somebody opened the passenger door. She tried to get out of her seat, but the closed seatbelt held firm. Perhaps nobody noticed that her entire body was in the throes of an adrenaline rush. Months had passed since Kennedy's last visit to Denver, a three-day stop to hand-deliver a valentine card and a bouquet of multicolored flowers. Months since she'd given or gotten a hug and scattered multi-colored flower petals all over her house. Months since they'd shared a bottle of wine, shared a bed.

All in good time. First, there'd be brilliant sunshine, R and R, and a warm pool. A pool where they would discuss pictures and the dead girl and who she was. She'd give Kennedy five or ten minutes to get the incident off his chest, and then she'd give him something a lot more fun to think about. And do. And all he had to do was chill the wine.

Sarah McGarrity stepped from the plane and welcomed herself to her first vacation in a year. Thirty feet later she met Kennedy Bracken with open arms.

11

Kennedy munched grilled shrimp in a coconut-mango-chutney sauce at Palapa Bar & Grill—built over the water—and considered Sarah's fourteenth question. The first thirteen had been rhetorical, all having to do with land, sea, and air, specifically the whys and wherefores of life on an island.

"Yes, we have a name," he answered, glad at least for the change of subject. "It's Azalee. A-Z-A-L-E-E. But I don't want to talk about it, about her. Tonight, in private, if that's OK."

Sarah had worked her way through most of her mixed-seafood platter without slowing down. She leaned her left elbow over the railing and watched over the side. "Amazing."

"I thought fish scared you," Kennedy said, also enjoying the show—the restaurant manager throwing small batches of raw shrimp at schooling jacks and tarpon that raced for the morsels and thrashed for each scrap.

"They do, but I find it amazing that I flew down

here early because I'm worried about you, and now you won't talk."

Kennedy wiped his mouth. Though he'd wanted to wait, he couldn't escape the topic. "I want you here, but not because I need to be comforted. Yes, I've thought of Azalee every day since I last saw her." He looked to the water. "You see scraps of shrimp and excited fish; I see body parts and feeding sharks."

Sarah dipped her head, looked over her shades. "Crap, Kenn. Get it together. You saw it happen. Took pictures. Reported it. The police identified her. There's nothing else you can do." She hoisted her glass of house chardonnay. "Here's to what's her name, Azalee, and the bittersweet joy you brought to her family, who never would have known her demise if you hadn't taken the pictures."

"Thank you," he said, "but with an important caveat. Barring a solo swim to her death, she ended up where I found her—without leaving a boat behind—which means somebody else was involved."

Sarah stared.

"But since they don't need my help, enough about Azalee." He reached for and raised his glass. "Welcome to Belize and a great vacation."

She tapped her glass to his. "To a great vacation. Thank you."

Kennedy walked Sarah along neatly cobbled Angel Coral Street—also called Back Street.

She stepped away from the curb to avoid a golf cart driven by a matronly woman hauling three kids. "Lots of golf courses?"

Kennedy held her arm and waited for a foursome of slow-moving carts to clear an intersection. "Not on Ambergris Caye, yet, but one's coming. Why? You want to learn to play?" He expected a quick "no way," despite her good coordination and trim body, for one reason—her absolute aversion to any form of exercise.

"Me? Golf? Sorry. No interest. But we seem to be in the minority, hoofing it down the street, everybody else riding in comfort."

"Here, other than walking, it's golf carts, bikes, or boats. There are a few taxis and —"

"And the problem with a golf cart is what?"

He flexed his arm against hers. "I'll rent one the next time we're in town, but for now"—he pointed toward the brightly painted lavender facade of his favorite grocery store, Super Buy—"we need to shop to stay on schedule."

Handmade tortilla chips, a bottle of Travellers 5 Barrel rum, a dozen limes, a loaf of whole wheat bread, and a bag of dog food—five of the six items on Kennedy's list. He held up his last item, a bottle of Lissette's Secret Sauce. "To die for. Anything you want?"

Sarah pulled a can off a shelf. "Do I want anything? Hah!" She zipped down a narrow aisle and dumped items into the cart. "Get some salsa to go with your chips. Then see if you can find hamburger and lunchmeat. And yogurt, with fruit. I'll be in the next aisle, where I saw spices, which you never have."

By the time Kennedy completed his assigned shortlist, Sarah had selected a bouquet of wine bottles, an assortment of toiletries, canned vegetables, a giant tube of sunscreen, and a dozen small bags of Peanut M&M's. "You have beer?"

Kennedy's cupboards were indeed full of stuff he'd purchased and never used, stuff that would impress Sarah, stuff like bottles of spices and cases of beer. "Enough for a day or two." He pushed the heavy basket into the checkout lane and made a show of looking at his watch. "We're done, by default."

Kennedy studied Sarah, fascinated by her diligence as she watched the cashier ring up every bar-coded item.

The cashier pointed to the screen. "Two hundred thirty-eight dollars and thirty cents. Belize." Her helper stuffed the last item into a plastic sack and tied it shut.

Kennedy, wallet in hand, showed three local one-hundred-dollar bills to Sarah. "The exchange rate is fixed at two Belize dollars for one—"

"Kenn, I get it. And these costs, all future costs, we split, fifty-fifty."

Splitting costs—they'd always done it. One or the other would pay and keep track, and eventually they'd battle through a day of reckoning. Kennedy, old-fashioned, would rather pay and forget it. Sarah, in her young forties for the past several years and more contemporary, had a quick-draw wallet.

He grabbed the tops of several bags and had Sarah do the same. "You're tough, but let's negotiate later. If we miss the boat, your luggage will get there without us and we're out of luck until five."

"Boat?" Sarah asked. "You mentioned it before, but isn't there another way. Like a road? Maybe a car? Or a golf cart?"

"Nope," he said, walking fast. "No road yet, so it's either the boat or a long walk through the jungle."

Sarah, too, walked fast and stayed right beside him. "There's something wrong with this picture, Kennedy Bracken—me hurrying to catch a boat." She huffed as she followed him across the sandy beach to the Blue Water Grill dock. "My guess is, before this trip is over, you're going to owe me big time."

He didn't have the heart to ask her if by *trip* she meant the walk to the boat, the boat ride itself, or her entire vacation.

Kennedy helped Sarah board the 30-foot-long, open-air passenger boat and introduced her to the captain and other passengers, fellow Bacalar Vista residents: Americans, Canadians, Brits, Germans—a mix of couples, single women, kids, guys with groceries. Most shared similar features—suntans and smiles.

He picked seats on the starboard side, mid-vessel—for the northbound shoreline view to the west—and lifted the seat cushions below which they stowed their grocery sacks.

After they were seated with only minutes to spare, he pointed out the twin 250-horsepower Yamaha outboards. "Way more than we need, especially inside the reef, but it's good to know if one goes down, we have a backup."

No response. Sarah's eyes were closed. But not asleep.

"Hey, you'll be OK," he said as one of the big engines purred to life. "Just enjoy the view."

He pocketed his hat as the boat left the dock and let the wind blow through his hair. For Sarah's benefit, he pointed out the reef—behind them, a half mile east of the shoreline—then westward to restaurants they needed to try, and resorts, and homes, and clear-water grassy flats where he had caught nice bonefish and lost a few big ones.

Kennedy gave thanks for the *National Geographic*-perfect day: warm and dry, a sea-breeze beauty, the flats between the shore and the reef clear as glass and free of chop. He looked forward to taking Sarah, perhaps on a small charter boat, completely around the twenty-five-mile-long island, but he'd first have to break her into riding boats in general.

"This is my commute," he told her. "Thirty minutes of bliss. No traffic except a few other boats and a few pedestrians on the beach. My biggest frustration is having to turn my head to keep my hair out of my eyes."

Sarah faced into the breeze of the twenty-five-knot ride and pushed her hair off her forehead. "Yeah, I know. Mine's about to beat me to death."

Kennedy laughed.

She scowled.

As they disembarked at Bacalar Vista, the resort concierge, as the perfect hostess, met the boat and welcomed first-day-guest Sarah with a complimentary rum punch. "How was your boat ride?" she asked, her voice soft, sincere.

Sarah gave it thumbs down. "The pits. And I'm glad I don't have to do it again anytime soon."

Kennedy had learned about Sarah's fear of the water, her nightmares about drowning in the ocean, only when he'd announced his then-imminent move to Belize. Those fears had interfered with every logical argument he'd ever posed as to why she should move south with him.

But as he watched her settle in and laugh with the crowd on the dock, he knew she needed the vacation. And by the time she finished her drink, she, the concierge, and two women from Mississippi chatted as if they were long-lost friends and made their way to the palapa, their four-way conversation focused on shopping, Maya ruins, and good restaurants.

That left Kennedy time to identify Sarah's luggage and their grocery sacks so staff members could cart their goods to his unit. He then joined the ladies in the palapa, where wine and laughter mixed well. Nobody seemed interested in the time until Sarah winked and rolled her eyes.

Kennedy checked his watch and then pushed back from the table. "We'll probably be back for dinner," he told the others, "but we need to put our groceries in the fridge."

Sarah took his hand as he helped her up. "And I can't wait to see your mansion and get these big-city shoes off."

Only then did one of the women place her hand on Sarah's. "Oh, I've been dying to ask. Did Kenn tell you about the dead girl yet? And the sharks?"

Sarah's eyes widened. She did an exaggerated double take and said, "Dead girl?" Eyes bulging, she looked at Kennedy, waggled her head, and did it again, as if on stage. "What dead girl? What sharks?"

Kennedy moaned, followed Sarah's lead, and rocked back and forth. He wrapped his hand around Sarah's. "We better go. This might take a while."

Behind them, as they exited the palapa, a woman's voice, driven by a strong Southern accent, pierced the silence: "My God, Greta, you are one dumb broad."

Kennedy and Sarah laughed to themselves.

She wrapped her arm in his. "You said you wanted to talk about the girl—"

"Azalee."

"Azalee, tonight, in private. I say we split the difference."

"How so?"

She tightened her grip. "Azalee, no. Not yet. Private time, yes. Now."

He picked up his pace.

12

Kennedy kicked off his KEENs, where they joined a pile of ancient tennis shoes, well-used fishing boots, and three mismatched flip-flops.

Sarah stepped out of her sandals and held them while Kennedy opened the door.

Krash went spastic.

Sarah dropped to her knees, where she reunited with her forever girlfriend. They hugged and cooed, as only a woman on her knees and a ninety-pound adrenaline-driven chocolate lab can.

Kennedy could only smile, Krash having taken no notice of him.

Krash shook with excitement, but Sarah talked to her and got her to settle.

Kennedy helped Sarah to her feet and then moved in, face-to-face. He didn't wait for her to tour his condo, mess with groceries, unpack clothing. He placed his hands gently on the sides of her face, leaned forward and kissed the woman with whom he wanted to share his life.

Later, Kennedy watched as Sarah decorated her face in the bathroom mirror.

Working on her eyes, she said, "I need to see your place."

He reminded her she'd already seen the master suite. "The second bedroom and bath look just like this one. Floors are tile, walls are hurricane-proof concrete block, and all the woodwork is solid mahogany. The kitchen stuff is all stainless. There are comfortable chairs in the living room, and the couch makes into a bed, though I've never had to open it. Same shutters on all the windows as in here."

Sarah finished her lips. "I recommend you never consider being a Realtor. I'll take the tour myself."

Kennedy and Sarah made their way to the palapa just before nine. He counted four tables of four and a party group of eight, as evidenced by after-dinner drinks and a couple of down-breeze Cuban-cigar smokers. He suggested a table for two against a low wall that faced the sea.

Sarah read handwritten notes on a whiteboard and said, "All the choices look good."

"If we're not too late." Kennedy turned his attention to the approaching headwaiter. "Alberto, good to see you. Meet Ms. Sarah. Sarah, Alberto's the boss in here. Anything you need, he'll help you out."

Alberto shook Sarah's hand, pulled a chair from an adjoining table, sat, and then spoke just to her. "Mr. Kenn's not normally this nice, so he must like you a lot. May I get you a drink, and maybe something exotic to eat?" He pointed his thumb Kennedy's way. "We'll let him fend for himself, maybe chips and a beer."

Sarah laughed and beamed as Alberto bantered and explained her dinner choices. She chose the special—grouper baked in coconut gravy—and a glass of house chardonnay.

Alberto turned to Kennedy. "Mr. Kenn, I'm sorry about leaving you alone on Tuesday. I was late for the lunch schedule, and then I went in on the four-o'clock boat. I didn't get back until Wednesday morning. If I'd known about—"

The memory rushed at Kennedy. He and Alberto—Kennedy's diving, fishing, darts buddy—had loaded their tanks onto two kayaks late that morning. Alberto wanted a hogfish to take to town for dinner with his family, so they started off free diving—no tanks. Alberto used a Hawaiian sling, the only legal way to spearfish in the Bacalar Chico Marine Reserve, which included the Basil Jones Cut and the entire shoreline to the Belize/Mexico border. Kennedy, free diving for the exercise, tried to get pictures of big snappers, but could not stay down long enough. He signaled Alberto, and then went back to his kayak to get his scuba gear. Alberto, all smiles, showed Kennedy his hogfish and had wished him well before going to shore, leaving Kennedy to dive alone.

"Not a problem," Kennedy said. He shook Alberto's hand. "I should have gone with you, but I'm glad I stayed. Now if you've got another special, please make mine the same as Ms. Sarah's."

As soon as Alberto delivered their drinks, Kennedy took Sarah's hand and they table-hopped. Introductions, questions, and short stories went both ways. Where're you from? Did you hear about the hurricane that skirted the Florida coast? Any plans to snorkel at Shark Ray Alley?

"Snorkel and sharks?" Sarah's eyes popped wide open. "Great oxymoron, which means it's a no for me."

Kennedy assured her no form of snorkeling was on their agenda, though he felt the atmosphere of the group shifting toward the inevitable.

Sure enough, a loud voice from ten feet away: "Kenn, did they identify the woman?"

Even the white noise of the reef seemed to join the intense silence of anticipation that spread throughout the palapa. Kennedy gave his practiced answer. "The police have a name, but it's not yet public."

Someone asked her age. Others wondered how she died. Was she Belizean? Maya? Guatemalan? A tourist? To each, the same answer, and Kennedy gave up a little of his enthusiasm for the evening.

Relieved to see Alberto deliver their steaming plates, he nudged Sarah back to their table.

She unwrapped her silverware and said, "They just want to know, same as you."

"Want and need—two different things." He placed his napkin in his lap, dug his fork into his entrée, and spoke softly. "As with any death, they'll get their answers when the police make an announcement." He chewed a bite of tender grouper, equally as good as the best he ever had. "For me, I'm just glad to be out of the picture, with the police running the show."

Sarah nodded, but her attention was on her plate. She forked a small bite, lathered it in gravy, and placed it carefully in her mouth. She worked her jaws. Then something happened to her eyes, their focus difficult for Kennedy to read. She looked down at her plate and seemed to speak directly to it. "This is so good I could cry."

Kennedy cracked up.

Napkin to her lips. "What?"

"That's the second time today you said those words."

She cocked her head, sported a wicked grin, and hoisted her glass. "You're right, so this is to a heck of a lot more crying yet to come."

They clicked glasses, sipped their wine, and dug in.

Sarah said, "You haven't mentioned your book since I got here."

Kennedy laid down his fork and rested his chin in his right hand. "Because I learned my lesson."

"You're too sensitive," she said. "I didn't say you

couldn't talk about it."

"No. Just that you had no interest in reading and helping me edit the same fifty pages more than a dozen times, which in truth was only thrice."

"*Thrice*? That's a word? I mention your book for the first time in months and you pop off with *thrice*?"

Kennedy forked another chunk of grouper and spoke while chewing. "For your info, I'm done. First draft complete, months ago. I'm editing, cutting, rewriting with everything I've got. You'll get an autographed copy when it's complete and ready for an agent."

"I still want to know. Is *thrice* really a word?"

He pointed to her plate with his fork. "Get busy, or I'll finish that for you." An idle threat. He'd learned long ago not to reach for anything on Sarah's plate, as her reaction would be akin to a weed whacker.

Minutes later, plates clean, neither wanted dessert.

Kennedy folded his napkin. "Something you need to see before we go in." Arm in arm, he led her to the pier.

"You going to throw me in?" she asked as they neared the far end, a hundred yards from the lights of the palapa.

"No. Just wanted you to see the stars, maybe a few fish, listen to the waves breaking on the reef." He waited for a smart-ass retort.

Instead, she pointed north. "It really is lower."

Clueless, he looked to where she pointed. "What?"

"The North Star," she said. "Polaris. It's just above the horizon."

"Rumor has it that if you're at the North Pole, it's directly overhead." That got him an elbow to his ribs.

Sarah sat on the edge and dangled her legs, her feet just above the water, softly illuminated by lights under the dock. "The most stars I ever saw," she said, "was from an unlikely spot—somewhere in Mount Rainier National Park."

"Why unlikely?" he asked.

"Because Rainier can be awful. Cold. Snowy. Lots of bad weather. I took an executive MBA course through the University of Washington, and a small group of us drove up to a visitor center called Sunrise, supposedly the highest road in the state. We toured the museum, ate lunch, and, for whatever dumb reason, started climbing. We climbed two, maybe three hours, but we couldn't get down before it got dark." She leaned back, elbows on the deck.

"You spent the night?"

"Almost," she said. "Even so, the sky was the most beautiful sight I'd ever seen. The Milky Way, horizon to horizon. We pointed out to one another dozens of constellations and shooting stars while freezing our butts off. A search-and-rescue team found us about three in the morning and escorted us off the mountain. The guys weren't too happy with us, but one of the rescuers later became my husband. And a year later, my ex."

"So, finally," Kennedy said. "The origin of the

infamous George. Very romantic."

She sat up, leaned against his shoulder. "Looking back, not very romantic at all. Just like the water." She looked down and waggled her feet, inches above the surface. Small fish darted into and out of the light.

Kennedy figured it wasn't a good time for a ten-pound jack to explode onto the scene, chase prey, and break the surface under Sarah's feet—heart attack, guaranteed.

"Let's go back to the condo," he said. "I've got a few limes that'll go bad unless we preserve them in rum."

"Good. Then you can tell me who Azalee is, where she's from, and how she died."

In the privacy of his unit, Kennedy asked Sarah what she'd like to drink, and she jumped at the chance for a homemade mojito. He squeezed limes over ice, crushed a sprig of mint, spooned sugar, added soda water, and tipped the bottle of rum to fill her cut-glass tumbler. He sipped her drink, considered going mojito for the evening—a brief thought—and made himself a rum and lime.

He handed Sarah her drink, toasted her presence for the third time that day, and related what he'd learned. The helpful Sergeant Gutierrez. Parents Rosella and Terryl Castillo. The parents' daughter, Azalee.

He pulled a note from his pocket. "Azalee Rosella

Consuelo Castillo. I'm glad she has a name, but I hurt for her parents. From what I saw, they're good people. Strong Catholics."

Sarah sipped her drink and then placed the tumbler on the glass-top coffee table. She slid her hand into his. "The parents are Catholic?"

"Devout. Why?"

She nodded slowly. "Then I need to show you something in your pictures."

"We don't need to look at the pictures. Just tell me."

"It'll be better if I show you—because the parents may have a problem."

Kennedy turned on the couch. "Don't do this. Just spit it out."

"I'm guessing the dead girl's not Catholic. She's Jewish."

13

Kennedy stood behind Sarah, hands on her shoulders, as he had imagined almost a week before.

She scrolled through almost half his original pictures, the ones downloaded from his camera, and then stopped on a shot not unlike the others. The photo was not one of the seven she had worked on. She zoomed in on a small shark, its pit-bull jaws latched to the young woman's calf.

"Wow," she said. "The hi-res clarity's awesome." She took a deep breath and pointed to a tiny object on the screen. "This is where I first noticed it and got concerned."

In the upside-down view, something, maybe a charm, hung from an ankle-bracelet chain. Kennedy had no clue what he was looking at.

Sarah tabbed deeper into the file and stopped on a second picture. When magnified, it showed an almost-frontal view of the trinket. She pointed with the mouse cursor. "Looks like a *hamsa*, with something in the middle, maybe a little jewel."

Kennedy recalled looking for rings and earrings during his photo shoot and seeing none.

Sarah centered the object in the screen, fiddled again with the zoom, and retraced the blurry outline with the cursor. "Definitely a hamsa," she said.

"And how's that special?"

"My roommate at Colorado State University wore one and never took it off. She's Jewish. She claimed it's a Jewish symbolic hand that wards off evil."

Kennedy dropped to his knees, eye to eye with the screen, and studied the tiny trinket. "No Catholic equivalent?"

"Maybe"—Sarah leaned forward and pointed at the pendant on the screen—"but this one's Jewish."

"Maybe," he said, thinking, "Azalee bought a second-hand trinket she didn't understand. Kids sell stuff up and down the beach. Black coral, beads, sharks' teeth, anything they find."

"And if she didn't get it from a kid?"

Kennedy liked the kid scenario, but Sarah had him in a corner. "So . . . good-Catholic Azalee Castillo," he said, "either converted or had a closet Jewish boyfriend."

Sarah turned in the chair and looked at Kennedy. "Then it might be nice if her parents know about it before they go through a Catholic funeral. Which is when?"

"No clue," he said. "We can go to town tomorrow and ask the police."

Sarah tensed. "To town? Like on the boat? Crap.

I just got here. If you want to talk to the police, call them. And don't tell me this place doesn't have a phone."

"Several," Kennedy said. "My cell works from the dock, there's a local line in the palapa, and I have Skype, but this topic should be handled in person. And for me, it's no big deal. If I want something from San Pedro—groceries, a jug of rum, or a word with the cops—I get on the boat and enjoy the trip."

"Count me out," she said. "Give me a town anytime with me in the middle."

He wrapped his arms around her and nuzzled in. "Then I'll move to San Pedro Town and buy a house. You can join me."

Sarah returned the nuzzle and snatched a quick kiss. "Not funny. Get a condominium—a house's too much to take care of."

As much as Kennedy cared for Sarah, she had a way of changing the subject, making him come to her conclusion. But the hamsa, the *Jewish hamsa*, combined with the brutal visuals he couldn't forget, bothered him more than she knew. He got to his feet and helped her up.

"Bottom line," he said, "you want to go in on the morning boat, about eight, or the noon boat?"

She pulled free. "You don't get it. I'm here to be with you, and I'll help all I can, but please don't take me for granted. I don't need to go to town to talk to the police. And since I'm not going to Azalee's funeral, I don't need to know when it is."

Kennedy collected the empty drink glasses, turned on the hot water, and spoke from the kitchen. "I'm not going to her funeral either, but the cops need to know about the trinket, and tomorrow morning's none too early."

Sarah rubbed her eyes. "Why?"

He turned off the water. "Because the person she got the hamsa from might know how she ended up in the water. And if the bastard threw her overboard and left her alone, unreported, to go through what I saw, then I'll do everything in my power to see his ass fried."

14

Kennedy waited for Sergeant Gutierrez while Sarah shopped at Super Buy. One hour, he'd told her, and then he'd meet her at Blue Water Grill for a beer before getting back on the boat for departure at two.

Fifteen minutes later, Sarah, out of breath, entered the San Pedro Police waiting room, a grocery sack in each hand. "I got what I need—hustled all the way. Have I missed anything?"

Kennedy looked at his watch, amazed. "Not yet," he said. Glad for her company, he took her bags. "Have a seat."

"Nobody's in a hurry here," Sarah said. She scanned the room, her typical attack-the-day persona pumped to the hilt.

"You're right, and that's good, but only if you slow down to match their pace of life. Also, it's Sunday, so we need to be glad Gutierrez is in the office."

Sarah grumbled through puckered lips. "We're wasting hours of sunshine. It's probably blowing snow in Denver, and here I am, in Belize, a tropical paradise, camped out in a police station. If you lived in San Pedro, I'd be at the pool."

"An August snow in Denver? Then be glad you're here. And if you're really interested, our next visit can be to a real estate agent. I'll have us a place to live before—"

A heavyset policeman interrupted: "Mr. Bracken? Sergeant Gutierrez will see you now. Please follow me."

The meeting with Sergeant Gutierrez, who welcomed Sarah to Belize, started off cordial, if not obsequious, both sides polite to a fault . . . until Kennedy explained what they'd found.

The officer leaned back in his chair. "A good-luck charm? A young girl, Azalee Castillo, with a good-luck charm. And for that I'm supposed to call her dear mother and tell her to stop the memorial service?" He shook his head. "I will not do that."

Sarah, who'd been quiet, spoke up. "The charm is Jewish. It keeps evil away."

Kennedy added that Azalee may have gotten it from her boyfriend.

Sergeant Gutierrez sat up tall in his chair. "A Jewish charm for evil. In a country with few Jews, no Jewish churches, and for Belizean girls, no Jewish boyfriends."

Sarah dipped her head so deep, Kennedy reckoned she had to look through her eyebrows. "Synagogues, sir. Jewish churches are called synagogues."

Sergeant Gutierrez ignored her. "In Belize, we have more Catholics than all other religions combined, including Muslims, Mennonites, Jehovah's Witnesses, and even some Methodists. Only once did I meet with a Jew, and that was to tell him his brother in the States had died. When he left Belize, he never came back. So now, with him gone, we have even fewer Jews in Belize, except maybe during the high season." He looked at Sarah. "That's when all the tourists come."

"What if I told you I'm Jewish?" Sarah asked.

Kennedy shuddered, not liking the wisp of acid in her words.

Sergeant Gutierrez leaned forward in his chair and spoke to Sarah. "Then I'd say you are probably a tourist, madam, and that you are most welcome to enjoy the hospitality of our small country." With perfect diction and the slightest touch of an English accent, he said, "We give this hospitality freely to all visitors in good standing, regardless of their faith. Further, even though I think you are not Jewish, I appreciate the help you gave toward identifying the object on Miss Azalee Castillo's ankle. I do not know the trinket's origin, and perhaps we shall never know, but I cannot take the burden of its mystery to the Castillos' home two short days before they are to bury the memory of their daughter."

Kennedy hoped Sarah got the message. Sarah, the born-again agnostic who believed religious extremists formed the roots of all wars. Sarah, who attended church only for weddings and funerals. Sarah, who—she'd told Kennedy—had prayed every night since she was a little girl: *Now I lay me down to sleep* . . .

Gutierrez had Sarah pegged—tourist, not Jewish—and he ended the visit cordially, though Kennedy knew Sarah seethed even when she shook the officer's hand.

On the boat trip back to Bacalar Vista, Sarah put her head on Kennedy's shoulder and spoke against the wind. "I'm impressed by how many locals speak English. Even Sergeant Gutierrez."

Kennedy hugged the grocery sacks between his feet and leaned in, his mouth close to her ear. "Belize isn't Mexico. Here, with thanks to the country's hundred years as British Honduras, the official language is English. But there's also Mayan, Creole, Spanish, and Garifuna, so there's a mix of cultures and customs."

Sarah didn't respond. Her head didn't move.

He peered, saw closed eyes.

Pleased with her comfort, he leaned back and soaked up the Sabbath sun—his every thought focused on Azalee Castillo's very Catholic Tuesday funeral.

15

Kennedy, humped over his laptop, sipped rum and lime. "According to the ISAF—the International Shark Attack File—the Caribbean side of the Mexican Yucatán has seen five shark attacks in the past hundred years, all fatal. The report does not include a woman who fell overboard a week ago while chumming sharks."

"Chumming?" Sarah asked. "Like, friendly?"

He rotated his chair. "No. Chumming is where you throw bait in the water to attract fish, including sharks."

Sarah fiddled with her hair. Think mode. "Does the Yucatán include Belize?"

"It used to," he said. "Folklore says the Maya cut a trench, called Boca Bacalar Chico, across the southern tip of the Yucatán peninsula, to gain back-bay access to the Caribbean. North of the cut it's all Mexico, and the cut-off piece of the peninsula is part of Belize."

"Like Baja Yucatán."

"Yes," he said. "But it's called Ambergris Caye. And

you're diverting the subject."

"Which was about shark deaths," Sarah said, "a nice cocktail-hour chat."

He ignored her and turned back to the screen. "Though I suspect their data may not be perfect, the ISAF reports Belize hasn't had a recordable shark-attack death during those same hundred years, except for last week."

"So maybe the barrier reef's a barrier for sharks too."

"Not from what I saw," he said. He plugged in more key words, his goal to make comparisons and track down deaths and dates and circumstances. "And maybe it's just sharks on a rampage," he said, "caused by overfishing." He waited for her laugh but felt her stare instead. He turned in his chair, looked up slowly, and found her eyes, lasers, focused into his.

Arms crossed, she stood in the living room in front of the seven-foot-tall mahogany television cabinet.

Krash, head down, butt up, stared up at her as if expecting a treat.

"Kenn," Sarah said, "she's dead. Soon to be buried in absentia. About which you can do nothing." She held up her glass. "So, if you'll top me up, we'll toast the good life we hope she led before she died."

Hands on his knees, he rose, assumed the position of attention. "Yes, ma'am." He took Sarah's glass and went into the kitchen. "I want to find her boyfriend," he said. "And assuming he's Jewish, that shouldn't be too hard. The cops don't seem interested, but I need to talk to him and either get him off my mind or find out what he knows about Azalee's death."

Sarah slumped into a seat, and Krash's head found her lap. "So now, Mr. Accident Investigator, you want to chase somebody you don't know, contrary to the police, in a foreign country."

"We just find the boyfriend," he said, "and ask him a few questions."

"We?" she asked, stretching the word like bubblegum.

He handed her a full wine glass. "Unless you want me to go by myself."

"You'd do that," she said, "and leave me here? Crap. I'm beginning to wonder why I came."

Kennedy sat beside her. "You planned to come to Belize," he said, "long before the girl's death. You came *early*, by several days, because you felt sorry for me. Me? I'm comfortable I did my job by giving Azalee's pictures to the police. And beyond my curiosity as to how she ended up in the water, there was nothing else for me to do, until you found the hamsa."

Sarah nosed the bouquet of her drink, took a tiny sip, and licked her lips. "Maybe you're just looking for an excuse to stay involved."

"Call it what you want," he said, "but I saw Azalee after she died, and it wasn't pretty. And even if the police are still investigating, I won't be able to sleep until I know how she got there. I'm hoping her boyfriend can enlighten us."

"So where do *we* go from here?"

Kennedy held up his glass, tapped hers. "To where Azalee worked. Punta Gorda. The locals call it *PG*. It's a hundred miles south of Belize City, just north of the Guatemala border. I've been there, fishing. It's a tiny town, half the size of San Pedro. Tropic Air will make a short stop at Belize City, and then it's down to PG and back in one day."

Sarah swirled the wine in her glass. "Kenn Bracken, first, there's nothing going to be easy about you getting me back on a puny little boat or dinky little plane. So, when I say I'll go with you, it's not because it sounds like a fun day out; it's because I don't want to be left behind, where I might end up having to get on the boat without you. And second, you're a crappy estimator of time."

Only because days are limited to twenty-four hours, he'd often told himself. "We get this behind us," he said, "and we'll have something for Sergeant Gutierrez to chew on while we get lost at Bacalar Vista. Vacation things, that kind of stuff."

Yeah, right, the firm set of her face said.

Neither was his heart in the words, not when his gut told him to get his ass to Punta Gorda to chase Azalee Castillo's ghost, regardless of where that visit might lead.

16

Sarah considered it a boat trip from hell, though Kennedy had told her the stiff sea breeze and choppy waters were normal. While she worried about every engine noise and slap of the hull, Kennedy, happy as a puppy, pointed to and described everything he saw—giant coconut palms, a triad of white-stucco homes built in only the past year, kids and their dogs playing on the end of a dock—as if she were blind.

Regardless of scenery and homes, she could have puked, constantly concerned about tipping over, catching fire, crashing into coral rocks.

Though Blue Water Grill's dock led to dry land, it proved anticlimactic. Yes, the beach was safer than the boat, but a taxi awaited her. A taxi that would take Kennedy and her on a short ride to the airport, where one of those dinky-ass planes had her name on its manifest.

She wondered if Monday-morning pilots flew with weekend hangovers.

At the airport, her pits glistening but not from

heat, she lucked out with her body-mass seat assignment and got a single in the back—nobody yakking beside her. Kennedy sat two seats forward, next to the window, a twelve-year-old girl next to him, her mother in the single seat across the aisle. Sarah kept her eyes closed, not even remotely interested in viewing dots of clouds or the sea she had just escaped.

They changed planes in Belize City, where she rejoiced that the second craft was not dinkier than the first.

Forty-five minutes later, the soft bump of tires on the runway was a pleasant surprise—another successful flight, no crash. Outside her window, Punta Gorda. What she could see looked like San Pedro, just a lot less of it.

Kennedy pointed out and offered her one of the town's complimentary bicycles for the short ride to the restaurant. "It has to be on the beach, five or six blocks."

Nope. They walked to the Coral House Inn.

Sarah had used her time on the plane to shake off her self-proclaimed pity party. Good timing, because lunch at Coral House Inn—conch ceviche, grilled snapper, sliced fruit, and rice with coconut sauce— left no room for emotions other than those related to taste.

Kennedy spoke to the server, a young boy, and asked if he could meet the owner.

A man, bald, perhaps sixty, came to the table,

hands folded in front of his chest. He said, "I'm Carlos, madam, sir. Is everything OK?"

Kennedy shook his hand. "Yes, of course," he said. "The lunch was excellent. Please join us, and may we buy you a glass of wine?"

"That would be nice. Thank you."

Kennedy identified himself as a journalist writing a story about Azalee Castillo—to which Sarah gave a nod of approval.

The owner spoke quietly. He was fully aware of Azalee's death, her parents' trauma, the funeral yet to come. When asked, he insisted Azalee's boyfriend, a young waiter at the same restaurant, was a devout Catholic.

Kennedy continued his role. "Would you mind if we interview him?"

"Interview him? Not possible, señor. I have not seen Christopher since Azalee disappeared. His parents and I fear something happened to him too."

While Kennedy continued, Sarah saw red flags— one named Azalee; another, Christopher. Something wasn't right. Her interest was piqued. She watched and admired her skilled partner, who asked simple questions without intimidating the owner.

To a Kennedy question, the owner said, "Azalee? A Jewish friend? Like from America or Israel? None that I know, señor. No Jews live in Punta Gorda."

Kennedy twirled his wine glass and shifted to small talk—fishing, flies, flats. Ignoring the men while they exchanged macho grunts about heroic fishing successes, Sarah cataloged what she'd learned. Three strikes: Catholic Azalee dead, Catholic boyfriend missing, no Jewish friends.

She needed one-on-one time with Kennedy and silently cheered when the manager excused himself and went back to work.

Kennedy checked his watch. "There's a plane that leaves in sixteen minutes," he said. "Let's try to make it." Before she could answer, he went to the men's room.

Instant butterflies. She looked at her own watch, calculated the number of seconds before takeoff, and pictured the humbug little plane that awaited her for the first leg of the three-legged trip back home. Home? No, not home. Kennedy's place, on the other end of a half-hour-long, most-undesired boat ride.

She cursed herself. With another day of her perfect vacation about to be lost forever, she proclaimed to herself that the next morning would be the start of Sarah's Day. A full day at the pool, Kennedy at her side, good book in hand, cold drinks a finger-waggle away. Tomorrow.

When Kennedy returned, she said, "Tomorrow's mine, and don't even think about changing it."

Stunned eyes brought joy to Sarah's heart, and not a sound came from his open mouth, which was even better.

She grabbed his arm. "Let's go. We have a plane to catch."

17

Kennedy had little to say on the flight back to Belize City. Sarah—seated across the aisle—cringed the entire way, so he kept his thoughts to himself. Everything seemed to fit together, except for two small details: the ankle bracelet and the missing boyfriend. Otherwise, Azalee's parents, with their daughter identified, caught up in grief and mourning, had just begun to feel the pain Kennedy knew would never heal.

Visions of his own dad's funeral had forever eluded him. Car accident, he'd been told, off a seaside cliff, no physical body to view, no goodbyes, no logical explanation. Just the facts—which changed with his mother's moods. He remembered missing school—eighth grade—for days. And crying, his mother hugging him, her crying too. An asshole counselor telling Kennedy to get over it, which he never did. But of the funeral—if there really was one—he remembered nothing. And as an adult, he needed only the slightest reminder—like thoughts of Azalee's parents, thoughts about an unresolved accident, thoughts about not getting to say goodbye—for him to sorely miss his dad.

Sergeant Gutierrez had explained that Azalee's funeral, a memorial service in her name, would take place the next day, Tuesday. Equally important, Kennedy pondered, Gutierrez had apparently written off the case as an unfortunate drowning, the body lost at sea.

But something tore at Kennedy's gut.

Something wasn't right.

By the time the plane touched down at Belize City, Kennedy knew that he and Sarah would not be on the next flight to San Pedro.

18

Sarah repeated, "San Ignacio? Is that a restaurant, a town, or a country?"

"San Ignacio Town, to be proper." Kennedy sounded like a tour guide. "It's just west of Belize City, in the foothills, near Guatemala. It's where the Castillos live."

"The girl's parents," Sarah said. "And we're going there for what?"

"It's a good tourist town, close to cave tubing and to zip lining, tree to tree, in the jungle. You'll enjoy the area. And the parents may be able to help us find Azalee's young friend."

"Kenn, if you consider my fear of water and heights, what else about cave tubing and zip lining do you think I'd like?" She shook her head. "Don't bother answering that. Isn't the funeral today?"

"No. Tomorrow."

"Convenient," she said. "We wouldn't want to infringe."

In charge of virtually every aspect of her life—

social, physical, career—Sarah cringed every time Kennedy, the master of non-communication, changed a plan on the fly. He'd told her the "just west" fifty-mile bus ride would cost a mere fourteen Belize dollars round trip, each.

To Sarah, cost was irrelevant. *Round trip* was the key phrase. "Pay in advance," she said. "I want the return ticket in my pocket before I get on that bus."

An hour later, Kennedy told a San Ignacio cab driver he needed to go to the home of Terryl Castillo, on West Street—the only detail he could remember from the brief meeting in Sergeant Gutierrez's office.

The cab driver put his decade-old minivan in gear. "For the wake, of course," he said. "Azalee Rosella Consuelo Castillo. Such a beautiful girl. Such a good Catholic. I have known her momma and papa since we were kids. Five minutes, I'll have you there."

Sarah, still trying to get her brain around the girl's multisyllabic name, caught Kennedy's look of bewilderment as he mouthed, "Wake?"

Around the Castillo's home, in San Ignacio's low hills, flowers bloomed everywhere. A giant bougainvillea, with red-blush blooms, covered an entire side of the home. Sarah stood back while Kennedy knocked.

He addressed the woman who answered. "We're looking for Terryl and Rosella Castillo."

"Yes, of course," the woman said. "Please come

in." She escorted them toward the center of the small living room.

Two people, Terryl and Rosella Castillo by default, Sarah concluded, acted surprised to see their uninvited guests. Then they recognized and welcomed Kennedy into their home. Sarah received the same hospitality as soon as Kennedy introduced her.

"Please welcome Mr. Bracken and Ms. McGarrity," Terryl Castillo announced to his other guests. "Mr. Bracken is the gentleman who took pictures of our Azalee that were shown in the papers."

Mr. Castillo had made his announcement to a house full of people—relatives, neighbors, Azalee's school friends. This, Sarah had learned because she met each of them, each dressed in black, the polar opposite of her butter-yellow blouse, white shorts, and white tennis shoes. The women captured her, surrounded her, asked questions she'd heard before. Where are you from? How long will you stay? Are you at a resort? Did you know Azalee? The last question was the only mention of Azalee Castillo, as if avoiding the topic would lessen their pain.

Sarah felt as if she had insider information she couldn't share. These people knew Azalee, they had watched her grow up, perhaps had gone to school with her. Not Sarah. She'd been privy—by proxy—to only the last few sad minutes of Azalee's bodily existence. And what she'd seen of Azalee, these people never needed to see.

Sarah smiled to herself, as she watched Kennedy endure the same greetings, his outfit a blue-and-white-striped golf shirt, dark blue shorts, and sandals—a sporty contrast to his male counterparts' somber dark suits. She'd tried to get his attention, to have him take off his sunglasses so he didn't look like a Hollywood dork, but gave up. No, not a dork. She loved the total package—lanky body, confident poise, manly mannerisms, and a head taller than the men with whom he visited.

While Kennedy spoke quietly with Mr. Castillo, Sarah wandered toward a table covered with Azalee's pictures. She watched the child grow, picture to picture, from baby, toddler, energetic child, to high school, standing with classmates. Each girl wore a white blouse and dark skirt; the boys, white shirts and dark trousers.

Then, as a young adult, Azalee appeared alone, in group shots, and with her parents. Sarah saw a beautiful, mature young woman. Different from the pictures, the gore, that Sarah had seen less than a week before. Different from pictures she had studied, cried over, edited, and would never forget.

Sarah studied the photographs.

Different, she thought.

Very different, indeed.

19

Back on the bus, Kennedy made sure Sarah sat next to the window.

"Did you learn anything about Christopher," he asked. He'd learned a little about the young man during the wake, but not enough to be elated, and certainly not enough to be able to find him.

Sarah, more quiet than usual, shook her head. "Didn't mention him."

Kennedy felt the chill but reckoned it best to ignore her mood swing. "The parents never met him," he said, "though Azalee apparently talked about him every time she came home. Said he was six inches taller than her father, which made him a giant among Belizeans. Maybe a six-footer."

His statements of fact garnered not even a nod.

Following the George Price Highway—aka the Western Highway—from San Ignacio back toward Belize City, the bus passed through Belmopan, the capital city of Belize, but he reckoned Sarah might not be too interested in a geography lesson.

He got back on track. "Azalee had planned to quit the restaurant, leave PG, and get a job in San Pedro." Then he answered the question Sarah had not asked. "Better pay, more tourists, more tips."

Sarah—either self-absorbed or upset—gave him a patronizing nod.

He'd learned long ago to never ask her what she was mad about, for fear of making her even madder. But he kept going, as if he were the lead in a one-man play.

"Scared me to death when we barged into the wake," he said, "us so casual, them so dressed up."

Not even a nod.

He kept going, not to be mean but hoping to touch on something that might bring her around. "I was amazed by the respect I got when they heard I'd taken the pictures. Like they were more concerned for my feelings than for what the sharks had done."

He stared out the window, replaying the scene in the Castillos' living room. A mile of jungle whizzed by. "Nobody asked a morbid question," he added to the one-sided conversation. "And nobody queried details."

He peeked at Sarah's profile. Stoic. Or deaf.

So he rambled on, words he needed to say, though missing feedback. "Her father got teary," he said, "when he told me about Azalee not showing up at home during her days off. He'd tried to comfort his wife, but she'd insisted something was wrong. He said he hadn't even been worried until the neighbor blindsided him with the newspaper."

Sarah didn't move.

Kennedy leaned forward in his seat and looked into her face. "This is stupid. Are you awake?"

She stared ahead, as if watching a movie. "I took a picture," she said.

"You brought a camera?"

"No," she said. "Took, not shot." She folded her hands in her lap and rocked back and forth, her face scrunched, her eyes glistening. "I stole a picture off the table. A picture of Azalee."

Kennedy's right foot jerked left and stomped on a nonexistent brake pedal, as if to stop the bus. "From the wake? A picture? For what?"

Sarah pulled a framed picture from her bag. She placed it in her lap, face up, and then tilted it toward Kennedy.

"Azalee Castillo is not the person in your pictures."

20

While waiting for the boat to Bacalar Vista, they drank Belikin Beer and shared chicken quesadilla at Pineapples @ Ramons Village. Kennedy had picked the restaurant based on Sarah's complaint that she'd experienced Mexican-food withdrawal symptoms every day since leaving Denver.

He spoke with his mouth full. "Tell me about the picture. Your conclusion."

She chewed and swallowed, took another bite, and then chewed and swallowed that too. "I told you. Not until we're at your place, please."

He leaned across the table, grocery sacks at his feet. "All I want to know," he said, "is where the hell you're coming from."

Over the next half hour of hushed-tone argument and second-guessing, he repeated three times: "Her mother and father identified her. Sergeant Gutierrez was there. I was there. The parents know their own daughter. The only issues are the boyfriend and the hamsa. Otherwise, case closed."

Sarah shook her head. "I agonized at the wake with what I should do," she said. "Tell Azalee's mother? Tell you? No. Take the picture. Dumb decision. As soon as I did, I wished I hadn't, but it was too late. I considered dumping the picture and never telling you, but there's—"

"Sarah. Forget the picture. Case closed."

"No, damn it. It's not." She leaned across the table, hissed her words. "I know women's faces. Subtle differences a man will never see. And I just spent a long night looking at every detail of Azalee Castillo's disappearing face." She flashed the stolen photo. "If this is Azalee, she's not who died."

Kennedy, working hard to keep his cool, got up from the table, talked to a waiter, and returned with a copy of the days-old newspaper. He folded the front page to put Azalee's "best picture" on top.

Sarah, not missing a beat, laid the stolen photo beside the newsprint picture.

Kennedy looked, made the comparison. "Clones," he said. "Or identical twins." He pushed the paper and photo to Sarah. "Or maybe even the same person."

Sarah pursed her lips. "We'll see."

Headwaiter Alberto met Kennedy and Sarah at the Bacalar Vista dock. Krash, tied to a short, bright-yellow poly line, danced beside Alberto. "She got out early this afternoon, Mr. Kenn. Probably something happened—maybe maintenance or the cleaners left the door open. But we had fun."

Kennedy squatted, face to face with his canine pal, and massaged her ears. "Yes, Krash," he said. "All's forgiven. Let's go home." He returned the rope to Alberto and let Krash run free so he could carry the grocery sacks.

Krash ran circles around fellow residents, chairs, the pool, but never too far from Kennedy and Sarah, whom she ran back to every few seconds as if to make sure they hadn't abandoned her again.

But something wasn't right. Krash limped.

Kennedy went to his knees, and Krash bounded to him. He patted her down, found two tender areas— left ribs, right hindquarter. He rubbed each spot lightly, but she twisted away from his hand, otherwise ready to play. "Is there a story?" he asked. "You fly down the stairs again?" He let her go, watched her run, shook his head.

"I like Alberto's take on it," Sarah said. "'Probably something happened.'"

At the condo, Kennedy slipped off his sandals, his hands loaded with plastic bags.

Sarah prodded his ribs to get him out of the way so she could open the door.

Krash ran in and barked. An angry bark.

Kennedy saw inside, froze. His living room deep in papers. Desk contents, scattered. File drawer, upside down. He listened for Krash—nothing.

Sarah grabbed his arm, moved in close. "Don't go in," she said. "They might still—"

"Krash stopped barking. Nobody's here."

"Robbery?" Sarah asked. "What's worth stealing?"

Fishing gear came to mind, but Kennedy noted the mess was central to his desk. "The pictures."

"Of the body?" Sarah said. "I don't understand."

He didn't answer as he weaved around and stepped over rubble, carried the groceries into the kitchen, and opened the fridge. Mind racing, he stuffed meat and cheese into one drawer, vegetables into another. The rest—bottles and cans still in plastic sacks—he crammed onto a shelf above the sink as a pressure in his head hissed for release. Open palms slammed against the countertop.

He faced Sarah. "They run the goddamn article, name me as the photographer, and give my address. The pictures have value because there's a market for gore. What's not to understand?"

Sarah bristled. "You, yelling, damn it. I didn't do this, so back off. And if you want my help, ask nice."

Kennedy held up his hands, nodded his apology.

"Is your system password protected?" she asked.

Kennedy shook his head. "Not since I left the States."

"Figure out what's missing," she said, "and then we'll know."

Teeth grinding, he left her in the kitchen, righted his desk chair, and turned on his computer, expecting it to be fried. His screen saver blossomed with a new message: **ADIOS AZLEE**.

Hah! Definitely after the photos. But Azalee—

misspelled? Accident? On purpose? Could be anybody. Even the boyfriend.

Finding his computer in seemingly good health, he allowed optimism to edge its way into his rage. Then he found his empty photo files. He checked "Trash" and found it empty too. His external-hard-drive-backup system, also without a password, was as empty as the day he bought it. Anger rebuilding and no longer looking for photos, he checked his personal files: taxes, medical records, investment accounts, email records—gone.

Thirty-eight short stories—gone.

His *Blood Ruins* manuscript file—three hundred and thirty pages of fiction, dozens of hard-earned revisions, all backup copies—gone.

Sarah tapped his shoulder and handed him a mojito, a strong mojito.

He knew it was strong because he inhaled half a swig down the wrong pipe and coughed like a smoker on a binge. When he finally gagged an almost normal breath, Sarah waved her hand in front of his face. He gave her a thumbs up.

"What's the verdict?" she asked, and then sipped her own drink.

Kennedy spoke in a barely audible rasp. "Double the rum. It'll be perfect."

Sarah laughed—the first Kennedy had heard all day.

"And the computer?" she asked.

"Empty."

"What about your backup harddrive, CDs? DVDs? Thumb drives? The thumb drive you hid from the police?"

He pointed to an empty shelf. "Gone."

"Seems like they went to a lot of trouble," she said, "if they only wanted the pictures. Where's your camera?"

In its special place. He looked at the spot on a corner shelf. The empty spot. "It's gone."

"How about money? Cash?"

Kennedy shrugged, not remotely interested.

Sarah pushed harder. "Let's check."

He trudged to the master bedroom, to the safe in his walk-in closet. He punched in numbers and looked inside, Sarah behind him. "Undisturbed," he said. "How about your stuff?"

Though they shared Kennedy's king-size bed, Sarah had moved her belongings into the guest bedroom. She went directly to a black, soft-sided briefcase. "It's been opened," she said, "but hard to tell if anything's missing."

While Kennedy watched, she pulled out her laptop, booted it without problems, and checked a few files. "Seems OK," she said. "So why so rough on your system without bothering mine?"

"I had what they wanted . . . pictures of Azalee."

"Or . . . not Azalee," she said.

"And now we'll never know."

Sarah squinted. "You're kidding, of course."

He mustered a shrug.

Quick with her hands, she again opened her laptop files, inserted a thumb drive, downloaded the photos, ejected the thumb drive, and handed it to Kennedy. "Now you have all the photos, originals and edited, if nothing else."

"Yeah, right," he said. "If nothing else."

"Before you spend another hour beating yourself up about this, and since it seems to be related, you'll recall our discussion about clones and twins. You ready to hear what I have to say?"

Kennedy would rather have taken the next hour to find and pay back whoever had trashed his computer, but said, "I need a pit stop first."

"I'll check my email," Sarah said.

"Good luck getting a connection," he said as he closed the bathroom door. Inside, he wished he had been home an hour earlier, or that Krash had been able to—

He stopped cold. Krash. The bastard kicked her. Rising blood pressure throbbed in his temples—

Sarah spoke from just outside the door. "Kenn, I need to show you something." *Now*, the tone of her voice seemed to say.

She was still there, in the hallway, when he finished drying his hands. "You OK?" he asked.

"No." She led him back to her laptop, sat and pointed.

A short email filled the screen: **BOTH GO HOME BITCH OR YOUR CHUM TO**. It was signed **EL TORRO**.

Kennedy read it again. "Doesn't make sense. Who's it from, and when?"

Sarah pointed to the screen. "El Torro is all I know, and it came from *your* email address to me, about three hours ago."

"Mine? That means—"

She said, "It's from the bastard who trashed your place."

"That, I get," he said, "but why the hell would he threaten you?"

Sarah stood hard from the desk chair, tipping it to the floor. "Well, Kenn, I just don't know." She shoved the toppled chair with her foot. "But I'd say this growing pile of bullshit—a dead body, robbery, vandalism, and now a death threat—stinks just a bit too much for me. What do you say I just pack up my stuff, go home, and get the bastard off my case."

Kennedy righted the chair. "Sarah, you have that right because a threat's a threat. But if all he wants are the pictures, he's got them, and that's the end of the story from our side."

Her face hardened. "Lock the front door; we don't need company." She pushed the chair back to Kennedy's desk. "We need to talk about Azalee. Right now."

While Kennedy watched, she opened the first of the seven edited pictures, its clarity pristine, and placed Azalee's equally pure portrait, from the wake, beside the screen. Then, point by point, she compared the noses: length, width, perkiness, nostril orientation. "Even ignoring the gunk in her nostrils," she said, "they're different noses."

Kennedy studied the picture. "They should look different, with her skin all puffy and wrinkled, plus the underwater distortion. I know what my hands look like after an hour in the hot tub."

"Could be," Sarah said, "but despite the unnatural wrinkles, they're still different noses. And speaking of hands, I need to show you her hand, so remind me later."

The eyes and eyebrows—width, length, tilt, fullness—got Sarah's same comparative attention. "Conclusion," she said, "different eyes, regardless of the water."

He shook his head, seeing details only as Sarah described them, but having no basis for debate.

She continued. "Let's talk about teeth." She pointed to the "best shot" of the dead woman. "That dark line is a gap between her front teeth." She opened three other frontal partial-face shots and zoomed in. "Four for four," she said. "A gap between her two front teeth." She then pointed to Azalee's picture from the wake. "Perfect teeth. No gap."

Kennedy shook his head. "So why didn't her parents notice something so obvious?"

Sarah held the front page of the newspaper under the light and compared the primary picture to the image on the screen. "Even without zooming in," she said, "a lot of detail disappeared between your digital pictures and the blurry front page, including the space between her front teeth."

Kennedy scanned the picture on the screen—the digital picture he had taken—and sucked in a deep breath. "So, unless being submerged changed the spacing of her teeth," he said, "the dead woman's not Azalee."

"Definitely not Azalee," Sarah said, "though they could be sisters."

Kennedy could only whisper, "Tell me about her hand."

Sarah opened the big file of pictures, clicked through a dozen, and then stopped. She shifted the focal point to get a toothy barracuda out of the way and focused on the right hand. "I meant to mention it the night you sent me the pictures," she said. "Her hand and the remaining fingers are lacerated and torn. Lots of little cuts, and some big ones."

Kennedy studied the picture, seeing the small wounds for the first time. "Those aren't fish bites," he said. "That's from coral."

"Her knees and feet are the same," Sarah said.

He pulled up a chair. "Show me more."

The superficial injuries Sarah brought to the screen were trivial compared to the carnage wielded by the sharks. But Kennedy had seen such cutting wounds before—on his own hands, knees, and thighs after a wave washed him into the coral wall and he'd hung on just long enough to escape back into deeper water. And even one coral cut, he recalled, hurt like a sonofabitch. The deep coral cuts on the woman's body—right hand, knees, feet, hips—meant one thing: "Whatever her name," he said, "she fought to survive the coral, and she fought to keep her head above water, for a damn long time."

Sarah wiped her eyes. "I can't imagine how scared she must have been."

"Makes me think she might have started outside the reef," Kennedy said, "but made it to the coral. Based on all her cuts, she fought to hang on, but the swells eventually carried her over the coral and into shallow water." He put his hand on Sarah's shoulder. "She had to have been dead by then, or hurt too bad to make it to the beach. Either way, when I first saw her—her body—she was headed *out* the cut, with the tide, into deep water."

"So close to living," Sarah said, "only to die."

Kennedy stared into the screen, his focus beyond pixels. "And we know only one thing about her. She's not Azalee. Which means we've got a good-news-bad-news problem for Azalee's parents."

"I get the good news. What's the bad?"

He sat up straight. "Tomorrow's her memorial service."

Sarah got out of her chair and leaned back against the kitchen counter. "Yeah, that needs to get fixed, but there's this other little problem" She spread and waved her arms to encompass the debris-strewn room. "This break-in is obviously *not* about Azalee."

Kennedy, too, glanced around the room, pictured the intruder, pictured walking in his shoes. "Which means somebody doesn't want me—or us—to find out who the dead woman is."

Sarah, glass in hand, picked up Kennedy's tumbler. "I'm doubling my rum, too, big guy, so you better watch out."

At two in the morning, Kennedy held her close, his hand coursing up and down the small of her back. He nestled her head in the crook of his arm and stared into the blackness of the room.

"Spit it out," she said. "I know when you're not with me."

He adjusted his arm, moved her closer. "The guy knows who I am," he said, "where I live, and that I took the pictures he worked so hard to steal. Which tells me that he—or the person who hired him to steal the photos—knows who the dead woman is. And now, by chance, he knows who you are and that you are with me."

Again, he flexed his arm. "He's on the offense, Sarah, and the only way we can change that is to find out who he is."

Nothing for a long beat, and then her words were soft, driven by baby-warm breath. "I love you, Kenn Bracken." Her hand stroked his chest. "But I'll love you even more when you quit chasing ghosts."

Chasing ghosts? he wondered. The dead woman? Maybe. But someone out there was alive, and he'd gotten Kennedy's attention.

Sarah snuggled in closer and stopped moving her

hands.

Kennedy got the message and yielded to the night. He let himself go, glad for all they shared, glad for their time together, glad she was so easy to love.

But he couldn't shake the thought that at the top of his never-forgive list was somebody who had likely killed a woman, threatened Sarah's life, assaulted Krash, and wiped out his computer.

21

Sarah considered her Tuesday morning options and recommended breakfast in the palapa. They shared fry jacks dipped in honey and drank black coffee before walking the dock to catch the early morning boat. She delayed getting aboard, as the stiff sea breeze warned her the ride would be bumpy. Imagination running wild, she pictured herself bounced around, thrown overboard, chopped up by the propellers—*screws*, Kennedy called them.

Kennedy took her arm and pointed to a guy fishing in shallow water near the dock. "Sarah, I need to get you out there. Women take to fly-fishing better than most men do. They more easily find the rhythm, are more patient, and don't depend on muscle to manage the rod."

"Yeah, right," she said. "And they walk around in the ocean, which is full of grass and sponges and crabs, and try to sneak up on fish, which I'm not about to do. Ever."

She hoped that ended the subject.

As soon as they boarded, Kennedy pointed to a small, unoccupied seat in front of the steering column. "It's called the princess seat because it's the best place to ride." He sat facing her, on her left, so he could watch the shoreline during their trip to town, his thoughts, no doubt on the break-in, on Krash, on the photos—

By Sarah's measure, the water was rough. Those passengers in the front of the boat held on with each bump and tried to duck the spray. Kennedy, in the middle of the port side, got wet, but the smooth-as-a-kiss ride in the princess seat, she rapidly concluded, wasn't so damn bad.

Sarah held Kennedy's arm as they dodged golf carts down Front and Middle Streets and walked into the police station. She wondered if Sergeant Gutierrez would throw her in jail for stealing the picture.

Kennedy had apparently thought about her concern. "You're welcome to talk," he said, "or just listen."

"Me?" Sarah said. "The sergeant's favorite Jewess? Not talk? We'll see."

His chest and shoulders sagged. "Please don't go there."

Before Sarah could answer, a young male officer beckoned them to follow and escorted them into Sergeant Gutierrez's office, where handshakes and reintroductions took only a moment.

Gutierrez folded his hands on his desk and looked directly at Kennedy. "How can I be of service?"

"First, somebody broke into my condo last night. My computer files, all the photos you saw, my camera—everything was either deleted or taken."

Sergeant Gutierrez leaned back in his seat. Lips puckered, face hardened, he shook his head and nodded a couple of times, as if mixing a martini. "Without knowing why they broke in, or why they would steal the pictures, you should have left the thumb drive with me. What else?"

While Kennedy pulled a folded piece of paper from his shopping bag, Sarah said to Sergeant Gutierrez, "I have an idea. Maybe you can find the thief and, you know, like arrest him." She smiled her biggest smile.

Gutierrez nodded to Sarah. "Maybe." Then he turned to Kennedy. "What else?"

Kennedy unfolded and handed the paper to the officer. "Second, whoever broke in left a threatening note. An email."

The officer read the note and then turned the paper over like there might be more on the other side. "And you found this paper where?" he asked.

"The message was sent to me," Sarah said, "from Kenn's computer. As soon as we read it, we made that copy."

Gutierrez looked at Kennedy. "Did you send the note, Mr. Bracken?"

"No, sir. It was time-stamped three hours before

we saw it. I presume it was sent by the guy who broke in."

"About whom we know at least two things," Gutierrez said. He paused and studied the note, as if waiting.

Sarah couldn't wait. "And what might those two things be, officer?"

"Well, he wants *you* out of town, which means he could be almost anybody, and he's illiterate, or pretending to be."

A pressure built in Sarah's gut—

"Sergeant Gutierrez," Kennedy said, "that's all we know about the note. Perhaps our next topic will show you its significance."

He pulled the framed picture from the shopping bag and placed it on the officer's desk. "Azalee Castillo," he said.

Sergeant Gutierrez looked at the picture. "Beautiful young woman." He looked at his watch. "They bury her memory today. A memorial service in her name."

Sarah held her breath as Kennedy leaned toward the officer.

"There's a problem, sir," Kennedy said. "We believe the dead girl, the person in *my* pictures, is not Azalee Castillo. And that's why somebody broke into my place . . . to take, and probably destroy, the photos, as the only evidence of the dead woman's true identity."

Sergeant Gutierrez moved not a single muscle.

Kennedy continued. "If you load the seven pictures of the woman's face, we can show you differences, many differences, that—"

"No!" Gutierrez, his face brilliant red, stood slowly, as if by levitation, his eyes locked on Kennedy's. "I will not hear of this," he said, articulating each word. "You defile the memory of Miss Castillo. You insult a mother's ability to identify her own daughter. You come forward on the very day the memory of the child is to be laid to rest." He clinched his fists, leaned forward, knuckles on his desk, as if a silverback gorilla. For the first time, he moved his head, looked fully at Sarah, and then back to Kennedy. "First a trinket and mysterious Jews, and then a robbery and an idiot's threatening note, and now you want me to insult the girl's family on this holy day."

He handed the note and photograph back to Kennedy. "I do not know what game you are playing, Mr. Bracken, Ms. McGarrity, but do not take me for a fool. This office is not a playground, and I am not your playmate." He pointed toward the door. "Enjoy your day."

Bullshit, Sarah thought. She scrunched her face and threw Gutierrez her evilest eye, unable to condone his lack of action. She believed in action. Action-reaction. Let him push—she'd rebel. Let him do nothing—she'd rebel even more.

Kennedy lightly gripped her arm and guided her to her feet. "No harm intended," he told Gutierrez.

"We'll be back when our evidence is more convincing."

"Don't hurry, Mr. Bracken," Gutierrez said. "I won't be waiting for you."

Sarah's face burned and her skull throbbed, but she followed Kennedy's silent lead down the hall and into the street.

Twenty feet of dodging golf carts was all she could take. She stopped, turned Kennedy toward her, and did her hissing whisper trick. "Doesn't anything ever piss you off? You could've at least pounded his desk and made him look at the picture—but, no, you practically apologized, as if we're the ones who screwed up." She stopped, but only to breathe.

"Every accident," Kennedy said, "and every death I ever investigated was ultimately resolved." His voice was soft; his words, firm. "Never once in all those years did I need Gutierrez's help." Then something harsh Sarah had rarely seen crossed his face. "And we don't need his help with this one either."

"We?" she asked, enjoying a thrill she hadn't felt in a long time—witnessing Kennedy exuding emotion outside his bedroom.

"Yes," he said. "We. You're included in the threat, which we damn sure need to resolve."

"Now we're talking," Sarah said, unable to quell her excitement. "Any man who calls a woman a bitch and himself El Torro is a lost-cause idiot. And if we can just figure out who the hell he is, I'll give up an hour or two of pool time and help you kick his ass."

Kennedy grinned and held up the flat of his hand, which she met with a vigorous high-five slap.

Feeling tough, she hugged his arm. "Buy me a beer and maybe a gun, big guy—I may have to pack heat to get through this." She refrained from laughing on the outside, because she was so damn mad on the inside, and laughing might push her fear-filled bladder over the threshold.

22

"Sorry I missed that," Kennedy said, glad that Sarah had finally quit ranting about Gutierrez.

She showed him an ad in a Belize magazine as they walked down Front Street. "If you're going to feed me, how about the Coconut Cafe?"

"Great fish dishes, curries, and Indian food, as good as it gets, especially for dinner. For an easy lunch, though, the Blue Water Grill has excellent seafood."

"That's good to know, but put the Coconut Cafe on my vacation-in-paradise dinner agenda." She stopped, bugged her eyes, and opened her mouth. "Oh, wait. Paradise? How can that be?" The animation disappeared. "Since so far it's been abysmal, most of our time spent on doomed-to-failure detective work, with a couple of hours of private time as the only exceptions."

Kennedy wanted no part of the topic other than how to fix it, which for Sarah meant food. "Then it's the Coconut Cafe for dinner," he said, "tomorrow night, Wednesday. We'll take the Bacalar Vista dinner boat round trip. I'll make reservations."

Sarah's face sagged as soon as he said *boat*, so he forced a smile.

She didn't return it.

For lunch, Sarah ordered black-bean-crusted snook, smothered in a caramelized banana-curry sauce. "And coconut rice," she added.

Kennedy stuck to his favorite—Japanese spiced grouper in vinaigrette gravy.

The weather, the sea breeze, the open-air decor— such was the small talk that filled the time until their drinks arrived.

Sarah sipped and complimented the tangy coolness of her lime drink. "Between the hamsa and the wrong identification," she said, "I don't think Sergeant Gutierrez likes you. I have a few thoughts, but do you care to share your plan?"

Kennedy wrapped his hand around his beer. "There's something going on that we're missing."

"Yeah, I'd say something's going on. They're burying somebody without a body, and for good reason. And what might that be? Try this: she's not dead."

Kennedy checked on the waiter and made sure they were alone. "You and I know this isn't about Azalee," he said, "who's maybe just MIA. It's about somebody who abandoned a swimmer, or dumped a body, and reported nothing. They might have laughed when Azalee's parents 'found their daughter' because by then the corpse was already digested. I once thought somebody might steal the pictures to make a buck, but now it's obvious they're covering up the dead girl's real ID."

"MIA?"

"Missing in action," he said. "Azalee off doing her thing. Not dead."

"Since she's alive and Gutierrez doesn't care— why should we?"

"Because if we were related to either Azalee or the dead woman, there'd be no way we could, or would, walk away."

"Be serious," she said, "we're not related."

"Right, but now throw in a death threat, demanding us—*you and me*—to quit, hide, and run away. Sarah, I don't take threats lightly. I'm not running away, whether or not Gutierrez helps, and I assume you won't run either."

Sarah threw in a crooked grin and nodded.

Good enough, Kennedy thought. "Welcome aboard, partner."

23

They stayed in the Bacalar Vista pool until the sun dipped low and the temperature dropped into the upper seventies. Kennedy noticed Sarah hugging herself, shivering. "A real cold front," he teased as he wrapped a thick beach towel around her shoulders.

"Temperature's OK," she said, "but the breeze gives me chicken skin."

"Then let's get dried off and have the dinner special in the palapa. Or do you want to shower first?"

"Hot shower now," she said, "and a nap. We can eat later."

Later, they lay side by side on their backs. He checked the wall clock. "It's eight twenty," he said. "You down for the count, or ready for dinner?"

"Exhausted but famished," she said. "Let's eat here."

"Then how about something special? I'll cook."

She leaned on her left elbow. "And the chef's

offering what choices?"

Kennedy thought about it too long, which got him a jab in his ribs. He grunted, rubbed his side, and faked pain. "Be easy," he said, "the chef's just going over all the stuff you bought, matching the ingredients with my gourmet cookbook."

"I'll give you a hint—your fridge and cabinets are full."

"Then it's either oatmeal, or bacon and eggs."

"Crisp bacon, eggs over easy, fruit salad, coffee, and nut bread toast. How long do I have?"

"Three or four minutes. Maybe ten."

Kennedy leaned back in his chair, plate empty, appetite sated. "So if it's not Azalee's body, whose is it?"

"Normally," Sarah said, "the victim's known and the killer's hard to identify."

"Whoa. Killer? What happened to Gutierrez's accident?"

Sarah steepled her fingers. "First, the Castillos aren't even involved, because the dead woman isn't Azalee. Second, if it was an accident, somebody would have raised an alarm or filed a missing person report. Third, somebody stole the evidence, your photos. So, in conclusion, I say it wasn't an accident. Maybe suicide. But probably murder."

Kennedy nodded, a fan of thoughtful logic. "I can't go with suicide, but if she fell or was pushed off a friendly party boat and couldn't be found, it would have been reported. But if somebody pushed her overboard and then took off . . . that's no accident. Based on the coral cuts, she tries to survive, but she drowns, and the sharks eventually get her."

"That's murder," Sara said. "And nobody knows she's even dead. There's no reported accident, and nobody's reported missing, until your pictures hit the street."

"And what a godsend—the Castillos are convinced the dead girl is their daughter, and the police aren't willing to think otherwise."

Sarah didn't answer, her face white.

"I'm sorry," he said. "I know sharks aren't your favorite topic."

"I'm OK, but do you think the sharks were planned, or a convenient accident?"

Kennedy shifted and got more comfortable. "Sharks are attracted to protein, whether alive and thrashing around, like the woman in Mexico, or dead and floating, like the body I saw here. And to the sharks, the path the Belizean woman took to enter their food chain didn't matter. She was there; they were hungry."

"Then why aren't there more shark attacks?" Sarah asked. "You said Belize never had a reported shark death until this one."

Kennedy, too, had questioned why. "I'm telling you a lot more than I know," he said, "but maybe there's so much food here, natural food, the sharks aren't looking for new stuff, stuff that doesn't look right—like people."

"Then why two deaths in two days? Here and in Cancún."

"I don't know," he said. "They're obviously unrelated, but there's something niggling about the timing—only a day apart."

A long pause before she said closed her eyes and faked a snore.

"Me too," Kennedy said, wide awake

Kennedy pushed a button on his watch—2:25—the night black outside his open window. Unable to sleep, he'd thought about the timing coincidence for almost an hour, his mind a kaleidoscope of unanswered questions.

He disengaged from Sarah's inside spoon position. Snoring, she didn't move. Making stealth moves, he poured a cup of cold coffee into a mug and zapped it in the microwave. He opened the microwave door just before the countdown hit zero.

Sipping the brew, he fired up his computer and typed "woman, shark attack, Mexico" and then read several new articles in detail. Not because he wasn't interested in the Belize death, about which he knew more than the press would ever know, but because the articles about the death in Mexico and the Cancún police investigation that followed made such a big deal about the family's tragic loss.

Fueled by the news reports with more information, old thoughts rumbled and festered and refused to go away: a woman—sailing with her husband, two college kids, and a friend—had died chumming sharks for fun.

He'd chummed for catfish as a kid—so he could catch them. He'd chummed for wahoo and other game fish when deep-sea fishing—so he could catch them. He'd had a barracuda take a hooked snapper, and then a shark took the barracuda while he was trying to reel it in—chum not needed.

So, chumming sharks? Driving them into a frenzy? While sailing?

Beyond stupid.

Kennedy had spent his formal work years in zero-tolerance construction projects. Do nothing stupid. Make no mistakes. Do everything right the first time. Mechanical failures, injuries, deaths—accident investigation—all a big deal to him. Not only after something bad happened, but on paper, *before* it happened. His forte was the "What ifs." What if *this* goes wrong? What if *that* fails? What if *somebody falls overboard into a shark feeding frenzy?*

Had nobody in the family wondered, "What if?"

Back in bed, eyes open, he pictured the mother in the water, father and kids screaming, sharks moving in. *That scenario* the family would have seen.

Kennedy reckoned that what followed, after the mother disappeared below the surface, had been every bit as brutal as what he had seen in Belize.

He missed the logic of what the family had done, and he needed to understand what had gone wrong. He needed to understand the accident.

And he needed to know if the chumming tragedy in Mexico was in some way related to the poorly written email note sent to Sarah—"*Both go home bitch or your chum to.*"

24

Kennedy made coffee. "I got us flights to Cancún," he said. "Eight-o'clock boat, in time for Tropic Air to Corozal, on the border. There, we'll take a taxi into Mexico, to Chetumal, where we'll catch a flight to Cancún. Couple hours talking to the police, and we'll come back the same way. What would you like for breakfast?"

Sarah—looking gaunt, draped in a white bathrobe, and standing stone-still in the hallway by the kitchen—did a double take, as if noticing she wasn't alone. "Good morning," she said. "How'd you sleep? What day is it?"

Kennedy waved his hands before her face and asked if she was OK.

"If you're cooking"—her voice cracked—"oatmeal with raisins, and a small fruit salad."

"I'm cooking," he said. "I slept OK, though not a lot. And it's Wednesday." He pulled out a bowl and a zip bag stuffed with oatmeal. "Have a seat. I'll get your coffee. And we've got plenty of time before the eight o'clock boat."

She squinted her eyes. "The boat? Again? Why? Shopping?"

"No. Cancún. Me and you. Investigating a chummy little shark attack."

Sarah collapsed into a seat at the table and made a two-handed grab for the cup of coffee Kennedy handed her. A half-dozen sips later, an aura of awareness, marked by flared nostrils and deep breathing, told Kennedy she was now fully awake.

She tilted her head, eyes drifting, as if visualizing a world map. "Cancún?" she asked. Something in her face evolved from inquisitive, to perplexed, to pissed. "What the *hell* are you talking about? I came to Belize to see you, to enjoy the hype you've thrown at me for a year. I've had two meals in the palapa, three hours at the pool, a dozen boat trips to and from town— twice to see the police—plus my fill of dinky-ass plane trips and bus rides to God knows where."

Kennedy pulled the steaming bowl from the microwave and held it toward her, showing off the finished product. "Oatmeal with raisins," he said. "What would you like in it?"

"Cinnamon and a sweetener, no butter," she said. "Why Cancún?"

Kennedy held up the coffee pot. "Need a refill?"

"Yes," she said. "But you're ignoring me. Why Cancún?"

Kennedy topped off her cup and sat beside her. "I don't know," he said. "Maybe for naught. But I spent the night trying to figure out why anybody would chum sharks."

"Maybe they were drunk."

"It was a family," he said. "Mother, father, two teenage kids. And a guest, a woman."

Sarah wagged her head. "And the mother fell in."

"Which doesn't make sense," he said. "If you're sailing, you're careful not to fall overboard. And if you're like any normal person, petrified of sharks, and if you're feeding them into a frenzy, you'd be even more careful than usual."

"Count me out," Sarah said. "You chum for sharks. I'm staying home."

"That's my point. For the story to hold water, the mother had to be either drunk, stupid, or physically dysfunctional. None of which was mentioned in the dozen articles I read online in the middle of the night."

"So, other than raw compassion for the shark-bait mother, why do you care?"

Kennedy moved his plate and folded his hands. "Because sharks ate an unidentified woman in Belize last Tuesday. On Wednesday, two hundred miles north, near Cancún, another woman disappeared, and she was presumed eaten by sharks. And all we know is that she was someone's mother. Neither woman's body will ever be recovered."

"Once again, why do you care?"

Kennedy nodded. "Three reasons," he said. "I want to know *who* died in Belize. And I want to know *why* someone died a stupid chum-related death in Cancún . . . right before our photos were stolen and we got a warning note about being chum too. And I hate coincidences."

"What coincidence?" Sarah projected her voice, her face strained with skepticism. "Are you thinking the body you found on Tuesday was the woman who died on Wednesday?"

"I don't know what I'm thinking," he said. "Maybe the Mexican date is a typo and the mother fell in on Tuesday."

Sarah's shoulders slumped. "Kenn, give me a break. The Mexicans might screw up the date, but how do you intend to erase the little two-hundred-mile problem?"

Yeah, the two-hundred-mile problem was one of several he'd thought about during the night. A woman in Belize, not Azalee, her age unknown. A mother of college students in Mexico. A day apart. Those were the facts.

"Sarah, I don't know," he said. "I'm up to my ass in memories I can't shake, internet news reports, bits and pieces of police statements, and crap from unnamed sources quoted in the media. I'm grasping for meaning, trying to get this behind me. I'm hoping I can do that in Cancún, by talking to the police, which is why I'm going. And I'd like you to go with me."

Sarah wiped her mouth on a floral-pattern table napkin and then folded it neatly and put it beside her empty bowl. "To Cancún," she said. "In the middle of my Belize vacation." She folded her hands, her fingers interlocked, her knuckles white. She looked at the wall clock. "I'll be ready in twenty minutes, but you owe me big time."

Owing Sarah didn't scare Kennedy—they'd worked out their differences before. But if the trip north imploded, she'd head back to Denver. And if that were to happen, she'd likely never set another foot in Belize.

He wondered about the odds of it being a wasted trip. A Cancún nightmare. Her reaction explosive.

Fifty-fifty at best, he thought.

Good enough.

25

Kennedy paid the Cancún cab driver, and he and Sarah once again entered a police station, this one Mexican, some sort of headquarters, as recommended by an officer at the airport. The place was full of people, and each person fit into one of two groups: those dressed for the business of the day and those not so well composed. Some with sad faces, others in custody, still others waiting to visit with someone of high authority.

A rock-solid, uniformed officer sat at a reception desk and looked up, ready to help.

"I'm Kennedy Bracken, and this is my assistant, Sarah—"

The officer politely interrupted. "*No hablo ingles. Un momento, por favor.*"

Sarah held up her thumb and index finger about an inch apart. "*Un poquito español.*"

Kennedy, impressed with Sarah's hidden language talent, could only listen as the young officer rattled on about something, his hands wagging in concert with his snare-drum-paced response to Sarah.

When he stopped to take a breath, Sarah held out her hands, exasperation on her face. Again, up came her thumb and index finger, this time the tips almost touching. *"Muy, muy poquito español."*

Well, Kennedy thought, maybe it's a *minor* hidden talent.

The officer's face died. He picked up his desk phone, punched two buttons, and spoke rapidly.

Almost immediately, a matronly woman officer walked directly to the reception desk and listened as the young officer handed over *"Señor* Bracken," as if Kennedy were alone.

The officer spoke to Kennedy. "Come with me, please." She exited the area and scurried down a hall—Kennedy and Sarah close behind—and into an office, where she closed the door behind her guests.

"Please be seated," she said. "How may I help you?"

"I'm Kennedy Bracken, and this is my assistant, Sarah McGarrity." The words flowed smoothly as he sat in one of two guest chairs facing the officer, who sat at her desk. "We're freelance journalists doing a job for *Sports Illustrated*," he lied, "and we're writing an article about shark attacks. We'd like to speak to you, or to one of the other senior officers, about the recent tragic incident offshore Cancún."

The officer stiffened. "And you come here," she said, "into deep Mexico, expecting us to speak English, as if we're sitting in an office in Kansas City? Next you'll expect us to teach English in our schools, make our road signs in both English and Spanish, and treat you as if you are Mexican citizens."

Heat engulfed Kennedy. He opened his mouth—

"No, ma'am," Sarah said. "We like Mexico just the way it is." She sat forward in her seat. "I've studied Spanish, which I love, and I work with Hispanics every day. But this assignment is different from articles about baseball and golf, and I'm afraid I'll misunderstand other senior officers, and even the commandant, when they talk about the case. I just don't know the Spanish words for shark, drown, panic, fear, and so many more words I'll need when we talk to those officers who speak no English, as you do so well."

Kennedy nodded.

The officer seemed to deflate. "My apologies, Ms. McGarrity. No offense meant. I will take you to Capitan Lobos. Federico Lobos. He was in charge from the time the first call came in. May I see your business cards, please?"

Sarah dug out what Kennedy knew to be her official business card, showing her company— PNQ Inc.—address, phone, email, fax, and her impressive title *marketing director*. Kennedy's card gave his name, an email address, a PO Box in San Pedro, and a title *writer*.

The officer read the cards. "Please wait here," she said.

As soon as the door closed, Kennedy gave Sarah his best I'm-impressed look. "I'm impressed."

"My Spanish vocabulary?" she said. "You just heard all I know."

"That too," he said, "but I'm impressed you knew *Sports Illustrated* covered things like baseball and golf."

That got him an elbow.

Kennedy thanked the officer as she left her boss's office, and then he sat beside Sarah.

Captain Federico Lobos, less fluent in English than his subordinate, carefully read Kennedy's and Sarah's business cards. He queried Kennedy's Belize residence and Sarah's marketing job.

"I write about Caribbean activities," Kennedy said. "Articles about fishing, new properties, music, entertainment. Ms. McGarrity is a marketing specialist. We make a good team, especially with articles like the *Sports Illustrated* assignment."

Captain Lobos said he loved *Sports Illustrated*, especially the swimsuit edition. "*Muy impresionante*" were his words of choice each time he named from memory a model and the color and cut of her suit.

When the subject fizzled, he folded his hands and asked, "How can I be of service?"

Kennedy told him about the Belize investigation, the underwater photographs, the shock to the young woman's family. "We have copies of all the Belize police reports," he lied, "so that we can ensure accuracy of the article when published. And of course, the article will be worthless unless we do a good job in comparing it to the tragedy here in Mexican waters, which the Mexican authorities so capably handled."

"*Gracias, amigo.* We tried to find the body, to comfort her family."

Sarah opened her notebook. "Can you tell us what happened?"

Kennedy appreciated Sara taking notes. Teamwork.

"Yes, of course, *señora.*" Captain Lobos sat tall in his chair, pulled a file from a stack on his desk, and flipped pages. "The call was Wednesday night, from the husband, a few minutes after nine. We sent help. They searched in the dark and all the next day. They called off the search the second night."

"That had to be a difficult call for the husband," Kennedy said.

"Yes," Lobos said. "We have text of the radio call."

While the officer flipped pages, Kennedy could only hope Sarah would get the important parts.

Lobos read, "Mr. Perry: 'Emergency. Mayday. Send help. My wife fell overboard. Sharks are everywhere.'

Lobos continued. "Dispatcher: *'¿Cual es su ubicación?'*" He added, "I'm sorry, that means where are you located? I will translate the rest."

He returned to the transcript. "Perry: 'We left Cozumel two hours ago, headed north toward

Cancún. We're a fifty-two-foot, twin-mast catamaran, white, drifting, and we need help, now.'"

Lobos read silently, and then said. "Mr. Victor Perry reported his GPS latitude and longitude. Then there was a break in the call while our dispatcher reported the emergency."

Kennedy, intent on every word, glanced at Sarah, who was busy writing.

"Dispatcher: 'We have *Armada de México*, the Mexican Navy, in a patrol boat, on the way to your location. They will come from the south, maybe twenty minutes. Look for strobe lights. Flash your mast lights when you see the strobes. Now, please tell me about the accident.'"

Lobos continued. "Perry: 'We were chumming sharks.'"

"The dispatcher," Lobos said, "added a note that Mr. Perry was crying as he spoke."

Forget the crying, Kennedy thought. Get to the details.

Lobos: "Perry: 'The kids were cutting fish, throwing it to the sharks. My wife slipped and fell overboard. She screamed, and I stopped the boat as fast as I could, but we cannot find her.'

"Dispatcher: 'How old are your children?'

"Perry: 'Our kids are grown, in college. They're in a small runabout, circling, using a spotlight.'"

After a delay, Lobos said, "Mr. Perry's last words to the dispatcher were, 'I see the strobe lights. They are coming. Pray for my wife. And for my family.'"

Kennedy felt deprived—not nearly enough information for him to know what had happened.

Captain Lobos continued. "The *Armada de México* patrol boat escorted the sailing vessel into Cancún harbor the next day, where I personally met the family and began our investigation. We called off the search just after sundown that night, on Thursday."

"I thought the mother's fall was *accidental*," Sarah said. "Why the investigation?"

"As we might with any death at sea," Lobos said, "we put their boat in quarantine, and they were allowed to go to a hotel while we completed our study. Both children are in university and were anxious to get home. Though we released Mr. Perry and the boat, he contracted a company to sail his vessel to Tampa, in Florida. He and his kids, and the other lady, flew back yesterday morning."

"Why were they here so long?" Kennedy asked.

"Just a precaution, you understand, since the family is from *Los Estados Unidos*, where accidental death is commonly honored with a lawsuit. Here, in *México*, death is more often honored with prayer and respect."

Sarah spoke up. "You speak beautiful words, *Señor Capitan*. May I quote you on what you just said? I want American readers to know what a good job you and your fellow officers did both throughout the tragic event and with the investigation."

"Of course, *señora*. Thank you for your kindness."

"And because we know you're a busy man,"

Kennedy added, "and you don't have time to talk to us all day, would you be so kind as to let us read the file, or perhaps give us a copy that we can read during the next few days?"

"We can even mail the copies back to you," Sarah added, "if you need to have them returned,"

Captain Lobos studied Kennedy's eyes, as if looking for a hint of subterfuge. Then, without moving his head, he looked at Sarah. Kennedy guessed it was no time for her to blush.

"No copies, of course," Captain Lobos said, as he stood and buttoned his uniform jacket. "But I will put you in a room and let you look at the entire file until I return from lunch, in maybe two hours. If you leave before I am back, I will look for your story in *Sports Illustrated*."

Kennedy reckoned he wouldn't need more than a half hour. "Two hours," he said, "is very generous, captain. We'll leave your files in good order."

Minutes later, they sat in a small room that had open glass walls to a busy hallway and Captain Lobos's file on a table. They divided the paperwork, Kennedy with the first half of the file, Sarah with the rest. They scanned pages and discovered the bitter truth within seconds.

Sarah turned a page upside down. "Crap. Not a word in English."

Kennedy flipped pages. "I'm good at *uno* and *dos*, "but I don't see any. We need a helper."

Sarah looked through the glass wall. "Then find

somebody," she said. "Lobos is gone."

Kennedy liked her thinking. He stuck his head out the doorway, and after three tries found a young officer who spoke English. Well, almost.

Kennedy wrote on his palm with an imaginary pen, his gestures exaggerated. "Copy, for notes. For Captain Lobos."

"Yes. I make good copies."

Kennedy handed him the file and went back into the room.

Sarah closed the door. "Why didn't you go with him? What if he doesn't come back?"

"If I'm with him," Kennedy said, "we get questions we don't need. And if he doesn't come back, and we never see the files again, then I probably won't get thrown in jail today."

Kennedy clicked his seatbelt just before they departed Corozal for San Pedro. "Hang tough," he said. "One more flight, one more boat ride, and we'll be home."

"Speaking of home," Sarah said, "if you play your cards right, lying about *Sport's Illustrated* when you could be telling the truth, you can get the police in Belize and Mexico so mad you'll have to move back to Denver just to survive."

"Maybe," he said. "But telling Lobos about the Belize pictures will contribute nothing to us understanding the hard-to-believe chumming story.

26

Kennedy, carrying his small overnight backpack with the police reports inside, took a shortcut out the north gate from San Pedro's Tropic Air terminal, Sarah on his arm.

He managed small streets, headed west, until they arrived at the lagoon side of San Pedro, lined with small restaurants and boat docks. He pointed toward the boat they would take across the lagoon to dinner.

Sarah's jaw dropped. "The big black one?"

"No," he said. "That's the *Thunderbolt*. It's for high-speed commutes to and from Corozal, Mexico. We could have taken it today, but I thought you'd rather fly. For tonight, we get the little pontoon boat next to it . . . the one named *Pontoon Boat*."

"Good thing," Sarah said, "or you'd be eating alone."

Kennedy checked his watch. Conflicting emotions fought for his time. They had agreed to keep the bootleg copy of Lobos's file under wraps on both flights back to San Pedro, though he'd rather have foregone food and gotten down to reading. But with Sarah focused on dinner—a dinner she deserved—that wasn't an option.

He wrapped her arm in his. "Time to go," he said.

The free boat ride, headed west into the glow of sundown, delivered them four minutes later to a pristine dock, Coconut Cafe perched on the end. Kennedy held out his hand to help Sarah from the boat to the dock, where restaurant staff welcomed and escorted them to a table next to massive glass windows.

Kennedy leaned his backpack against his right foot and inhaled deeply. The Indo-Caribbean spiced aromas settled in his jaws, unleashed endorphins, made his mouth water. Perhaps waiting to work on the reports wouldn't be so bad after all.

Sarah wrinkled her nose. "What's that smell?"

Kennedy did an involuntary double take. "It's—"

"Just kidding," Sarah said. "It's lovely, and the view of San Pedro could be on the cover of a magazine." She reached across the table and held his hands. "It's wonderful to be in a nice restaurant, where we can take our time and just chat."

Kennedy's idea of chat lay at his feet—pages stolen from the Mexican police. No, he thought. Back off. "Yes," he said. "Tonight. Just you and me."

A petite waitress offered drinks. Sarah settled on a Jewel of India, enamored by its pomegranate liquor, vodka, and other *secret* ingredients.

Kennedy preferred rum and lime, but ordered a

Brahma Blue, picked not for its contents, but its name. Brahma. Bull. *El Torro*. Since the sonofabitch was on his mind.

Minutes later, Sarah sipped, looked down into the rose-colored drink, and inhaled deeply. "This, my friend, could get me in trouble."

Kennedy tasted his Brahma Blue. It made his jaws ache, the good kind of hurt. He sipped, and then sipped again, felt it slide down his throat, his taste buds pulsating as if drenched in a mix of fire, ice, and passion fruit. He hoisted his glass, licked his lips, and said, "If it's trouble you want, woman, count me in."

A second waiter listed the ingredients of every entrée, as if he'd tasted each bite he described. He talked Sarah into the chef's special for the day, a medium-spicy chicken tikka masala.

Kennedy ordered his favorite, the curried lamb marinated in red wine—plus an extra portion of sauce on the side. He ordered four pieces of naan, spiced with garlic and coriander. Sarah would want only one piece, leaving three for him to dip into the curried sauce he'd dreamed about on the way home.

The waiter recommended two local wines: a pinot chardonnay and a red zinfandel, both from San Pedro's Rendezvous Estates.

Sarah shrugged. "I've not heard of either blend, but I'm feeling brave. Let's try both."

After being served—faced by lights across the lagoon and surrounded by drinks, wine glasses, side dishes, and steaming entrées—Kennedy held up his glass. "To you, Sarah. Thank you for coming, for being here, for sharing your life with me." They clinked their glasses.

Sarah's eyes twinkled. "That was sweet. This is the vacation, the Belize I pictured, and I'm so glad I'm here."

Kennedy, unable to fight the urge, tapped the stolen booty with his foot to make sure it was there. "*Bon appétit.*"

Sarah wasted no time and tried both dishes, hers and his. After each, she carefully wiped her mouth on the linen serviette, sipped her drink, and tried both wines, again.

"Wine's OK," she said, "and my dinner's great, but yours"—she licked her lips, her eyes glassy—"is so much better."

Kennedy hated to ask, knew the answer. "Would you like to trade?"

Barely were the words out of his mouth before Sarah handed him her plate. "My pleasure," she said, and made the exchange.

Kennedy talked, listened, and savored every bite of the good-but-not-as-good chicken dish. With Sarah on an endorphin high, he watched for her to leave behind any of the used-to-be-his lamb dish.

Not a chance. She cleaned her plate. Finished her second piece of naan. Left barely a tablespoon of the spicy lamb sauce in its small bowl.

Kennedy eyed the prize. "Are you—"

Sarah, her nostrils flaring as if vacuuming up the

delicate aromas, her eyes darting dish to dish, didn't even look up when she interrupted: "May I have a small piece of your bread? I need something to sop up the rest of the sauce." She pointed first at the gravy in her bowl, and then to Kennedy's naan. "Maybe about half a piece?"

Kennedy broke the naan and shared it.

Though his dry half went down well, Sarah's, soaked in the last of the lamb sauce that had once been his, could have been a brain elixir—his.

"That was fantastic," Sarah said. She spoke fast, as was her wont after a few drinks. "I love sharing with you."

For dessert, they had coffee and split a single order of gulab jamun—warm dumplings—served Belizean style with coconut ice cream.

Fully sated, Kennedy checked his watch and nudged the backpack with his ankle. "We've got almost an hour to kill," he said. "Would you—"

"Perfect," Sarah said, her eyes sparkling. "That gives us enough time to walk through town and see which stores are still open."

Kennedy reminded himself to be patient. He wasn't pushing a construction project along some critical path—this night was Sarah's. He forced his shoulders to relax and said, "We might even find a little music, maybe a bar, close to the dock."

A short boat ride and fifteen minutes later, they found Pages Bookstore, across the street from the Catholic primary school. Sarah bought a photo journal of ancient Maya ruins, while Kennedy discovered and purchased a well-used copy of James O. Born's *Field of Fire*, a mystery loaded with cops, bullets, and bad guys. He'd read it and knew Sarah would also like it.

The books went into the backpack, but the closest they got to music and a bar was the xylophone player outside Elvi's Kitchen on Middle Street.

At 8:55 p.m., passengers already seated on the nine-o'clock boat back to Bacalar Vista welcomed Kennedy and Sarah. The jovial passengers compared stories about where they'd eaten, the bars they'd haunted, shopping at the Emerald Mine. The word "emerald" seemed to capture Sarah's attention.

Kennedy—one arm around her—bided his time and talked bonefish strategies with a recent arrival to the resort. Kennedy's other arm rested on his backpack—later, he thought, but soon.

The boatload of happy returnees stopped at the palapa, where they met with those who hadn't gone to town. Within minutes, the groups merged and the palapa overflowed with rowdy laughter. In the background, drink blenders roared. Three guys played darts for drafts in a spot adjacent to a rum-tasting table. Butted up next to the low wall that defined the edge of the blue-lighted pool, a foursome of bridge players tried to shoo away a jolly, cigar-smoking kibitzer.

Kennedy and Sarah fit right in, but his "later" became much later.

By the time he opened the door to his condo, Sarah had snuggled deeply into his shoulder, a mixture of passion and gravity. The former was out of the question; the latter, a matter of physics.

Before he went to bed, where Sarah lay, her limbs sprawled like she'd taken a hard right hook, Kennedy retrieved the police reports from his backpack. The file contained no pictures. He flipped through almost thirty sheets and found names, but the rest of the words, in Spanish, meant nothing to his monoglot capabilities. Worse than he had expected.

He held the pages to his chest, and then placed them on the table. On the top page, he stared at a woman's name, repeated often throughout the reports. Remembering what he'd thought some days before, he spoke softly to the reports, as if the name had a face.

"Madrilène Perry," he said, "my gut tells me you didn't die because you were dumb."

Kennedy washed his face and brushed his teeth. Exhausted, but hyper, he stared at the bed, where Sarah hadn't moved.

Driven, unable to sleep, he returned to the internet and searched "woman, shark attack." A new reference caught his attention, sent him to another site. A site with pictures. Sixty-two pictures, he guessed, since he'd seen them all. Hell, he'd taken them all.

As he moved frame-to-frame, anger evolved to rage. Not a rage that warranted a yell or a pounded fist, but one that tore at his guts. A number of the pictures had crude titles—*DINING ON DELTOIDS . . . SNACK ATTACK . . . GLUTEUS UNGLUED*. Kennedy missed the humor.

He searched the file for information, but the posting was anonymous, and the body was not identified. The photographer, to Kennedy's small joy, was not credited.

The last shot was numbered fifty-three, whereas Kennedy expected sixty-two. With nine missing, he went back and looked for the seven pictures he'd designated as Sarah's face shots—none. Perhaps, he wondered, the two other missing pictures had also been face shots—partial face shots—that Sarah hadn't used.

So, Kennedy thought, the sonofabitch steals and posts the pictures. But excludes the ones with faces. Perhaps a *nice* sonofabitch?

Hah. Not a chance.

Unlike the "best-partial-face" posting in the newspaper that had led to Azalee Castillo's innocent misidentification, these pictures were selected to make sure the body was *not* identified. That, he knew.

Before he turned off his computer, Kennedy found the picture he wanted and zoomed in. The hamsa filled the screen. He asked it a simple question: "Who the hell were you attached to the day she died?"

He got no answer but swore he'd find out.

27

An entity nested in Sarah's skull. It lived, it breathed, and it pulsated when she moved her head, so she quit doing that. Her last memory was a tequila shot in the palapa when she'd tried to keep up with Kennedy. She inventoried body parts by commanding key muscles to twitch. Everything worked except her eyes. The insides of her immobile eyelids appeared a dark pinkish gray, which meant morning, or perhaps midday.

She stretched out her left arm feeling for Kennedy. Empty sheets meant she'd slept alone, or he was up. Remembering how to make her lungs and nose work, she sniffed for the telltale clue.

And there it was, coffee, the mandatory catalyst that would start her day.

She opened her eyes, sniffed in a weak breath. "Hello." The word came out raspy, her throat dry, as if she'd been screaming for hours, spurring on the Denver Broncos.

Dead quiet.

She yelled again, upped the volume. "Hello!" Instant pain signaled she'd dislodged something in her brain. Driven by acute caffeine-withdrawal symptoms, she grabbed her head in both hands, and yelled a bit more cautiously. "Anybody home?"

Kennedy walked in, wearing shorts and a tee, a heavy mug in each hand. "If you can sit up, I've got coffee for you."

Sarah ignored her throbbing temples, fluffed her pillow against the mahogany headboard, and scooted up the bed.

Kennedy sat beside her.

The first two tiny sips—igniting some magic combination of chemical and psychological tonic she'd never bothered to question—told her she would survive.

"How'd you sleep?" he asked.

"No clue. I didn't even dream. How about you?"

"Played detective all night and shot bad guys. I think it was the chicken masala."

"Ha. More like rum and tequila shots. If this is Thursday, I bet your blood and sweat are still flammable."

"Might be," he said. "But let's make a deal. You get ready, and I'll make breakfast."

Sarah sat across from Kennedy at the breakfast table. "So, what's next?"

"Two things on my agenda."

"Translations and what else?"

He worked his jaw, exhaled from the bottom of his lungs. "Our pictures made the internet."

Sarah sipped hot coffee, swallowed hard. "Your originals or my seven?"

"All but nine of the originals. The missing pictures are the ones that show any part of her face."

Though they weren't her pictures, Sarah felt like an insider, an insider who'd been violated. "I'm sorry. I know you tried. Is there an address for the source?"

"Nothing. Not that I can see."

Sarah had seen barren websites before. "I have a friend who might be able to help. She does IT-consulting work, tracking down folks who don't pay their bills. Show me the site. It's all she'll need."

Kennedy went to his desk, booted his computer, and pulled up the pictures.

Sarah copied the site address and looked at her watch. "In the time it takes you to refill my coffee, I'll send her an email, ask her who posted the pictures."

"Free refills on the coffee." He patted the stack of papers he'd heisted in Cancún. "And then we've got a lot of translating to do before the Mexican police beat down our door."

Sarah: "Between scrawled notes, police jargon, and my limited language skills, I need help."

Kennedy looked over her shoulder. "How about a manicure?"

"Yeah, like that'll help. You giving up?"

"No. Mianna, the woman on staff who does nails, speaks Spanish."

"She Mexican?"

"Sarah, this is Belize, not Mexico. She's Belizean. Her heritage is Garifuna. Her first language is English, but she also speaks Spanish and French. She's studying marine biology at the University of Miami, working toward a PhD, and has a deal with Bacalar Vista to live here while she's finalizing her dissertation. Something reef related."

"Convenient," Sarah said. "What kind of deal?"

"She's our assistant chef and also does nails."

"Sounds perfect. Maybe you should marry her."

"I thought about it," Kennedy said, "but her husband carries a lot of weight in his well-defined chest and is surrounded by weapons that slice, dice, and chop. As the other half of the Mianna team, he's our chef."

Sarah rested her left foot on a stool while Kennedy— as the photographer who had helped identify "Azalee"—summarized for Mianna what had happened to the woman who'd died in Mexico.

Mianna—Sarah thought it interesting that Kennedy had mentioned neither her raw beauty nor the midnight blackness of her skin—absorbed it all, her excitement evident.

"I can translate and read the reports to you in

English while I work," Mianna said to Kennedy, "and you can write or type as we go." To Sarah, she added, "Of course, with me translating, your pedicure might take a while."

Kennedy waggled his index fingers. "I'm not the greatest typist," he said, "but I can keep up if you don't go too fast."

"Some of it might be explicit," Sarah said.

Mianna soaped Sarah's foot. "If it has to do with sharks, it won't be a problem. I did my thesis on the use of bioacoustics to repel sharks. There's no limit to what they'll do for a meal." She seemed to catch herself and looked at Kennedy. "Sorry, Mr. Kenn. I didn't mean to be insensitive. I know that what you witnessed had to be difficult for you."

Kennedy nodded. "I just happened to be there with my camera," he said. "But it got me interested in the death of the woman in Mexico."

With Mianna gently massaging her foot, Sarah said, "Let's get started before I fall asleep."

Mianna worked two hours to finish Sarah's feet and toes, interrupted by short breaks to read and translate. For another hour she worked on Sarah's fingernails, continued translating in short spurts, and ended by hand-painting tiny roses on each of twenty nails. Then Sarah suggested that she and Kennedy change places, so Mianna could translate while Sarah typed.

"Sorry, ladies," Kennedy said. "I don't need a pedicure."

The women conferred, and his rampant case of cracked heels became their focus of revulsion.

"Funny, funny," Kenndy said. "Now I'm serving lemonade and iced tea, but only if we can get back to the translations."

Sarah said, "I'll pass on the drink, but I need a potty break."

She made the stop and then checked her email. The reply from her IT friend was succinct: "During previous twenty-four hours, pictures (how horrid!) downloaded to a dot.com site sharkattack-photos. Source is not named but the email address at MSN is knowillpower. First registered early September two years ago in Kentucky. Current location unknown."

Sarah sent a copy to Kennedy and rejoined the twosome.

"Another hour," Mianna said to Kennedy, "your feet and hands will be beautiful, and the translations will be done. We'll wake you before I leave."

Kennedy rolled his eyes and mouthed, "Yeah, right."

He was asleep, head back and snoring, before Mianna finished his right foot, during which she'd interrupted the process a half-dozen times to feed the final translations to Sarah as she typed. Mianna finished Kennedy's left foot in minutes, though he had no clue it had happened.

As soon as Mianna put away her equipment and left, Sarah, only half amused by Kennedy's unconscious state, focused on the translations.

She finished by typing a set of notes that described a police psychologist's interview with the victim's grown children. The daughter, Racine, the report said, had taken her mother's death as the end of the world. The son, Rick, conversely, held his emotions inside, as if they were a carefully guarded secret, likely to his own psychological detriment, the doctor had reported.

Sarah's eyes were dry as she typed the words, but she hurt for the family's loss. For the trauma they had witnessed. For the trauma the mother had suffered, in the water, with sharks.

Sarah reached up and put her hand to her chest, felt her own pounding heart. Realized she was hyperventilating. That she was the one in the water. That the sharks—

She made it to the bathroom in time to minimize the mess.

28

Kennedy had typed eleven of thirty-three pages of translations, Sarah the rest. After their light dinner, he cleaned up typos, clarified ambiguities with Sarah's input, and read every word to himself, his mind in turmoil.

He skidded back his chair, ground its legs against the floor, and carried his empty cup into the kitchen for a refill.

"My, my, temper, temper," Sarah said. "Neighbors are gonna think daddy's in a bad mood."

Kennedy ignored her, poured coffee, added creamer, and nuked it for thirty seconds. Cup in hand, he sat across from Sarah. "Your turn," he said.

"To what?" she asked. "I heard it all when Mianna translated, one sentence at a time. And I typed a good bit of it."

"And what do you think—the big picture?"

Sarah dog-eared a page of *Field of Fire* and closed the book. "First, I like the book. Thanks for letting me read it."

"Second, my thoughts are straight from the police

reports. You have a family on a yacht, having fun. They'd been in Cozumel and got carried away throwing chunks of fish overboard to feed the sharks. Mom fell in, yelled, screamed, and disappeared. The father and an employee—Eloise, I think—told the same story. The kids didn't do too well. The daughter was catatonic, as I probably would have been, and the son, though not much of a talker, tried to help his mom—according to the police report—and got hurt in the process—"

"And after several days," Kennedy interjected, "the Mexican cops declared it an accident and sent the survivors home to Tampa. End of story. I read the same notes, but I asked you about the big picture."

Sarah's face hardened—like it had when he'd first told her he was moving to Belize. "You're screwing up my vacation, Kenn Bracken. The key words, your words, are 'End of story,' but you're not listening. You saw a dead person in Belize and took pictures. And now you're chasing another corpse, who might as well have died skydiving, and you're trying to combine the cases." She folded her arms and slipped her feet off the coffee table as if to stand. "They're unrelated, damn it, and I'm about fed up with all this crap. Which means you can either join me in the vacation spirit or chase ghosts on your own."

Kennedy knew her well enough to know she made few idle threats. "Before you pack up and go home," he said, "hear me out."

The look on her face did not improve.

"Something's missing in the reports," he said. "Something about—"

"*Earth to Kenn!*" Sarah bellowed. "*Do. You. Hear. Me?*"

Krash had. She looked up and then just as quickly laid her head back down.

Her neck scarlet, Sarah continued. "It doesn't goddamn matter what's missing. It's you who's the problem. You have a feather up your nose about Azalee not being Azalee, and instead of looking for the guy who broke into your place, you're grasping at straws hundreds of miles away. So count me in, *just me*, and get rid of both dead woman, or I'm out of here."

Kennedy could either yield . . . or watch Sarah go home. But he liked neither choice and couldn't help himself. "The police found no chum on the boat," he said. The words that had plagued him, that should have remained cerebral, had popped out.

Sarah looked into his eyes, but her normal intense focus wasn't there, as if something had fizzled.

"Either the police reports are incomplete," he said, "or somebody's lying."

"I'll get my tickets online," Sarah said, detached. "If I'm on the first boat in the morning, what's the earliest I can get into Belize City?"

They were the words he'd never wanted to hear. No goddamn way, he scolded himself. He went to the kitchen, considered a swig of rum, tossed down a small glass of water instead, and steadied himself against the counter.

No, he thought. Doesn't end like this. Arms folded across his chest, he assessed his adversary. Wrong word, not his adversary—the woman he wanted to marry—the woman who wanted to marry him. Well, maybe.

Sarah hadn't moved, still staring at the spot where he had sat only moments before.

He reclaimed the seat, got back in her field of view. "You can take any commercial flight after about eleven," he said, "but I hope that's irrelevant."

His words seemed to wake her up. She nodded.

He looked at the wall clock—almost nine—and leaned forward in his seat, hands folded on his knees. "And that means," he said, "I have very little time before morning to help you change your mind."

Sarah, too, glanced at the clock. "Then it'll be by telepathy," she said, "because I'll be in the guestroom. Alone." And with that she scratched Krash's ears and walked down the hall.

The heavy thunk of the solid-mahogany door closing at the end of the hall left Kennedy no doubt he'd be sharing his pillow with his second-best friend—Krash.

29

An hour later, Kennedy sat at the palapa bar, fiddled with a stack of coasters, and ordered rum and lime. "Five Barrel, if you have it." His dilemma was simple. Two choices. Pursue the love of his life . . . or his home-grown obsession with death resolution.

But he wasn't interested in *or*—he wanted *both*.

Lots of empty tables in the palapa, he noticed, but a couple of diners ate slowly, enjoying their late-evening meals.

He and Sarah should be doing the same. Instead, he inhaled the Caribbean aromas of the night, at least part of his decision made. "Is Mianna in the back?" he asked the bartender.

Within minutes she leaned across the bar and dried her hands. "How are your feet, Mr. Kenn?"

He hadn't thought about them since she'd left his place. "Perfect," he said. "Couldn't be better. If your husband's here, may I buy you both a drink?"

She looked at her watch. "Yes. We're off at ten, about three minutes ago. A draft beer for him, while he closes the kitchen. A white wine for me."

Kennedy ordered the drinks, and Mianna carried the draft back into the kitchen, her wine still on the bar. When she returned, she thanked Kennedy on behalf of her husband and lifted her glass.

"I'm glad I could help today," she said. "Do you have enough for your story?"

"Yes, thanks," he said. "But I do have a question for you. About sharks."

"My favorite subject."

"Chumming. How the hell would you chum for sharks?"

"I wouldn't," she said. "I'd never kill a shark. Why?"

"My story. I just need to understand how it's done."

Mianna gave in. "They're predators," she said. "They smell blood in parts per million. Give them the scent, and you can't keep them away."

"Which means, chum with something bloody."

"Anything bloody will work. A commercial shark fisherman might use slop from a slaughterhouse, whatever he can get. He can cut and chop, put it through a grinder, or hang it in a chum bucket, but only if he doesn't mind losing the bucket. If you're out fishing, anything you catch—needlefish, jacks, triggerfish—will make good chum. Just chop and toss. As soon as the sharks show up, bait your hook with the same stuff and hang on. Unfortunately, most shark fishermen don't believe in catch and release."

Kennedy's mind raced.

Mianna twirled her glass. "How's this relate to Cancún?" she asked. "To the woman who died?"

Very perceptive. Madrilène Perry. Chumming sharks. Assumed consumed. "The woman in Mexico fell overboard while chumming sharks," he said. "Not to catch them, but for fun. And I'm just trying to picture an entire family doing something so utterly stupid that it led to her death."

Mianna nodded and sipped her wine. "I felt the same way when I translated," she said. "Now may I ask you a question?"

"Sounds serious. This about sharks?"

"No," she said. "Sarah. She seems sad. Is she having a good time?"

Kennedy swirled his drink. "She's miserable, and I haven't helped."

"Is she special to you?" Mianna asked. "A good friend?"

"Way beyond a friend. We got close to marriage several times, but work, our jobs, always got in the way. And that's still the problem."

"I thought you retired."

"I did," he said, "from the job where I'd been a twenty-four-seven, world-traveling problem solver. Construction. Accident investigation. But then I hired on as a writer, self-employed. Now I write fiction, tell lies twenty-four-seven. Sarah's job is in Denver. She worked hard to get it. It's untouchable. So, as long as my work's here in Belize, we'll never be—"

Mianna put her hand on his arm, leaned to look over his shoulder, and finished her wine in one gulp. "Mr. Kenn," she said, "if it's right, it'll happen. And if not—" She shrugged. "Gotta go. Papa's waving to me."

"Thanks, Mianna," he said. Then, under his breath, to her back, "for everything."

Kennedy looked into his glass at the single floating chip of ice. *If it's right.* He finished his drink and then munched and swallowed the ice.

And if not—

30

Kennedy's nightmare had him thrashing in bed—until he realized his eyes were open and it wasn't a dream. Another dilemma. Another problem. Too many missing puzzle pieces. Too much unseen, unsaid, unreported.

His bedside clock indicated Sarah had four more hours to sleep before she'd get up, pack, and leave. He reckoned that even as angry as she was, he could probably join her in the guestroom and get her to at least listen.

He collated his thoughts, made up his mind.

Guestroom empty—so much for stealth.

He checked the hall bathroom—also empty.

He found Sarah on the couch, on her side, scratching Krash's ears. "I couldn't sleep," she said. "And we need to talk."

"I'll make coffee," he said.

"No," she said. "Just listen. Then I'll listen to you."

Kennedy, itching to tell all he knew, all he suspected, yielded the floor.

"I love you, Kenn," she said, "and I'd like to spend my life with you. But I'm afraid that's never going to happen. Though you haven't touched your book since I got here, you're married to it. And you're a polygamist to every whim that comes your way, like moving to Belize, and this shark thing. And you can't stay focused on anything long enough to really matter, certainly not that I've seen."

Kennedy measured his response.

"Don't say anything," she said. "Just let me finish. My week ends tomorrow, but I came here fully prepared to stay longer if what I found showed me there was hope for us in the long term. And by long term I mean more than three hours of bonefishing by yourself."

Unfair, he thought. I haven't fished in a week.

Krash raised her head and nosed Sarah's hand.

"All I wanted," she said, "was a week with you in paradise. No work. No phones. No schedule. But you found something to take your mind off all that. Something bad, I admit. But something you had every right, perhaps even the obligation, to forget about once you took the pictures to the police. And with our week now almost gone, you've again weighed your choices—her or me. And the way I see it, the dead woman's winning the race."

Kennedy replayed her words, words that stung, words that told the truth. Truth, the operative word, his only way forward. "My goal, too," he said, "was a perfect week for you. I wanted you to love this place, with me, and never want to leave."

Krash sparked Sarah's hand back to life.

Kennedy continued. "I know that's not possible, probably never has been. But I still wanted your trip to go well." He offered no defense, no excuse, and yielded the floor.

"And since I'm not willing to move here," she said, "you're willing to watch me walk out the door. Goodbye forever."

Kennedy heard no voice inflection to indicate a question. "I hate doors," he said, "whether one or many, when they separate us. Belize versus Denver—many doors. Here—just one door."

Sarah shook her head, scrunched her face. "And what door's that? To the guest room?"

"No," he said. "The dead-body door. I've been yanked through it, but you're reluctant to step over the threshold."

Sarah sat up, and Krash immediately joined her on the couch, her big head in Sarah's lap. Sarah's jaw muscles expanded and contracted, as if tiny beating hearts. She spoke slowly. "I said I'd listen," she said. Her face devoid of emotion, she looked at the clock. "You have a couple of hours."

"It won't take that long," he said. He waited for a nod but got a blank stare, instead. "I'd like to know who died the day I saw the body. The body that was never Azalee Castillo. Unfortunately, the police don't give a crap about what we think. Then another woman dies, and again sharks are involved."

"And you don't like coincidences," Sarah said, "or unexplained deaths. Like for your father." Sarah's words, the language of her face, something that flashed across her eyes, spelled mockery.

"Please don't go there. This isn't about my dad."

Her tiny shrug, half nod, and slowly closing eyelids said she believed otherwise. But her mouth said, "I'm listening," while her hands scratched Krash's ears.

Kennedy wanted, needed, to unburden himself. Yes, goddamn it. His caring about the case—every case he'd ever worked on—and about life in general was about his dad. No. Not about. Because of. He'd never forgiven his mother because of his dad—"Gee, I don't know," she'd said, drunk, two years after they'd found his burned-out empty car thirty feet down, buried in kelp, the "funeral" a sham. "Accident? Suicide? Murder? Who the hell knows? Or maybe the bastard just ran away." Yes, Kennedy cared about the two shark deaths—two *unresolved* shark deaths— about death resolution, because of his dad. But he'd told Sarah not to go there, as he'd told her before, and he wasn't about to chase the lure she flashed in his face.

He spoke carefully, picked his words. "I believe the cases are unrelated: younger woman versus older, Belize versus Mexico, Tuesday versus Wednesday. But I need the Mexican case to go away. I need to get it out of my head. I need to quit seeing the kids' mother in the water, going through exactly what I witnessed, her body gone forever."

Sarah steepled her fingers, cracked her eyes open, rolled her head his way. "Kenn, the Mexican case is closed. The family's gone home. What more do you need?"

"Answers," he said. "Information. More than we have. The police inventoried the entire boat. Two pages of items, room by room, every cabinet, every closet. You typed the list."

Two palms up, eyebrows erect: "And?"

"No fishing gear. No poles. No live well. And most important, no chum."

Sarah ducked her head and looked up at him. "And that's keeping you awake?"

"Yes," he said. "The mother was supposedly throwing chum and fell overboard. She went in among the sharks. The police say four people saw it happen, told the same story. But there was no chum."

"So they pulled fish from the freezer," she said, "and threw it overboard." Sarcasm laced her words. "They threw it all, so none was left."

"No," he said. "Mianna says sharks will go after chum. *Bloody* chum. And I don't think frozen shrimp or processed mahi-mahi fillets are in that category."

"So what?" Sarah's words, up an energetic notch, echoed in the small room. "Why the hell do you care?"

"Because, goddamn it, if a family's dumb enough to chum sharks and someone falls overboard, and the whole world turns to a shitstorm panic attack while ol' dad calls the Mexican cops, nobody in the dumbass family is going to clean the boat while they're waiting to be boarded. And if the family's forte for fun is chumming, accompanied by the ultimate price for failure, then on a very personal basis, I have to question the email you got, which just happened to use *chumming* as a threat." Hands on hips, he sucked wind.

"You don't have to yell," she said.

"Goddamn it. I'm—" Ready to explode, Kennedy held up his hands, palms toward Sarah, and looked her square in the face. "Sorry."

"Me, too," she said. "And for the last time, why do you care?"

"Sarah, damn it. They . . . were . . . not . . . chumming." He'd said the words without yelling, words Sarah needed to hear, words that showed how important resolution was to him. He added, "Somebody's lying. And if four people can lie about something that simple, that tragic, then I have to wonder what other bodies are in their closets." He sat back, convinced she now understood.

Sarah shook her head ever so softly. "And if you, Kenn, are more concerned with those people and their lies than you are with making a one-week vacation nice for me, then I don't need to stay."

Closing arguments made, he thought.

As simple as that.

Case lost.

31

Sarah stepped around her suitcase and laptop bag, stooped by the front door, and hugged Krash.

Krash's chocolate-brown body waddled in harmonic rhythm with her wagging tail, her right front paw up, her face nuzzled to Sarah's, looking for love.

Sarah broke, cried great, chest-heaving sobs, and fell to her knees. She used both hands to scratch Krash's ears and jabbered baby-talk words to perhaps her closest best friend who had never let her down.

Krash gave her a tongue-lashing in return.

Drained, Sarah reached for the doorknob to stand but couldn't get past Krash.

Kennedy helped her up and held her tight.

She managed squeaky words, "Don't you dare say you're sorry."

He didn't. But he held her to his body and rocked slowly, as if time didn't matter, which it did.

Which pissed her off. She lifted her left foot and,

afraid she'd kick Krash, vented a rousing dose of frustration into the side of her suitcase, which fell against the support column for the dining table. Krash jumped and barked, the table tilted, plastic apples flew, and Kennedy exploded into manic survival mode. He pushed away from Sarah, dove for the table, and saved the plate-glass top just before impact with the tile floor.

"Holy shit," he yelled, his butt up, his head down, his arm pinned beneath the heavy glass. "What was that about?"

Sarah cracked up and squealed like a sixth grader at a slumber party. A new wave of fun tears met the old sad ones, and she laughed all the harder.

Kennedy groaned. "Sarah, damn it. Help me."

"Me? Help?" She bent, laughed even more, held both hands to her stomach. "You've done everything for a week all by yourself. Why should I help you now?"

"Here's a reason," he said. "Either help me get the glass off my arm or get ready to see lots of blood."

Sarah tapped the glass with the manicured nail of her index finger and noticed that the small, hand-painted rose could use a little touch-up. "Kennedy Bracken, you're a wuss. You want my help, beg for it."

"What?"

"Beg," she said.

"Goddamn it. Help me."

"Beg," she repeated. "Grovel."

Kennedy's face reddened. He lifted his arm, tried

to lift the glass, to no avail. "Please."

She put her nose next to his.

Krash moved in, made it a threesome nose fest.

"Please, what?" Sarah asked.

Kennedy got a face full of Krash's very pink tongue. Pinned to the floor, playing dodge dog, he shook his head and managed the smallest of laughs. "*Please* will you help me? I need your help. I can't do it alone. I'll die without your help."

"Aha," she said. "Finally. Now those are the words I wanted to hear." Sarah rolled the heavy glass top off Kennedy's arm and onto the soft side of her suitcase, located where the base of the table normally stood.

Kennedy scowled and rubbed his arm. He opened and closed his hand in jerky movements, as if it were a bionic attachment, and then wiped canine slobber off his nose and mouth.

Sarah figured he was a bit miffed. She leaned the glass top toward him. "I think this is yours," she said. "Do you need help with it?"

He didn't answer. In a show of brute strength, he grabbed opposite edges of the thick glass and hefted it onto the base.

Sarah applauded. "And to think just a moment ago you needed my help, and then, like a miracle, you didn't."

"There are some things I can do myself," he said. His words were controlled, and Sarah knew he was holding back, though he wasn't entirely successful at keeping the grouch out of his voice.

"And with other things—" She let the accusation hang.

"You're pushing me," he said. "And it's getting late. Maybe already too late."

"Maybe all you have to do," she said, "is admit there're things for which you need my help."

"Your help? How about just now," he said, "since there was a guillotine about to cut me to shreds."

Sarah folded her arms across her chest. "Some guillotines are glass—others, self-imposed."

Kennedy's face exhibited deep-think mode.

Sarah knew he was trying, trying to understand, trying to put the pieces together.

His lips tightened into a straight-line smile, his nod almost imperceptible. "I was that bad?"

"Worse," she said. "And you *can't* do it alone."

"You mean, like I might need your help?"

"It feels nice to be needed," she said. "And I bring a lot of skills to the table."

"You know this means I can't let you go."

"My week of vacation ends tomorrow," she said. "You have just fewer than twenty-four hours to convince me I need an extension."

Kennedy picked up the suitcase and glanced at his watch. "We missed breakfast. And the eight o'clock boat. Get ready, and I'll buy you an early lunch in the palapa."

32

Kennedy munched chips and bean dip. "I've got two things on my agenda, mutually exclusive."

Sarah worked on spicy conch ceviche. "Let me guess. You want to throw me overboard so I'll learn to swim, and you want to live until sundown."

"You want to learn to swim?"

"Don't even think about it. And let me tell you about mutually exclusive: ceviche and *coffee*."

In less than a minute Alberto delivered to Sarah a draft Belikin served in a cold glass.

"Thanks, Alberto," she said, "and you can have this." She handed him her still-full coffee cup. To Kennedy: "What're your agenda items?"

"Find Azalee's boyfriend, then talk to Madrilène's husband."

"Oh, that's easy," Sarah said. "Maybe Alberto can call and have them join us for lunch."

"I'm serious. Two things happened, and neither has a valid conclusion. Azalee's boyfriend, what's his name—"

"Christopher."

Kennedy waved a chip at his bona fide partner and nodded. "Christopher's a key player in the Azalee mystery. We need to talk to him."

"Isn't it possible," she said, "even logical, that the good Sergeant Gutierrez, even without us helping, is already looking for Christopher? Azalee's on the books as dead, even buried, if in name only, and Christopher disappeared the same day she did. Appears a little suspicious, wouldn't you say?"

Kennedy didn't want a logical argument, but he needed to keep Sarah happy. He let a slight nod answer for him.

She handed Kennedy a chip piled high with ceviche. "Gutierrez has every resource he needs, so we can back off. What's your second point?"

For the partnership to work, Kennedy would have to yield at least something, and Christopher was a good card to slough. He spoke with his mouth full. "Madrilène's husband, Victor Perry. He's either hopelessly dysfunctional or playing some kind of game. And what he did, what he allowed to happen to his wife, was mighty close to what I saw in Belize. Way too close for comfort."

"Since the Mexican police closed the case," Sarah said, "why's Victor on your list?"

"Because his family's tragedy is the only link we may have to chumming, which, as I recall, was the threatening part of the email you got."

Sarah rolled her eyes. "Then call him," she said.

"Call from San Pedro if you need privacy."

"Even if I could get a call through," Kennedy said, "I need to talk to this guy face-to-face and watch his eyes when he tells me about his wife."

"So it's Tampa? Like Tampa damn Florida? Are you suggesting we—"

"You can take your luggage," he said, "in case you decide not to come back."

"Trust me," she said. "If we're going to chase lost-cause Victor Perry to wherever he lives, I'm not coming back here. Maybe ever."

Kennedy pumped his fist. "You gave me twenty-four hours. You still packed?"

"Suitcase and briefcase," she said. "Ready to go."

"Then I'll be back in five minutes," he said. "See if you can find the concierge. Tell her we're trying to get to Tampa, probably through Miami."

"First flight in the morning?" she asked.

"Hah," Kennedy said. "Tell her we'll be on the noon boat—that's in fifteen minutes—then the first flight to Belize City. Her job is to get us seats on the earliest available flight to Miami."

Sarah sat speechless, mouth agape.

Kennedy enjoyed the micromoment of silence, and then turned and sprinted to his condo to get Krash. Running fast, breathing hard, feeling good, he considered his goals. Find Victor. Suss out the truth. Keep Sarah happy.

The first two were no-brainers.

The third would need a miracle.

33

Sarah abhorred unplanned boondoggles. She liked structured, day-to-day, critical-path activities. At work, she was the organizer, the quality-assurance expert, the person to whom others turned when black smoke poured from bureaucratic kettles. So how, she wondered, as she watched Kennedy run back toward the palapa, had her day gone from packed and ready to go home, to a casual brunch, to a tête-à-tête with the concierge, to a haul-ass boat trip to catch a plane, to catch a plane, to catch a plane to Tampa damn Florida?

Kennedy dropped his overnight bag by the table, reclaimed his seat, and drained the last gulp of beer from Sarah's glass.

"What'd you do with Krash?" she asked.

"Neighbors. They'll be here for three more weeks, and they'd keep Krash forever if I gave them the chance."

"Three weeks should be sufficient," she said, "since you'll be back tomorrow. Next question: What do you plan to do when you get to Tampa?"

"Look up Victor Perry. Talk to him. Ask him a few questions."

"And how do you propose finding him?"

Kennedy pulled a slip of paper from his shirt pocket. "His address was in the police reports. We'll call him, meet him this evening."

"No chance," she said. "Our ETA's eleven-forty-five tonight."

Kennedy puckered his lips. "Then we'll call him, meet with him tomorrow."

"And you have his number?"

"Just his address. It's a P.O. Box."

Sarah lowered her chin. "That's not an address."

"I'll get it," he said.

"Then what? 'Hi, this is Kennedy Bracken with *Sports Illustrated.*'" She mimicked him, her voice a pitiful alto imitation of his bass rumble. "'Are you the Victor Perry whose wife died while chumming sharks?'" She shook her head. "The only answer you'll get is a phone hanging up or someone cocking a gun."

Sarah looked up from her seat in the Belize City airport departure lounge. "If you're looking for surname Perry, there're three hundred listings in Tampa and the surrounding areas."

Kennedy's jaw hung open, as if from a stroke.

"How about Victor or Madrilène?" he asked.

Sarah handed him her laptop. "Knock yourself out. You might want to look at all the listings for V Perry and M Perry. See if you can get an address to match."

Kennedy, hunched over in a small wooden seat, attacked the keyboard.

"Hey," Kennedy said. "I just checked my email and got your IT friend's note. What's with Kentucky?"

"No clue," Sarah said. "What you see is all I know."

"Kentucky seems a long way from the ocean and sharks to be posting my stolen photos."

"Point made, but it's also a long way from Tampa where I think we're still looking for the Perry family."

Sarah enjoyed watching him work . . . when he actually worked. He was a different kind of efficient. While Sarah made lists—and lists of lists—and planned in detail the process of getting from A to B, Kennedy skipped a few steps—like almost all of them. That's how he'd retired. That's how he'd moved to Belize. Head down, he'd charge into a swirling mess, grab whatever he could, raise it high as if a prize had been won, and dive back in for more. But in almost all cases, Sarah had long ago noticed, they'd both arrive at B, side-by-side, Sarah refreshed and dressed to the nines, Kennedy looking like Krash had won another wrestling match.

Sarah checked her watch while Kennedy pecked away at the keyboard. She stretched and smoothed the wrinkles from her skirt and matching jacket—everything black except her yellow silk blouse. "I'm going to the ladies' room," she said. "Don't leave without me."

"I wouldn't think of it." He patted an array of pockets in his freshly laundered but already-wrinkled khaki cargo shorts. "You've got the boarding passes."

Satisfied the plane was safely headed east across the Gulf of Mexico, Sarah nestled into her seat, her head perched against an American Airlines pillow on Kennedy's shoulder. "You sleepy?" she asked.

He spoke as he typed. "Nope. Got work to do. I'll wake you when we're close."

Sarah had no intention of sleeping.

The laptop's battery-life warning beeper startled her. She stretched her neck and moved the pillow to her lap.

Kennedy, head down, chin on chest, didn't budge.

She checked her watch. He'd lasted less than an hour. She reached over and turned off the computer.

Still no movement.

She looked around at sleepers everywhere and

asked herself what the hell she was doing on a plane to Miami when it would have been so easy to have gone straight to Houston and then to Denver. No logical answer magically appeared.

Screw it, she thought. Twenty-four more hours. She'd let Kennedy lead. Whatever he wanted to do to get his closure.

She stopped midthought. *Closure.* She'd heard it before, though Kennedy hadn't mentioned it during his tirade on chumming. *Closure*: a fervor that'd plagued him since his father's death wherein he never got what he needed to resolve his loss. His subsequent quest for "death resolution," for bringing closure to surviving families, had defined his accident-investigation career, kept him challenged, made him a lot of money, given him ulcers. She studied his tanned face and the day's growth on his broad chin, as a blister of drool threatened to tip over his lower lip.

And now, she thought, staring at him, as if speaking by telepathy, you're once again trapped by a beyond-control need for closure. She gazed out the tiny portal at damn sure nothing she wanted to see. But this time—remembering tough cases he'd described at length—his quest for closure lived on two fronts, for two victims.

She watched him sleep, loved to watch him sleep, and wanted to be with him for the rest of her life.

From his lower lip the wad of drool, an inch long and growing, threatened her keyboard.

"Yuck." She recovered and saved her computer, wondering which might come first: twenty-four hours or the rest of her life.

34

Ensconced in Concourse D at Miami International Airport, Kennedy, looking online for Perrys, eliminated a few V Perrys with phone calls. Frustrated, he placed Sarah's laptop in the adjacent seat and turned off his cellphone.

Sarah used a receipt to bookmark *Field of Fire*. "What'd you learn?"

"None of the addresses match the police report," he said, "which means I need to make more calls." He showed her his scribbled notes. "Eliminated some, got a few voice mails, plus others I can't get through to."

"And the plane," she said, "leaves for Tampa in forty minutes." She took his notes and ran her finger down the page. "You're looking for 'Victor and Madrilène. You can probably eliminate 'Victor and Carol' and 'Sandra and Vic.' Then there're three guys on an answering machine—'Vic, Rick, and Ray.' Sounds like they're either bouncers or Mafia." She pointed to another with her finger. "What's 'Vicky?'"

Man or woman?"

"A guy—deep growl with a sweet lisp. Could be, but I bet not."

"Then maybe work on the M Perrys," she said, reopening her book.

Twenty minutes later: "Got her," Kennedy said. "Maybe." He turned the laptop to Sarah. "It's a business. Central America X-M Ports." He looked at his notes. "A voicemail said the office would close July 19 through August 28. Yesterday. The message mentioned two names. Madi and Eloise."

"Madi for Madrilène," Sarah said. "How about Eloise?"

"Maybe DeLaney, Madrilène's assistant on the boat."

"Got a phone or address?" Sarah asked, continuing to play straight man, to Kennedy's joy.

"The Website physical address is for the business, but there are two cell numbers."

"Then check the V Perry listings to see if you can match either the address or one of the listed phones."

In seconds, Kennedy figured out that Vic, Rick, and Ray were Victor Perry—Boston accent on the voicemail—and his kids, Rick and Racine. The names matched those in the Mexican police reports.

"Which means," he told Sarah, "we have an address for tomorrow morning."

"To talk about chumming."

He shrugged. "A wonderful topic for *Sports Illustrated*."

Sarah put away her book. "Under false pretenses and using a magazine about sports, you plan to question this guy about his wife's death? Have you thought about what you'll do if he's smarter than a rock, catches on, and goes after you?"

"A quote from Charlie Brown," Kennedy said. "'There's no problem so big it can't be run away from.'" He gave Sarah a macho-man smile.

Which she ignored. "Charlie Brown never had to worry about guns in the hood." She pointed to the gate. "They're boarding our flight, but it's not too late to forget about the Perrys. I can get home from here tonight just as easy as from Tampa tomorrow."

Not what he wanted—Sarah looking for an out. "This isn't about guns," he said. "We're interviewing a family about an accident. You gave me the weekend, and I have no intention of quitting." He stood, boarding pass in hand.

Sarah wasn't as fast to stand, but they got in line together. Side by side. He followed Sarah onto the plane.

Miles apart, he feared.

35

There wasn't a bone in Sarah's body in favor of what she and Kennedy were about to do.

He had called the Perry residence and left a voicemail that they'd like to meet sometime before lunch and left his cellphone number.

"Nobody there and you still want to go to his house?" Sarah asked.

"No reason not to."

Wrong, she thought. Lots of good reasons not to.

On the road, Sarah used her phone to navigate Kennedy through considerable late-morning Saturday traffic, south to Apollo Beach and onto Cocoa Lane. Stately homes on both sides of the street backed up to canals. Canals with yachts.

"That's one big house," she said, as he drove the bright-red rental Ford Taurus by the Perry address.

"Two cars in the drive. Somebody's home." He stopped three houses down the street and dialed the number again. He let it ring . . . and then hung up. "Nobody's answering, but I bet there's a doorbell."

Sarah didn't answer, her mind cataloging how Kennedy's idea could easily turn to a pile of crap.

He pulled into a tree-lined driveway to turn around. "I'm OK with you staying in the car," he said.

"No way. My notebook's ready." She spoke the words, but her heart didn't buy them, as something cold crept its way across her back.

Kennedy parked in Perry's circular drive. "Stand close to me at the door. If they have a peephole or camera, I want them to see a couple."

"A couple now, " she said, "but as soon as we're done here, I'm on my way to Denver. So keep it short."

Kennedy nodded. "Ten minutes, max." He pushed a polished chrome button.

Chimes sounded from inside, as if echoing through a museum in Rome. Sarah silently hoped nobody would be—

The door opened. An attractive barefoot woman, spiky blond hair, midthirties, wearing a hot-pink lounge outfit, didn't introduce herself. "Y'all come on in. Vic's expecting you."

Sarah couldn't tell if the woman's brassy demeanor, voice, and accent were from cow country or cotton country, but she held open the door for Sarah and Kennedy.

The woman led them into a lavishly furnished great room that smelled of cigarette smoke and fresh flowers. "Vic," the woman said, "they're here."

A head turned—a cellphone pressed to one ear. A single rotund finger popped up and waggled above the chair.

One minute? Sarah wondered.

While the threesome waited, Kennedy and the woman spoke quietly, and Sarah scanned the beauty of the opulent room. Large windows, with sunscreen shades and open sheer drapes, framed a view of trees, water, and more homes in the distance. Oil paintings of ships at sea hung among magnificently horned and antlered trophies on the wall. Bookcases, photos, a university-crest lamp, soft leather furniture, deep cream carpet, and fuzzy throw rugs completed the scene.

Like I give a crap, Sarah thought, wanting nothing more from the encounter than a speedy exit.

Victor Perry climbed out of his chair and turned toward his guests. Six foot six and five feet around, the giant was dressed neck to bare feet in white.

Sarah thought of a bull-size sumo wrestler in Pillsbury Doughboy drag. Then, bull? El Torro? No, dummy, she scolded herself and dismissed the thought.

Kennedy held out his hand. "I'm Kenn Bracken, Mr. Perry, *Sport Fishing* magazine."

The big man shook it, though Sarah noted his face carried an edge of suspicion.

"And this is Sarah McGarrity," Kennedy continued. "Her job is to make sure I leave nothing out."

Victor, without so much as a glance toward Sarah who held her hand out for naught, spoke to the woman in pink. "Lou, who the hell are these people?"

"For crying out loud. You said it was the Realtors and to let them in."

Kennedy held up his hands as if in surrender and spoke up. "Mr. Perry, we don't want to intrude on you, but as I said in my voicemail, we're in Tampa for only another hour. We work for *Sport Fishing* magazine, and we're writing an article—"

"We heard about Madrilène's tragic death," Sarah interrupted, fearful Kennedy had already lost his audience, "from Captain Federico Lobos in Cancún. He recommended we talk to you, since you were such a great help during his investigation. We're writing a story about the two unrelated shark attacks in the same week. One in Belize, and of course your wife in Mexico. May we have a few minutes of your time?"

Victor scrunched his eyes, and then seemed to mellow on the spot. For the first time, he pulled the cigarette from his lips. "Yes, of course. Pardon my manners. It's been a stressful time, what with my wife's accident, her death. Let's start over. I'm Victor Perry, and this"—he hitched his thumb toward the woman in pink—"is Lou." He held out his hand toward Kennedy. "Please remind me your names."

Kennedy said, "Sarah McGarrity, and I'm Kenn Bracken."

Victor—his head cocked, eyes squinted, as if trying to place, or memorize, Kennedy's face and name—shook his hand, again.

Then, surprising Sarah, he shook hers, engulfing

it in his meaty paw, and repeated her name.

Something distinctive about his accent, she thought. Boston? New Orleans?

The big man spoke. "Please, have a seat, the both of you. Get comfortable. Lou, get 'em somethin' to drink." Then, to Kennedy, "What's your pleasure? Scotch? Gin? Lou, I'll take a refill." He handed the woman a half-pint glass tumbler that held a lone ice cube.

Kennedy said, "I'll take a beer, anything but Belikin."

"Right," Victor said. "Belize and Belikin. Can't get enough when I'm there, wouldn't drink one of them pissant little bottles for free when I'm home." He peered at Sarah. "How about you, little lady?"

Little lady? she thought. Restrained only by her desire to help Kennedy, she refrained from snapping back. While her brain repeated the mantra *quick exit, quick exit*, her mouth said, "First, I'm so sorry about your wife's death. This must be difficult for you. We appreciate your taking the time to talk to us, so we'll keep it short."

"Lou," Victor said, as she delivered his refilled tumbler, "she don't know what she wants. Make her one of those girly things you're drinking."

The tip of Sarah's tongue shuffled words— *condescending, arrogant, shithead*—and she readied herself to spit them out—until she realized the woman at the bar was talking to her.

Eyes on Sarah, the woman said, "You'll like it. It's

a mimosa spiked with cassis. Or maybe it's a kir royal spiked with orange juice." When she gave Sarah her drink, she whispered, "Thanks for what you said about Madi. She was special—"

Victor clapped his hands. "Lou, wake up. Get this man his beer. He's dyin' of thirst."

Victor was again on his phone.

"Ignore him," the woman said to Kennedy. "There's a dozen kinds of beer. Come on over to the bar, I'll fetch you whatever you'd like."

Kennedy kept his seat. "How about Coors? Bottle or can doesn't matter."

Sarah raised her wrist, looked at her watch, made sure Kennedy got the message, and continued her quiet cataloguing of collectables and memorabilia throughout the well-appointed great room.

The woman delivered Kennedy his drink—a Miller Light—and handed him a frosted mug. He asked how the kids were doing.

"OK, I guess, with all that happened."

Victor pocketed his phone and aimed words at Kennedy: "What'd Lobos tell you?"

Careful, Sarah thought, as she continued her stroll.

"He was saddened by your loss," Kennedy said, "but very professional, of course. He was concerned about sharing information you might consider private to your family. So not a lot, other than your wife fell overboard, and there were lots of sharks around, something to do with chumming. He suggested we meet and let you tell us the story."

"He's an ass wipe," Victor said. "He made me stay a goddamn week when me and my kids didn't do nothin' wrong. Good he didn't tell you anything. That way you get the truth, everything that happened, and it's *me* gonna tell it."

Which, by Sarah's watch, consumed exactly fourteen minutes and one more cigarette. Fourteen minutes to tell, verbatim, the story Victor Perry had told the Mexican police. Fourteen minutes of describing his wife's horrid accident and tragic death. Fourteen minutes, in Sarah's assessment, of emotion-free memory dump by the fat man in white.

"Victor," Kennedy said, "I'm sorry for your loss and admire your strength to go forward. You've given us a great rundown on a subject that has to be tough to talk about. But I'd like to ask a couple of questions that'll tell our readers what they might do to protect themselves from this kind of accident."

"Like what?" Victor asked.

Sarah read Victor's words, which were laced with sarcasm, not as a question, but as a demand for an explanation.

"First," Kennedy said, "a lot of our readers, wanting to catch a giant shark, use chum. As you know, it doesn't take long to attract the bad boys. Can you tell us what you were chumming with? And how?"

Now *that's* blunt, Sarah thought, feeling like an insider to macho-man talk.

"Dead fish," Victor said. "I got no idea what kind. Big chunks, little chunks, guts everywhere. Goddamn sharks went crazy."

"So nothing like buckets of blood from a slaughter house."

"Oh, Christ." Victor puckered his face and wrinkled his nose. "No buckets of nothin'. Just regular fish. You cut it in chunks and throw it overboard."

"I'm with you," Kennedy said, "so let's change the subject. One more question."

Sarah wanted to give Kennedy a thumbs up, but held off.

Kennedy lowered his voice, as if to share a secret. "We want to warn our readers about the downside of spilling chunks of fish, plus blood and guts on the deck. Now, since your wife slipped and paid the ultimate price, and your son fell and injured himself while trying to help her, perhaps you've got some advice about deck safety for the average boat crew."

Sarah caught the flaw—a small detail from one of the police psychologist's interviews in the copied police reports. She focused on Victor, who seemed short of breath, his face bulged and red.

"You know," Kennedy added, "stuff like washing down the deck, or—"

Victor erupted and slammed his glass onto the coffee table. "I said nothing to Lobos about my son. Who the hell you been talking to?" He shifted his massive body out of his oversized leather chair and clinched his fists at his sides. "Either you lied about what Lobos told you, or something's going on. Maybe insurance for all I know, but it ain't got nothing to do with chummin'."

Sarah tensed, the cheeks of her butt vibrating like a bass woofer.

The woman in pink, her hand to her mouth, said nothing.

"Get out of my house," the big man bellowed, his voice stentorian. "The both of you. Now."

Kennedy, his face impassive, hadn't allowed his ungracious host to stand alone. He reached for Sarah's hand and said, "No harm intended, Mr. Perry. We won't bother you again."

"And thank you, Ms. *DeLaney*," Sarah added as she reached the front door. "The drink was wonderful."

Victor, his face carved by rage, snapped his eyes back and forth between the two women. "What the hell's goin' on here?"

But his "Get the hell out of my house" wasn't quite loud enough, wasn't quite explicit enough, to override Eloise DeLaney's "My pleasure, y'all."

36

Kennedy cruised north toward the airport, rehashing words said and body-language messages. "Sonofabitch's awful sensitive about a couple of little lies."

"Perhaps because you did it so unconvincingly," Sarah said.

Kennedy looked for her smile. Nope. "So, you think Victor was chumming?"

"Don't know. His description of blood and guts sounded convincing. As if I have a clue."

As a writer, Kennedy forced his characters to cave in, answer questions, yield to the pressure. But real-life people like Victor could stand firm, avoid reality, tell Kennedy to piss off. "All talk in my opinion," he said. "Still no evidence either way. And speaking of evidence, did you spot anything interesting when you inventoried the living room?"

"Maybe. I saw only three photographs. Two were of a young man, the third of Victor and the same guy, whom I'd guess to be the son, Rick. No pictures of women anywhere—including Victor's wife or the daughter."

"Maybe they're in another room." He started to say the ladies' room but didn't want the elbow.

"What'd you think of Ms. DeLaney?" Sarah asked.

"DeLaney? Who's she?"

"Eloise DeLaney," Sarah said. "Your friend in pink."

"Lou? That was Eloise?" Kennedy almost sideswiped a tall pickup—eliciting a squeal from Sarah—before settling back into his lane. "Eloise from the boat? Where'd you get that?"

"Nicknames, like Rick and Ray, which Victor seems to like. She's Lou for Eloise. Plus, they knew each other more than just friends."

"Good Lord," Kennedy said, "are you psychic?"

"Not at all. I'd guess they're not lovers, but she's familiar enough with the house to know there're different kinds of beer in the fridge. Could be she's running Madi's business."

Kennedy knew what he'd seen: Saturday morning, barefoot, drink in hand. "Maybe, but if that was Eloise, they're shacked up bigger than hell. Why else would she be there a week after the accident?"

"Get your head out of the gutter," Sarah said. "He treats her like a maid, and she barely tolerates him."

"Again, maybe," Kennedy said, "though we'll never know. But at least we got the nicknames down. Madi for Madrilène. Lou for Eloise." He stacked his hand on top of Sarah's. "You reckon Victor's got a nickname for me?"

"Dead Meat, would probably work."

Kennedy sat with Sarah in a Starbucks before her flight back to Denver. The sucking, grinding, steam-jet noises of the coffee shop, as well as the constant barrage of people and baggage, detracted from the magnificent aromas.

He didn't want Sarah to go, but he'd long ago used up his bargaining chips. "I'm lost," he said. "I killed your vacation and came to Tampa because I didn't buy the coincidental deaths, and now there's more shit going on than I can sort out."

"Then let's make it simple," she said. "What'd you learn when we first got to the house? You chatted with Eloise, while I snooped."

Kennedy puffed his chest. "Let's just say it didn't take long for me to realize she was hot after my body."

"Oh?" Sarah said. "Shacked up with Victor and hot after you. Busy woman. What'd I miss?"

"Nothing specific," he said. "Just the way she stood, looked at me, asked questions about the housing market. Of course, I didn't know she was Eloise or that she thought we were Realtors."

"Yeah, right, Mr. Clueless," Sarah said, "definite signs she wanted to jump your bones. Back to my question. Did you learn anything useful?"

"I asked her how the Perry kids were doing," he said. "She told me the daughter, Racine, left for school yesterday—in Baltimore. Her brother, Rick, leaves this afternoon for—" Kennedy tried to remember the word. A single word. *Trance? Chance?* "I don't remember where."

"Rick to somewhere," Sarah said. "That's good. Think we might talk to him before he goes to wherever *somewhere* is?"

Kennedy shook his head. "Not if papa-bear Victor gets a vote."

Sarah, chin in her hand, squinted her eyes.

He'd seen her quite often in a similar daze, not unlike an eyes-wide-open, petit-mal stare. He sipped coffee and waited for her wheels of thought to grind out a new idea or two. He waved his hand in front of her eyes.

Sarah looked up, and a slight smile crossed her lips. "How about one more stop before I go home? You have any more airline miles?"

Kennedy knew she knew. And he knew she had miles too. But they both played the game. For their first four years together, pre-Belize, she'd questioned his motivation every week or so when he left for Djakarta or Brussels or Johannesburg to take over and turn around a failing construction project or investigate a disaster. Then, days or weeks later, after he'd return with another war story, she'd ask him if his gains had been worth the risk. No, he'd always say, but then he'd brag about the airline miles.

"Millions more to go," he said. "Where to?"

"Think Orioles."

"Cookies?"

"Way off," she said. "But *you* gave the clue. I saw a lamp in the entry with a university logo on a medallion. Big letters in the middle, BHU, but I wasn't close enough to read the wrap-around fine print. But I did pick up the middle word—*Hebrew*. Any chance, with Racine flying to Baltimore, there's a Baltimore Hebrew University?"

Kennedy exhaled, and then had to pull hard to refill his chest. "No clue. But if she's at a Jewish college, I need to talk to her."

Sarah's face betrayed her lack of excitement. "I get the feeling you're mixing up the players, and you're so wrong. Racine being Jewish, if she is, has nothing to do with Belize."

"You don't know that," he said.

"Damn it, Kenn. The cases are *not* related. I'm beginning to like the fun we're having following clues, so I'll go with you to interview Racine, but I'm out of there and back to Denver if you even mention to her what you saw in Belize, since it was the day *before* her mother died."

Kennedy waved his hand and shook his head to calm her down. "I know you're right. It just bothers me. The coincidence."

"Bullshit. You think there's only one Jewish woman in all of Mexico and Belize . . . and to solve your coincidental cases all she had to do was die twice?" She squinted her eyes, snapped her lips shut, and dragged a breath through dilated nostrils. "Damn it. That's not coincidence—it's convenience."

Back off, Kennedy warned himself. He wanted her help. Needed her help. "Baltimore's a long way from here. And a long way from Denver. Sure you want to go?"

"My eventual goal is north and west to Denver," she said, articulating her words. "This is just the northern leg."

Kennedy pumped his fist and then raised and waved his palm, looking for a high-five. He got only air until she raised her hand and he slapped her warm palm. "Yes," he said. "One more day and we're still a team. And yes, grovel, grovel, I need your help. And no more about coincidences."

"That's better," Sarah said, "but you can still use a little practice on the groveling."

Feeling good, albeit with reservation, he looked at his watch—almost noon. "If you'll dig out your laptop and look up BHU, I'll call and get us booked. If you're right, we'll track down Racine as soon as we get there, which shouldn't take more than an hour or two. And I'll get you a ticket for tomorrow, a midday flight to Denver. That'll screw up your weekend, but it'll give you half a day of rest before Monday morning."

"That's if we can find all the right tickets," Sarah said.

"Trust me. Megamiles talk."

But Kennedy wasn't worried about miles. In fact, though he often tried, he'd learned since retiring that it was near impossible to use airline miles for late bookings. His solution? American Express, which had sold him a plethora of tickets for his almost-always-last-minute flights, including the past few days.

And he wasn't worried about tickets or prices.

His bigger concerns were finding Racine and making sure Victor didn't find out.

37

Sarah, arms folded, waited for her luggage at baggage claim. "Baltimore," she said. She'd confirmed her guess about Baltimore Hebrew University, but now came the reality. She faced Kennedy. "What the hell am I doing in Baltimore goddamn Maryland? I'm supposed to be sipping a rum punch, soaking up sunshine, cooled by a sea breeze. Crap. It's hotter here than in Belize."

"Sarah, I'm no head doctor, but I've never seen you more frustrated. By everything. All week. Everywhere you turn, you're either pissed off, sarcastic, or depressed. Where's the serious executive you used to be?"

"Now that's a twist because you never mention emotions, mine or yours. Are you showing off or just trying to make me feel better?"

"Neither," he said, "but a few understandable problems got in the way of your vacation and in the way of me wanting to impress you with Belize. Fortunately, there's an easy solution if you ask me—

move to Belize and everything you've seen this week will seem normal."

"Hah! Never will anything I've seen this week ever be normal. But show me a good time, with a few days at a pool, any pool, and I might be more fun than you can imagine."

"You were half the decision to chase after Victor."

"And you're getting too serious. Maybe I should just go home, rest up tomorrow, go back to work on Monday."

"Help me find Racine, and we'll get you out of here tonight."

Sarah spotted her suitcase, her mind flashing visions of office work and stacks of stuff that would be waiting on her desk. She grabbed the handle and stood her bag upright. "You're no fun, Kenn Bracken. Get us an Uber to BHU, and we can be back here by six."

"Nope. We'll need a taxi and a driver with a clock, for destinations unknown."

The driver of the yellow cab—*Nick's Taxi* emblazoned on the doors—loaded the luggage.

Sarah, nestled in the back seat with Kennedy, asked the driver to take them to the Baltimore Hebrew University campus.

"Sorry," the driver said, "there's no such place."

Before Sarah and Kennedy could respond, he added, "It used to be *BHU* but changed its name in about 2010 to Baltimore Hebrew Institute—now *BHI*. Same school, same address."

Sarah said, "Works for us."

Kennedy gave her a thumbs up.

The driver took them to their destination and then named the avenues—Park Heights, Magnolia, Narcissus—as he circled and cut through the tiny campus.

"Stop here," Sarah said, when they were back on Park Heights.

"What's this?" Kennedy asked.

She opened her door. "I don't know, but the sign says Administration, and I see nothing that looks like a dorm. Wait here."

She went inside, but as soon as she saw the desk and thought about the questions she might be asked, she stopped two coeds instead.

"My niece, Racine Perry, is a sophomore, and I have no idea where to find her. Is there a directory I can look at?"

Both students knew Racine, and one was armed with a two-page address book. She read the address and apologized for not having memorized the entire booklet since there were only a hundred students on campus.

"A hundred freshmen?"

No, they told her. The entire campus.

Sarah said her goodbyes and recalled taking many classes at CSU, each with more than a hundred students.

Back in the taxi, she gave the address and added, "Near the corner of Glen and Narcissus Avenues."

Within minutes, they stopped in front of a quaint two-story Victorian with a high front porch that overlooked magnificent, big-trunk maples and oaks.

Kennedy handed the driver two twenties. "That's yours to keep, but I need you to wait and take us back to the airport."

He took the money. "Clock's running, folks. Take your time. I'll keep your luggage safe, and I'll be right here when you're ready to go."

Sarah held Kennedy's arm, climbed the steps, and read the names on a buzzer pad. She pushed the number four button—labeled *Stintz/Perry*. "You ready?" she asked Kennedy.

"Good reporters are always ready."

Thirty seconds later, the door opened, and a wild-haired, barefoot pixie answered, her wardrobe a bulky Baltimore Ravens sweatshirt and track pants. She acted as if she'd expected somebody else.

Sarah stepped forward. "Sorry to bother you. We're looking for Racine Perry."

The young woman kept eye contact with Sarah but closed the gap in the open doorway by a few inches. "She's not available. Can I give her a message?"

Sarah: "Ms. Stintz, we know about Racine's mother and the accident. We're journalists, and we just arrived here from Tampa after visiting with Racine's father, Victor Perry."

The girl opened the door and held out her hand. "Lizia Stintz. Come in. And he's Racine's *stepfather*... unless you want her to go ballistic."

Stepfather, Sarah thought. A sensitive issue, no doubt. With Kennedy at heel, she followed Lizia up two flights of stairs, the banister carved and polished, to an open doorway. The living room, combined with a small kitchen, sported two desks and comfortable furnishings. Two closed doors, Sarah surmised, likely masked bedroom and bathroom.

"Have a seat," the hostess said. "I'll check on Racine." She went to one of the closed doors and peeked in. "Racine, somebody here to see you." She stepped into the room and closed the door behind her.

When Lizia reentered the main living area, she sat, folded her hands in her lap, and spoke directly to Sarah. "She's a mess. When she got here yesterday, she could barely tell me about her mother. She cried so hard I thought she'd pass out. We were up almost all night."

"Mr. Perry told us what happened," Kennedy said. "Did Racine tell you?"

"She tried, but never got the whole story out. Some kind of sailing accident. Her mother drowned. Do you know anything more?"

Sarah shook her head. "You mentioned her stepfather. What's that about?"

"Hah," Lizia said. "Bad vibes there. Racine never talked much about him or her stepbrother, even before the accident. Now she can barely say their names without crying."

Kennedy leaned forward in his seat. "When we talked to her stepfather and Eloise DeLaney, I got the feeling he was anything but religious. Yet BHI is—"

"Racine's Jewish," Lizia said, "as was her mother. I don't know about Racine's stepdad—she calls him Victor—or his son, Rick, but Mr. Perry wears a cross. Eloise? I don't know, but Racine says she's really cool."

"Can you tell us about her mother?" Sarah asked.

Lizia's voice softened. "Madrilène was awesome, inside and out. She's an alum, when it was BHU, and loved the school. She treated Racine like a princess and insisted on good grades, being safe, and using her head. I got to be with her and Racine several times last year when she visited, and I loved her, a perfect Jewish mother. She invited me to join Racine and her on their summer buying trip—some kind of import-export business—to Panama, Costa Rica, all over Central America. Places I've never been. But I turned her down."

Sarah: "I can't imagine—"

"Racine told me her mom had bad vibes about the trip, about everybody being together for so long, but that it might be the family's last chance to all vacation together, before summer jobs, marriage, life stuff." She looked over her shoulder toward the closed door. "I can't help but think that if I'd gone along, maybe she'd still be alive."

"Why didn't you go?" Kennedy asked before Sarah could ask the same question.

"One reason." Lizia drooped her shoulders as if burdened by heavy words. "The whole family brought Racine to school last year and helped us move in. Victor was nice, but the stepbrother's a creep. He hit on me the first minute we were alone. Racine hates him, avoids him, and I wasn't about to get trapped with him on a boat with no way home."

"Victor and Madrilène," Sarah said. "Sounds like second marriages for both."

"Second for Madrilène," Lizia said, "and at least one other for Victor."

Sarah: "We'd like to ask Racine questions about the story Victor's helping us write, but we may have to catch her when she feels better."

"In the meantime," Kennedy chimed in," do you have at least a picture of Madrilène in case we need it for the article?"

Sarah tried to get his attention, warn him away from his coincidence game. His eyes avoided hers as Lizia went to a bookshelf.

"My cellphone's in the bedroom, but Racine has a few pictures in her yearbook that might help." She opened a skinny booklet, looked at pictures, and handed two to Sarah. "They're both Madrilène with Racine."

Pictures in hand, Sarah glared at Kennedy, knowing he'd want one or both photos. But when she focused on the pictures neither had enough quality to be useful in proving Kennedy wrong. Crappy photographer. Both too far away. Not enough light in one, too much backlight in the other. Madrilène's smile was big but tight-lipped in both. Neither picture showed enough detail to reveal jewelry, and Madrilène's pantsuits in both pictures precluded a view of—

Kennedy reached over and gently took the pictures from Sarah's hand. "Lizia," he said, "do you know where we can find Rick?"

Before Lizia could answer, a phone on one of the desks rang. She excused herself, picked up the receiver, said a pleasant hello, listened, and added, "She's asleep and asked that I not disturb her." Lizia then held the phone from her ear, and even across the room Sarah could hear the loud voice. Lizia answered, "I'm sorry, Mr. Perry. I didn't even wake her for the reporters."

Kennedy jumped up and Sarah panicked. She raised her hands and formed a time-out tee, but Lizia missed it as she turned away from her guests.

"Mr. Bracken and Ms.—" She lowered her head, apparently listening. "I'm sorry, sir. I'll do that." She turned, shaking, crying, and looked at Kennedy. With her hand over the receiver, she handed the phone to him. "It's Racine's stepfather. He wants to talk to you."

Sarah whispered, but only because she couldn't talk. "Be nice."

Kennedy found and pushed the speakerphone button. "This is Kennedy Bracken—"

Victor Perry's words vomited from the phone. "I know who the hell it is," he said, "and you're dead, asshole. Now get out of my daughter's house, and stay the hell away from me and my family."

Sarah couldn't breathe, her lungs blocked by fear.

"Sorry, sir," Kennedy said, "you must have the wrong number. I thought you were the cable guy."

The scream from the phone filled the room. "You're dead, Bracken. You and your bitch friend are—"

Kennedy tapped the speakerphone button and closed the connection. "Definitely not somebody I want to talk to." He returned the phone to its cradle.

Lizia supported her weight with both hands on one of the desks. She cried hard.

Sarah embraced her gently. "I'm so sorry. We didn't tell him we were coming."

Lizia shook her head, spoke between sobs. "Since they got back from Mexico, all his calls to Racine are like that. He yells and I cower. If I had caller ID, or even suspected it was him, I'd never answer his calls." She plucked a tissue from a box, blew her nose, and shook her head. "I am so glad I wasn't on his boat for a month."

Then Lizia laughed, all nerves, and to Sarah's surprise, segued back to the pre-phone-call topic. "All I know about her brother is he's into dope at a school in Transylvania. She calls it Transy."

"Where is it?" Sarah asked.

Lizia shook her head. "No clue. I'm hoping it's one

of those military schools for creeps with parents who can't handle them."

Kennedy spoke softly and handed the pictures back to Lizia. "Madrilène and Racine, at least in these pictures, could pass as sisters. I'm very sorry about her death, and we won't bother you again."

"They look alike," Lizia said, "and they're both about five-four. But Racine's skinny, almost frail, where Madrilène had a beautiful figure."

Sarah pulled a business card from her wallet and wrote Kennedy's name and cell-phone number on the back. "If you need either of us, or if Racine would like to talk, please call us at these numbers." She handed the card to Lizia.

"Thanks for your help," Kennedy said. He shook Lizia's hand.

Sarah wrapped Lizia in her arms. "Half of this hug is for you; the rest is for Racine. Please tell her we mean no harm, and that we'd like to talk to her when she feels like it."

Sarah spoke as she and Kennedy walked into late-afternoon sunshine and admired the view from Lizia's front porch. "You think Racine will call?"

"I hope so. I'd stay a week if I thought she'd talk."

"Are you glad we came?"

"Yes. Knowing nothing else, and making no assumptions, I'm impressed by how much Madrilène and Racine look alike."

Sarah, her arm linked with his, pulled his bicep tightly as they managed the high steps. "We need better pictures." She caught herself. "And not because I think the cases are related. I just want to know what she looked like."

Kennedy gave her a shit-eating grin, and then nudged the taxi driver's shoulder. "Thanks for waiting," he said. "We're headed back to the airport."

As soon as they were situated, Kennedy said to Sarah, "Boot your laptop, see if you can find Transylvania, or Transy. If we can find Rick, we'll get some answers."

The driver spoke over his shoulder and queried the nonquestion. "If you're headed to Transy, Transylvania University, I'll be glad to drive you."

Kennedy gave Sarah a thumbs up. "Maybe," he said. "You know where it is?"

"Lexington, Kentucky. Final answer. Great trivia question. But way too far to drive. Lots of folks think it's in the Transval, Romania, or that it has something to do with vampires."

At the mention of vampires, a flash of disgust crossed Sarah's face, and she gave Kennedy a don't-go-there look, a stern reminder she considered the subject of his book verboten in polite company.

Kennedy behaved. "So Transy's in Lexington, Kentucky, and I've never even heard of it."

The driver laughed. "Yeah, but I cheated. I've got a couple more degrees than I need for this job and trivia out the wazoo."

"Sounds like you could be a writer," Sarah said, enjoying the moment.

Kennedy mimicked Sarah's whoa-shit look and mouthed, "What?"

"Tried that," Nick said, "but I drank too much and almost died. Being a cabby fits my needs."

"So don't drink, just write," Sarah quipped. "No responsibilities. Live anywhere you want. Pour out the books. Sell for millions."

"Nope. My cab's my life."

Twenty minutes later, the driver pulled into the departures terminal and asked which airline.

"Don't know," Kennedy said. "We're going two different directions. One to Denver, one to Lexington."

"Then safe trip to both of you. I hope you find what you're looking for."

Kennedy paid and tipped the driver, and Sarah chipped another twenty into the tip kitty.

"I'm glad you're happy," Sarah told the driver. "I wish more people in the world had your attitude."

The driver whistled as he drove off.

"What was that about?" Kennedy asked, toting Sarah's suitcase into the terminal. "The writing thing?"

Sarah stopped walking and faced Kennedy. "Only this. You changed careers—accident investigator to writer—the day you turned fifty. You packed up and moved to Belize. To write. I've been with you a week, and you've written zip, not a word. Yes, bad news about your computer, but you've made no attempt to recover your manuscript. I'm getting ready to fly to Denver, and you might never see me again. So I ask you this. With no writing, and no me, just what the hell are you going to do tonight, tomorrow, next week, the month after that? Maybe being a cabby would make you happy too."

A crinkle of confusion contorted Kennedy's face, a look Sarah didn't often see but highly enjoyed.

"If that's not perverse logic," he said, "I don't know what is. Victor's pissed at us, so we got the hell out of Tampa, and Racine's catatonic, so I'm going to Lexington, where I hope to meet her dysfunctional stepbrother and flush the stink out of a chumming story that doesn't float. Though I totally screwed up your vacation, I'd still like you to go with me, but I understand why you can't, so I'm going alone. Now if you have any clue what airline you'd like to fly to Denver, we'd better get in line, unless you want to spend the night in, and I quote, 'Baltimore goddamn Maryland.'"

An elderly couple stopped beside Kennedy. "If I talked to my wife that way," the old man said, "I'd be dead by morning."

"Or sooner," the old lady added as they shuffled off.

Sarah laughed, grabbed Kennedy's elbow, and recaptured his attention. "You deserved that," she said. "And by the way, I'm going to Lexington with you, headed west, so don't argue."

Kennedy stopped—a two-second pause—and then pumped his fist. "Thank you. I truly do need your help. Time to divide the Perry family and conquer."

The divide part, Sarah liked, but she had reservations about the conquer.

38

Kennedy hung up his phone. "We're on US Airways at 7:55. We board in forty-five minutes. One stop in Charlotte, then Lexington about eleven thirty. Hope you confirmed we're going to the right town."

"Yep, Lexington. I got a hit at Transy. I asked the operator for student Rick Perry. She wouldn't ring me through but allowed me to leave a callback message on his house phone. Which means he's there."

"What message?" Kennedy asked.

"'Rick, it's me,'" she said. "Can't wait to see you. Sunday morning. Be ready.'"

"Maybe I should let you go in alone."

"Not a chance. If this guy's anything like his dad, I already don't trust him."

A half hour into the flight, Kennedy put his hand over Sarah's book and said, "Kentucky."

"Kentucky, what?"

"Kentucky. Your IT friend. Kentucky's where my

pictures got posted to the internet."

"Big state, and it doesn't matter unless you're still pushing coincidence."

"Or maybe," Kennedy said, "the stars are beginning to align."

During the stop in Charlotte, Kennedy called ahead and rented a car. Then he called the 800 number on his Marriott card and got through to the Fairfield Inn at Lexington's Blue Grass Airport.

"King, nonsmoking," he said.

"No kings left," the soft southern voice said, "but I have a king suite."

"Perfect," Kennedy said. He read off his credit card number to guarantee late arrival.

With Kennedy still on the phone, Sarah said she was hungry and would scout fast-food shops. She disappeared down a corridor.

Also hungry, he finished his call and caught up with her. "What'd you find?" he asked.

"You won't like it. It's a what-the-hell-else-would-you-expect burger joint in an airport lounge."

"Can't be that bad," he said.

It was.

"I've had burgers this bad before," he said, "but never worse. We should have waited for Lexington."

"No time," Sarah said. "You're going to be very busy tonight, and it doesn't involve food."

Kennedy's smile filled his entire face.

39

Sipping a surprisingly good cup of coffee in their suite, Kennedy studied the screen on Sarah's laptop. "Transy has eleven hundred students," he said, "ten-to-one bigger than BHI, and an impressive curriculum."

Sarah looked up from the front-page section of the Sunday *Lexington Herald-Leader*. "So once again we're looking for an address?"

"Yes," he said. "There's a good online map we can follow. I'll drive. You navigate."

"It's Sunday morning," Sarah said, "and classes start tomorrow. Is nine too early?"

"For a dopehead? On the last day of summer? Try ten. Or eleven. Maybe two."

"I'm not waiting all day," she said. "Let's go at ten, and he's either there or not."

Kennedy let Sarah out and parked his rental Chevy Malibu on Haupt Circle, which half-surrounded a small park with a gigantic T-shaped flowerbed in the middle of a lush grassy lawn.

Sarah chatted with four students soaking up the morning sun and then returned to the rental car. "Directory says he's in Rosenthal—218A. It's some kind of student apartment complex."

Kennedy, his thoughts already on Rick, handed Sarah her laptop, the screen open to the campus map. "Scan down the names of buildings on the left. If it's listed, you can give me directions."

"Or, we follow the directions I just got, since his apartment's just around the corner on Fourth. When you get out of here, take the first left"—she pointed—"and look for Rosenthal parking."

"That close?" Kennedy said. "Dare we stay parked and walk?"

Sarah closed her laptop and slipped it back in its case. "Walk? Like exercise? God forbid." She opened her door. "I'll lead. You follow."

Kennedy rang the bell.

The guy who answered pulled the door fully open. "Hi, I'm Will. Can I help you?"

Stunned, Kennedy thought of *Pook*, a character he had written into a short story about human attention-getters. Will had a flaming-red-tipped, chartreuse-based mohawk, a sleeve of neon tattoos on one arm, and miniature beer barrels stuck through his earlobes. But Will had spoken as if at a business meeting.

"Yes, you can." Kennedy made introductions. "We're looking for Rick Perry. Do we have the right place?"

"That's us. Come on in. Rick's in the shower."

The small suite was clean, with a loveseat, two chairs, two desks. Doors to two bedrooms stood open, a third was closed, and in the background was the sound of running water. Stacks of boxes, unpacked and empty, evidenced the new-school-year, move-in process. Kennedy wondered how long it would take them to trash the place.

"Rick in trouble?" Will asked.

"Not that I know," Kennedy said, before making introductions. "We just left Rick's sister in Baltimore and want to talk to him about his mother's death."

"Oh, wow," Will said, "that's a bummer. Sharks and all. If I'd been there, I would've died on the spot."

So much for first impressions, Kennedy thought. Will was already more mature than fictional *Pook* had ever been.

"Is Rick taking it hard?" Sarah asked.

"Actually," Will said, "he's doing well. Lot stronger than I'd be. If I'd seen my mother fall in like that, I would've gone after her, and we'd both be dead."

Kennedy noted the bathroom noise had changed from running water to a hair dryer. "I heard they were chumming the sharks," he said, unsure where his statement would lead.

"Yeah, dumbest thing I ever heard," Will said,

"feeding sharks so they'll come after you. That'd be like walking around the Serengeti with a dead gazelle on your back, hoping to get a picture of a lion."

Kennedy laughed. "Hadn't thought of it that way," he said, "and I'm sure the family didn't—"

Rick—Victor in every way except more hair, fewer wrinkles, and three inches shorter—walked out of the bathroom, his massive body bare-butt naked. He did a double take when he saw Sarah and Kennedy. In a single smooth motion, he made a military about-face, said, "Thanks, Will," stepped back into the bathroom, and slammed the door.

Will cracked up.

"Nice tan," Kennedy said to Sara, whose face registered zero reaction.

When Rick reemerged, a towel around his waist, he ignored the threesome as if they were invisible. Padding quietly, he went into one of the bedrooms and closed the door.

"It won't take him long to get dressed," Will said, "but he won't be too happy."

Minutes later, dressed in khakis and a button-down short-sleeve shirt, Rick stepped from his room, raised his arms, and flexed a set of impressive biceps. "Rick Perry," he said, "two hundred seventy-five pounds of blue steel at your service. Sorry about the earlier show-and-tell. I just wanted to see if you were awake." The big man laughed at himself.

Kennedy—despite the person he had been prepared to meet—saw a young man with a good sense of humor, who came across as anything but a dopehead.

Will jumped in. "Rick, meet Sarah and Kenn. Sarah's the pretty one."

The boys laughed, and Kennedy and Sarah exchanged handshakes with Rick.

Kennedy sat beside Sarah. "We visited with your father yesterday in Tampa, and Racine last evening in Baltimore, about your stepmother's accident. Please accept our condolences for your loss."

Rick's eyebrows stretched his eyes wide open as he turned around one of the desk chairs and sat on it backwards. "You talked to my *dad*?"

"Yes, for an hour," Kennedy said. "Beautiful home. We had drinks with him. He filled us in on what he saw, what he remembered, even your days with the police. Can we talk?"

"Yes, sure, though I don't know what I can add."

"Let me explain," Kennedy said. "We're writing about shark deaths and would like your perspective on what had to be a tragic night for everybody."

Sarah put her hand on Will's arm. "Will feels like I do about chumming for sharks. I would've been scared to death." She opened a notepad, readied her pen. "Can you tell us about that? How you enticed the sharks to come to the boat?"

"We, uh," Rick said, "as we told the Mexican cops, we cut up fish and tossed the pieces overboard."

"Big or little chunks?" Kennedy asked. "Or did it matter?"

Rick looked directly at Kennedy. "We had four big jacks—fifteen to twenty pounders. Caught 'em that day. I cleaned 'em and threw the guts in the water. My sister—or this other lady who was on the boat—screamed and pointed. When I looked, there were sharks everywhere. And then we all got in on the action."

Rick regurgitated the story, a repeat of what he'd told the Mexican police.

And an unsettling thought beat its way into Kennedy's consciousness: tell a lie, repeat it forever, and eventually it becomes the truth.

"I cut the fish," Rick continued. "Heads, big chunks of body, fat fillets, even the tails. Everybody helped. We just tossed the chunks and watched the sharks swarm. Some of 'em probably went after each other, like cannibals."

"Wasn't that messy?" Kennedy asked. "The blood and guts on the boat?"

Rick turned to some inner thought, his head lowered a notch, eyes down. "Yeah, and that was the problem. That's when she slipped and fell overboard. Took less than a second. She screamed, and we all went to the rail." Rick stared at the ceiling, as if peering into a memory. "My dad leaned over the side and tried to reach her. He got close, but the sharks didn't wait. When she went under, straight down, she never came back up."

In the silence that followed, Will used a casual knuckle to keep a tear off his cheek. Definitely not

Pook, Kennedy reckoned.

"Thanks for telling us," Kennedy told Rick. "It's got to be difficult for you to talk about. It was tough for your dad too. I have just a few more questions, if you don't mind."

Rick inhaled. "Shoot."

"At the time of the accident, were you guys under sail, or were you motoring?" Kennedy didn't suggest other choices, like *drifting* or *anchored*.

"We were"—Rick's eyes flickered with an aura of indecision—"motoring." Then he jutted his jaw with confidence. "Yes, motoring. That was one of the few nights we didn't have a strong breeze."

Gross lie, Kennedy thought. "So, ten knots, maybe fifteen?"

"More like ten. It was night."

"Chumming at night? Wasn't it hard to see?"

"Spotlights. Big spotlights."

Kennedy: "How long did it take to stop the boat after your mother's accident?"

"Stepmother. And I hit the kill switch myself, no more than a minute after she fell in—"

A phone rang and Sarah reached for her purse. Kennedy feared the call would interrupt the flow of the story, but Rick kept going.

"—we launched the skiff, my sis and me, and we never quit searching until the Mexicans came."

Sarah, phone in hand, wrenched herself off the couch. "Sorry, guys," she said. "I'll take this outside."

"Rick, one more thing," Kennedy said.

"I mentioned we're writing about shark deaths, plural. Sometime before your mother's accident, a young woman was killed in Belize by sharks. A diver who happened to be there photographed the shark frenzy. The pictures, very gruesome, made their way to the internet. As I told your dad, if you ever come across them, I suggest you don't open the file, because I'm sure it's something you won't want to see."

Rick, his face concerned and passionate, folded his arms across his big chest. "Yeah, thanks for the warning. I'll be sure to avoid 'em."

Sarah reentered the apartment palming her phone. She spoke to Rick. "That was Racine. She wanted me to tell you your dad wasn't alone when we visited him. He was with Eloise. Eloise DeLaney, your mom's—"

The almost-three-hundred-pound giant popped up from the chair like a bagel from a toaster. "I know who the hell she is."

Kennedy, on his feet, his hackles raised by an aura of déjà vu, found few differences between son and father and was glad he wasn't facing both. "Rick, you're out of line. We have what we came for, so—"

Rick looked down, pounded fist to palm, and mumbled, "Bitch should've been—" He froze, and then looked up just enough to home in on Kennedy. "I'm out of line? Get out of my house." He pointed to the door. "Get out. Now."

Kennedy put his hand in the small of Sarah's back.

"I'm just the messenger," Sarah said to Rick as

Kennedy opened the door.

Rick, still pointing, said, "Out. Both of you."

As soon as the door slammed shut behind them, Kennedy stopped Sarah. "Where did that—"

From inside the apartment, Rick yelled at Will.

Kennedy stopped to listen but Sarah yanked him from the door. "Forget the kids. Victor's on his way."

"Victor?" Kennedy scanned the street and saw they were alone.

Sarah yanked his arm. "Kenn, he's not here, but he's coming, now, from the airport."

Kennedy, his mouth suddenly dry, grabbed Sarah's elbow and headed toward the car, down the block and around the corner. Half trotting and breathing hard: "Where the hell'd you get that news?"

"The call was actually from Lizia. Victor called her a few minutes ago. He said he'd just landed—here, in Lexington—and was on his way to Rick's. He'd wanted to talk to Racine, but Lizia told him she wasn't home. Victor told Lizia he wanted Racine to call him at Rick's place. She called to warn us."

"So we have, like, exactly no seconds to spare." He looked over his shoulder, saw Rick. "Junior's outside," he said, "maybe on a cellphone."

"Then Victor knows we're here."

Around the corner, they untangled their arms and held hands for balance. Kennedy, feeling Sarah's not-so-gentle tug, was surprised he didn't have to pull her along. He plucked his keys from his pocket as they reached the safety of the car.

In seconds, he turned right off Haupt Circle. As they approached Fourth Street, he glanced left, down the block. Rick had his hands on the roof of a black sedan, talking into the passenger-side window.

"Maybe Victor," Sarah said.

"And somebody's driving him."

One minute later, Kennedy drove into a residential area, off campus, and stopped on a side street, half a mile from campus. His mouth was so dry he couldn't swallow. He let his body settle and made his legs relax.

Sarah leaned back against the headrest, huffing. "Holy wow. Running from bad guys is better than vodka in an IV drip."

Kennedy found his voice. "What was the bit about Eloise?"

"When Lizia told Racine about us, she mentioned that we'd visited with Victor *and* Eloise. Racine said something like better hope Rick doesn't find out."

Kennedy laughed. "And you made sure he did."

"Hey, Madrilène died, and for that I'm sorry. But this is one odd family that's working hard to destroy my vacation. I didn't think it'd hurt to spice up the stew."

"Then you got what you wanted. And what do you think about Rick's 'bitch' comment? Who was he referring to—Madrilène, Racine, or Eloise?"

Sarah shrugged. "No idea, but regardless of who Rick's pissed at, though it seems to have something to do with Eloise, the daddy seems to have forgotten the mommy's been dead for less than two weeks."

"I still say widower Victor and Southern belle Eloise are doing the dirty."

Sarah's elbow shut him up but did nothing to quell his growing curiosity about the dysfunctional Perrys and their secrets.

Secrets Kennedy was determined to unravel.

40

Kennedy parked in the Blue Grass Airport rental-car-return row but didn't get out, his thoughts whirling. Despite his offer for Sarah to stay another day, she'd booked a 2:10 p.m. flight back to Denver, which gave them only an hour.

"We talked to Victor and both kids," he said, "and got nothing except a blurry picture."

"And you still think something's going on," Sarah said. "Something that's too coincidental."

Coincidental had been a convenient word to describe how Kennedy felt after Azalee's mistaken identification and the unrelated death in Mexico. Now, his brain swam in a pool of too much disjointed information. He forced himself to think one step at a time. "Something damn sure happened on the Perry party boat, and Rick's story doesn't float."

"Like what?"

"Easy example. There's a simple math conversion that says if you're driving sixty miles an hour, you're going eighty-eight feet a second."

Sarah leaned forward, got eye-to-eye with him, a worried look on her face. "You having a stroke?"

"No. Hear me out. That means their cruising speed, ten knots, was about fifteen feet a second. Which means Rick's story has two problems."

"I think the problem's in the driver's seat."

"Hush. Listen." He faced her. "If you throw a chunk of chum overboard when you're making fifteen feet a second, ten seconds later the chum is a hundred and fifty feet behind the boat. And that's where the sharks would eventually show up. You can't chum while you're moving, unless you turn tight circles and chum in the middle."

"Why's it matter? The sharks get the food—"

"Why? Because they said they were chumming and sharks were everywhere. And that didn't happen unless they were stopped. As in not motoring."

"So maybe when she fell overboard," Sarah said, "the boat was going only one mile an hour . . . or wasn't even moving. No matter how fast or slow it was going, there had to be a lot happening while they tried to save Madrilène."

Kennedy focused his thoughts, unlocked his jaw. "Second problem. Rick said his dad leaned over the rail and tried to grab his wife's hand. Which is bullshit. If Victor had been standing right beside her when she fell overboard, there's no way he could have grabbed her. Not with the boat making fifteen feet a second and him as big as he is."

Sarah humped her shoulders. "So what? Like

I said, it could have been stopped."

Kennedy vigorously scratched his head, both hands. "Rick says they were motoring, no wind, and he killed the engines less than a minute after the accident. The original police reports said Victor shut down the engines and stopped the boat."

"Does it matter whether Victor or Rick stopped it?"

"Probably not," Kennedy said, "but it might matter which one, if not both, *lied* about stopping it."

Kennedy did more arithmetic. "But more important, if whoever killed the engine had taken just twenty seconds, rather than a minute, Madrilène would still have been a hundred yards behind the boat. And that's a football field. In the dark. Which, even with spotlights, is a long damn way for anybody to see her, and an impossible distance to see sharks."

Sarah nodded slowly. "So Rick lied."

"Rick and everybody else—they all lied."

Sarah closed her eyes, pinched the bridge of her nose. "Where in the hell do we go from here?"

We, Kennedy thought. Such a nice word.

41

Kennedy said, "Tampa."

A beat, before Sarah answered. "I stayed the weekend, and we learned a few things, but no way am I going back to Tampa damn Florida."

"We may not have to. Victor's here, with Rick. You think Eloise came with him?"

Sarah sat, quiet, thinking. "No. He came to see Rick, so he's alone."

"Then we need to talk to Eloise. If you've got the business number, we can get her direct line."

Sarah opened her notebook and gave the number to Kennedy. "When you get her online, let us girls talk."

Kennedy dialed, and a recorded male voice said, "You've reached the offices of Central America X-M Ports. Please leave a short message with your name and number, and we'll call you back. If you need immediate assistance, please call—"

Kennedy scribbled the number. "Got it."

One ring, and then: "X-M Ports, this is Eloise."

Kennedy puffed out his chest like he'd won a trophy.

Sarah ignored him, focused on her goal. "Eloise, it's Sarah. We met yesterday at Mr. Perry's house. I'm headed home and wishing I had one of your kir royale mimosas. How's Tampa?"

Kennedy pointed a finger down his throat.

Sarah snapped him a don't-screw-with-me face.

"Hot," Eloise said. "If you were here, we'd stay by the pool all day long. And you could bring your boss— make him hustle drinks for us."

Kennedy puffed up his biceps.

Sarah closed her eyes, didn't want to look. "He'd be good at that. I'll tell him about your offer. Now, Eloise, I know you're busy, so I won't keep you. I have a few more questions for you and Mr. Perry, and I'll be quick. Is he there?"

"No. His pilot picked him up this morning. He didn't tell me where he was going."

"His pilot?" Sarah asked.

"Vic uses a charter plane," Eloise said. "A Beechcraft according to the invoices. It holds six, and it's really fast. We rode in it Tuesday morning when we came back from Cancún. It would've been a fun trip except for, you know, Madi."

"Eloise, we have a deadline on our story, so I'm sorry I missed Mr. Perry, but maybe you can help. I'm trying to make sure we write an objective story about the accident, and I don't want to leave out or exaggerate anything. Can you tell me what you remember about that night, in your own words?"

In the void that followed, Kennedy shrugged.

"Eloise, you there?" Sarah asked.

"I'm here, but I hate talking about this," she said, her voice stressed and fearful.

Sarah said, "Take your time. I have you on my speakerphone, so I can type as you talk."

Kennedy, too, signaled he was ready, pen in hand.

"We were cutting fish and throwing it," Eloise said. Her second sentence confirmed the similarity to the police reports. Eloise's statements weren't exact, but they tracked closely with Mianna's translation of Eloise's deposition to the Mexican police.

In only minutes, as Eloise wound down her memorized story, Sarah shook her head.

Kennedy scribbled: "Change the subject to chumming."

Sarah pushed away his note and said to Eloise, "I can't imagine how painful that must have been for you. May I ask you a couple of questions?"

Kennedy flashed his note at Sarah, jabbed it with his finger. She refused to look, shook her head.

The voice from the phone said, "Sure."

"Since the family sailed," Sarah said, "I assume Madrilène was a good swimmer. Did she hurt herself when she fell in? Is that why she couldn't get back to the boat?"

"I don't know. There was a delay after the splash. Like maybe she was unconscious, or went under for a few seconds, before she screamed."

"Unconscious?" Sarah asked, not remembering the detail from the Mexican notes. "Did she hit her head?"

"I don't know," Eloise said, pleading. "I just remember the delay."

"Could you see her beside the boat?"

"She was maybe ten or twenty feet from the side, but I'm not good with distances." Eloise's answer verged on a soft wail. "Oh, Sarah, this is so difficult. Madi was my best friend. And it was my fault that..."

Sarah leaned close to the phone but heard only the faint sound of crying.

Kennedy, grimacing, leaned toward Sarah and again waved a note: *Sharks? Chumming? Ask her.*

Sarah focused instead on Eloise, afraid she'd hang up. "I understood it was an accident. What makes you think it was your fault?"

Then, as if there'd not been a single tear, Eloise spoke, her voice flat. "Sarah, thank you for calling. Come visit me whenever you want. Just not when Vic's here."

End of call.

Kennedy wrinkled his note. "Should have asked her about the sharks."

"Give it up. The sharks may have gotten Madrilène, but they're not the story."

42

Frustration oozed from Kennedy's throbbing temples. "The sharks aren't the story? Of course they're the story. Why the hell do you think we're here? Four key words. Chumming. Madrilène. Sharks. Witnesses. That's the story. Except you didn't mention sharks when you had the chance, with all the crying and blubbering going on."

Sarah faced him. "Sometimes you impress me with your compassion and kindness. At other times, like now, you're an insensitive clod, crude and cold."

Kennedy started to protest, but Sarah kept going.

"Eloise wanted to talk," she said, "to tell me something, maybe about what happened. But something's not right, even woman to woman, and we're not going to get it from her. And for damn sure, not from Victor."

"That leaves Rick and Racine."

"And Lizia," Sarah said. "And maybe Will."

He held up his phone. "More calls?"

"Beats flying," she said.

"Who first?"

"Not Rick or Will," she said, "since big daddy's either at their place or close by. Let's try Racine." She opened her day planner for the number.

"And I suppose," he said, "you're against some insensitive clod chiming in?"

"You said it, big guy."

"Then I won't," he said, "at first, but if I don't hear a question about somebody actually seeing sharks, I'll do the asking myself."

He caught Sarah's elbow on its way to his ribs and held on. "Damn it, Sarah. We'll never know the facts unless we get the truth from Eloise or from one of the surviving Perrys—like Racine. Which means now would be a good time to ask the right questions."

Sarah scowled and freed her elbow with a jerk.

Once again, Kennedy visualized working alone, no partner, making calls, asking questions. He'd been alone before, an entire career, and he'd done just fine.

She dialed and punched the speakerphone button. "In case you want to help me, *partner.*"

"In case *I* want to help?" he said. "I recall begging for your help, so please don't be too quick pushing me into the background. You go home tonight, but I'll still be 'chasing ghosts,' as you call it, trying to get a good night's sleep."

She held up her hand to cut him off. "Phone's ringing."

Yeah, he thought, squeezing the rental car steering wheel, itching to talk. *Phone's ringing.*

43

The phone quit ringing. No hello.

"Lizia, it's Sarah. Thank you for your call. We took off from Rick's apartment just in time."

"You're crazy," Lizia said, "and you're fooling with the wrong guy. And I don't mean Rick. If Victor catches you, there's no telling what he might do."

"We don't intend to get caught. All we want is to finish our article. In fact, we just spoke with Eloise, the other woman on the boat."

"I'm lost," Lizia said. "Is Eloise in Lexington, too?"

"No. We called her in Tampa. Now we're hoping we can talk to Racine, if she's feeling better."

"She's not," Lizia said. "She's scared to death Victor will come here. I'm taking her to my—"

A voice in the background interrupted Lizia.

"We're getting out of here," Lizia continued, "at least for a few days, to where we can feel safe, especially at night."

"Lizia, is Racine there?" Sarah asked. "Can I talk to her before you leave?"

A shuffle of noises, and then, "She's not here."

Sarah wondered if her own lies were that transparent. "Can you give me a number where she is? Or an address?"

"Sarah, I'm sorry. Please don't call us again." She broke the connection.

"Oh, a few more questions," Sarah said into the dead phone, her voice cranked up several decibels, her eyes on Kennedy. "How about the goddamn sharks. How many? How big? How—"

Kennedy's fingers found their way into her rib cage, and tickle-induced spasms made her drop the phone and clamor for survival. Between fits of laughter, torso convulsions, and gasping for air, she managed to say, "You'll get yours tonight, big guy."

He stopped cold. "You'll be in Denver."

She wiped her eyes. "No. I won't." She'd made up her mind. Something was wrong. And the wrong thing involved five people: one dead, one on a rampage, one in hiding, and two bad liars.

She pointed to the terminal entrance. "If you want to solve this case, Kennedy Bracken, get out your plastic. We're going back to Baltimore."

Kennedy, face frozen, didn't respond.

"You OK with going back?" she asked, puzzled.

He nodded, slowly, but his jaw muscles flexed as a flash of frustration crossed his face. "Going back makes sense to me. But you're driving me nuts with your last-minute changes."

"Well, crap," she said. "There's an easy damn

solution to you not wanting my help. It has two wings and leaves in a couple of hours. Headed west. Your choice. Time to decide. Am I in or out?"

"Sonofabitch," Kennedy said, "you want *me* to decide? I want and need your help, but your in-versus-out decision has to be mutually exclusive. If you're in, you're in all the way. If you're out, it's over. You had a week of vacation, which we both wanted to be a nice experience, but you hung its failure over my head every morning the sun came up. Now, days don't even count to you. You jump on a plane as if it's a game, and then reluctantly onto another, and another, always dangling the I'm-going-home-to-Denver threat to keep me in line."

Sarah cinched up her negotiating hat. "I'll repeat, 'Your choice. Time to decide.'"

Kennedy turned his head her way. "Wrong damn thing to say, Sarah, because I'm tired of your pissing and moaning, and I don't really care if you go home."

A pressure in Sarah's head screamed for release, but she let him continue.

Which he did. "If you want to quit—your decision—there's the door. But if you want to help, really help, then call your office and tell your boss you're taking a second week off. Two damn weeks—the company can survive without you. Buy tickets to go home next weekend. That'll give us tonight and five full days to figure out what the hell's going on. If we get done earlier, so be it—you'll be home Tuesday, Wednesday, whenever."

Sarah steamed, weighed his words, considered her options. She could pitch a hissy fit and storm into the airport, or—

She'd lost him once, to Belize, not just because he'd wanted to write, fish, leave footprints. More important, she'd lost him because her job dictated her life—their lives—around the clock.

—she could yield. Take a chance. She raised her chin, purposefully high. "You want to solve this case with me? Or without me?"

"I want and need your help."

"Then I'll use your words. You get my help only if I'm *in* all the way. Which means we do everything together, other than when you need to take the lead, at which time I'll step back. But when it's *my* time in the hot box, you get the hell out of the way and give me the same respect."

"Deal."

"Then we'd better get inside," she said. "You get tickets to Baltimore. I'll call my office."

Kennedy's face softened, and he nodded ever so slightly. He touched her shoulder. "Thank you."

"You're welcome." She opened the car door. "But I want you to know I've never in my life taken a two-week vacation."

And every bone in her body knew the second week of this one would be no better than the first. Starting in Baltimore. Again. Trying to get through to Racine. Again. A girl she'd never met.

Holy wow.

44

Kennedy and Sarah climbed the high stairs he'd seen before. "You ready?" he asked, glad to have his partner at his side.

Sarah delivered her answer with a single finger to the Stints/Perry buzzer button.

Somebody yelled.

Kennedy jumped.

Sarah screamed.

Victor Perry charged from the street up the Victorian steps, great heaving strides, his fists clenched, his body and face puffed with anger.

With the stairs blocked by charging Victor, Kennedy decided against the downhill, big-drop-off handrail to the left, grabbed Sarah's arm and pulled-pushed her to the other end, where the drop to the flowerbed was a mere seven feet. They climbed the rail and jumped together, flying as if choreographed, before landing side by side in a brilliant-pink rhododendron—Sarah standing, Kennedy on his butt.

"You're dead, Bracken," a voice from above said.

Victor looked over the rail.

Kennedy scrambled to his feet, glad Victor hadn't jumped, which was the only reason Kennedy was still alive. Out of breath, he asked, "Are you the cable guy? You kind of remind me of a gentleman I met just yesterday in Tampa."

Victor, also out of breath, spoke with a surprising calm. "You want to get through this in one piece, wiseass—and you too, missy—stay away from my family. And watch your backs."

Kennedy spoke from his position of relative safety, barring a jump-and-squish strategy by the big man. "Thanks for the advice, Victor. And by the way, did you actually see sharks, *real* sharks, before your wife disappeared?"

Victor hefted a beefy leg and kicked the pristine-white upper railing, which shattered and rained chunks of rail and spindles over the side.

Kennedy and Sarah moved fast, together, to get out of the way of falling debris.

Victor pointed a porky finger at Kennedy and spoke from the lofty, crudely remodeled, open-view veranda. "Like I told you, Bracken, watch your back."

With Sarah on his arm, squeezing tight, Kennedy said, "We'll see you around, Victor." He looked back and walked down the hill. At the curb, ever watchful of the giant he left behind, Kennedy opened Sarah's door to their rental car.

Neither spoke as they drove away, constantly watching over their shoulders and out the windows.

Victor, arms crossed—king of the hill on the porch of his stepdaughter's house—slowly moved his head to follow their departure.

In the post-adrenaline-rush calm that followed, Sarah spoke, her voice breathy. "What was that about?"

"I guess," Kennedy said, "that was the only way I'd get to ask my shark question. And after all that, for what?"

"The *'for what'* is simple and now confirmed. Victor's got something to hide, and Racine, Rick, and Eloise know what it is."

Kennedy digested her words and his own rumble of conflicting thoughts. "Then we're doing this wrong." He braked, pulled into a driveway, and turned around. "We're going back."

Using neighborhood streets, even as Sarah protested, Kennedy skirted Racine's house by two blocks and then closed in.

"Kenn, stay away from him," Sarah said. "This is stupid, and I don't want to wake up dead."

"I don't want him to be my buddy, but I want to know where he is and what he's doing." Kennedy picked a shaded parking spot half a block up the hill from Racine's place.

Victor sat on the top step, elbows on his knees, and stared toward the street.

Sarah mumbled, "Looks like a polar bear waiting for a seal to pop up through a hole in the ice."

"Or he's abandoned," Kennedy said, "and waiting

for somebody to let him in."

Sarah looked at the reflection in her outside wing mirror. "Or his driver dropped him off and nobody's home."

"You think the girls are hiding inside?"

"I had hoped they were," Sarah said. "But the way Lizia talked, and with classes starting tomorrow, she was leaving the apartment and taking Racine somewhere safe, like to a friend, a teacher, or maybe a relative."

Victor Perry was halfway down the steps before Kennedy realized a huge black sedan, maybe a Lincoln, had driven by Kennedy's position and stopped in front of the house. He nudged Sarah and pointed.

She'd already slouched down in her seat. "I'm watching."

Victor got in the backseat, and the sedan departed.

Kennedy started the car and pulled from the curb. "Get out your Avis map," he said, "and let's see where he's going." Following the sedan, he stayed back all he could and had to play catch-up each time traffic separated the vehicles.

"Where are we?" he asked, glancing at Sarah's map.

"Southbound on Hilton Parkway." She traced a finger down the page. "And the only things I see to the south are a bunch of interstates and the Baltimore-Washington airport."

"Airport's good enough for me. Bastard won't be bothering us tonight." A Marathon service station provided Kennedy a convenient turnaround spot.

But the station's name proved to be the catalyst for an unpleasant thought—the marathon race Kennedy seemed to be running, for which there was neither an end in sight nor a prize for the winner.

And just maybe, something worse.

45

Baltimore Hebrew Institute. Again. Sarah searched for talkative students and found two likely candidates in the administration building. But she soon learned she'd been lucky with the students who'd first helped her find Racine.

"I'm not doing too well," she told Kennedy. "The last guy I talked to looked like a student but was clueless about the school."

"Then let's eat. You have to be starving."

"Which means you're hungry. What do you want?"

Kennedy's entire face broke into a grin. "Steak's not too good in Belize."

"Then steak it is, unless we find Mexican first."

Sarah directed Kennedy through near-campus streets and found success on Park Heights Avenue. "Looks like your choices are Chinese and Italian."

Kennedy's face screamed happy. "Then it's gotta be lasagna."

Sarah pondered his choice. "Good. You get the

lasagna, and I'll decide if I like it."

The stunned look on Kennedy's speechless face made her love him even more.

Seated, they each ordered iced tea and Sarah checked out the other patrons—an elderly couple, a dating pair working on coffee and dessert, and a mom and dad with two young kids, one crying.

Sarah, soft voice: "Lean to your left."

Kennedy did, but leaned so far he almost fell out of his chair.

When he righted himself, she said, "BHI book bag. But they just signaled for their check."

"Then do your thing," Kennedy said. He stood, scanned the restaurant, and pointed. "Restrooms are in the back left corner."

Sarah commented on the bag to the young couple, which opened a conversation. During the next few minutes, she introduced herself and her absentee journalist colleague, Kennedy Bracken. And that led to the salient points of their short overnight visit: looking for Sarah's niece, Racine Perry, or her roommate, Lizia Stintz, since they seemed to be out for the evening.

The students knew Racine and Lizia and spoke freely about them, their friends, their relatives, and where they might eat. And the young woman's online address book filled in the blanks of who might be spending the night with whom.

"You mentioned relatives," Sarah said, when her written list was complete. "Any in town?"

"None that I know," the girl said. "I met Racine's dad when he helped her pack up for the summer break. I think he was from New York."

"That would be Victor," Sarah said. "But he lives in Florida."

"No," the girl said, shaking her head. "Her stepdad is in Florida. The one I met, her father, lives in New York."

"I didn't know that. Do you recall his name?"

"First name's Jack." The girl again went to her phone. "Racine is listed as Racine *Levine* Perry. He's Jack Levine."

Sarah made a note as Kennedy returned to the table.

Later, when the students again asked for their bill, they, and Sarah, learned that Kennedy had paid their tab as a thank-you for their help.

"Our pleasure," Kennedy told them, which led to handshakes and goodbyes.

"Thanks for doing that," Sarah told him. "Now are you ready to order?"

"Hah."

Sarah worked on a bowl of vegetarian angel-hair pasta. Though visually brimming with mixed spices and chunks of garlic, guilt rendered the dish tasteless. She picked at her food and promised herself she could never allow harm to come to Racine or Lizia, not when she'd gained access to them through lies and deceit.

Kennedy, in the meantime, demolished the antipasti they were to have shared, cleaned his plate of the last morsel of lasagna and steamed vegetables, and finished single-handedly the basket of toasted garlic bread.

Sarah watched, fascinated, as he scanned the table, his eyes focusing on her unfinished entrée.

She knew it was coming. It'd been four days since her Coconut Cafe coup de grâce plate switch. The look in his eyes said it was payback time. And if he could pull it off, he'd be as proud as a young footballer catching his first pass.

A tiny grin cracked his face, the face she loved. He held up his empty plate, moved it toward her, and spoke his words ever so carefully. "You want to trade?"

Sarah lifted her almost-full bowl of pasta, its spicy aromatics profound.

Kennedy's eyes gleamed.

"No, thanks," she said. "But I'll take one of those takeaway boxes when the waiter comes."

If the rest of her week were to crash and burn, the memory of the look on his face would have made it worthwhile.

Then she reneged and took back the thought, wanting no part of crash and burn. "Just kidding. It's all yours."

46

In response to Sarah's call to the third name on her
written list—while Kennedy leaned back in the
driver's seat and finished off her pasta—a lady
named Betty answered the phone. Sarah, with neither
introduction nor explanation, asked for Lizia Stintz,
expecting better odds of being put through without a
hassle.

Five seconds later: "This is Lizia."

"Lizia, it's Sarah. Two hours ago, Victor Perry was
on your front porch, looking for Racine. He had a
temper fit and kicked a big chunk out of the porch
railing."

Whispered words: "Just a minute."

Seconds passed.

Kennedy had parked down the street from Betty's
address. He scowled a what's-going-on look.

Sarah gave him something he would
understand—index finger to pursed lips.

"I'm sorry," Lizia said. "We were all in the kitchen,
so I couldn't talk. Is he still there? Does he know

where we are?"

"We followed him halfway to the airport, and we were glad to see him go."

Lizia spoke fast, her words clipped. "Sarah, this is bad. Racine got here Friday and told me her mother had died, which is why she cries and sleeps and doesn't eat. But I don't think it's just her mother. She's scared to death."

"Did she tell you why?" Sarah asked. "Something about her stepdad?"

"Him, yes," Lizia said, "but I've got no idea why. And she seems scared of everybody else too. She won't take a call from anybody, doesn't matter who it is. The only reason I got her to come here was because of Mr. Perry's call this morning."

"How about visitors? Will she see us?"

"Sarah, I hate to be blunt, but after what Mr. Perry said, even I don't want you to visit. Are you still at Transy?"

"Lizia, we flew back to Baltimore this afternoon. That's when we saw Victor at your house, on your porch. We're sitting in our car, just down the street from Betty's house. The same Betty you're staying with."

"Oh, God," Lizia said, "it didn't hit me you're here. I think I'm going to throw up."

"Just take a deep breath," Sarah said. "We won't bother you—"

"Trouble behind us," Kennedy said.

"Hold on," Sarah said to Lizia. Then to Kennedy, a whisper, "What's wrong?"

Kennedy leaned forward in his seat and looked into the driver's-side wing mirror. "There's a big sedan in the middle of the street. No lights. I think it went by us the other way a couple minutes ago."

Sarah, instantly hyperventilating, spoke into the phone. "Lizia, there's a car in the street behind us. It might be Victor. Don't hang up." She punched "mute" on her cellphone.

Kennedy whispered, "I need to start the car, but I don't want the lights to go on." He fumbled with switches Sarah couldn't see. "I think I've got the lights turned off, but we're about to find out." He turned the key, the starter motor kicked in, and the engine purred to life in perfect darkness.

"Keep your foot off the brake," Sarah whispered.

"Why are you whispering?" Kennedy asked.

"Because you did."

Kennedy shook his head. "Frick and Frack. Some detectives we are." He stayed focused on the rearview mirror. "If that's Victor back there and he somehow followed us, he doesn't know what we're doing. And even if he thought we were on the phone with Racine, he wouldn't know which house."

"What should I tell Lizia?"

"Have her get to a dark window and watch what the car in the street does when we leave. And if she has the slightest problem, have her call 911."

Sarah punched "mute" again and told Lizia what was going on.

"Oh, God," Lizia said, "I need to call the police right now."

"I can't stop you," Sarah said, "but you'll know a lot more as soon as we pull out of our parking space. Stay on the phone and tell us what you see. Have Betty call the cops if you need them. We won't be far away."

Though we might be dead, she thought.

47

Kennedy turned the wheel toward the street. "You ready?"

"Ever see the movie *Bullitt?*" Sarah asked.

"Yes, but I'm not looking for a chase scene. I just want to know if the car stays put or follows."

"Then you drive; I'll watch."

Kennedy pulled out and headed toward the stop sign, half a block ahead.

The black sedan, headlights on bright, was five feet off his tail before he'd gone twenty feet.

Sarah looked back. "They're following."

"No shit," Kennedy said. He turned on his headlights, flicked his turn signal, stopped at the stop sign, and made a right turn.

The beast stayed on his tail as if linked by a short chain.

Kennedy headed to Park Heights Avenue, the only big street he knew well. Three blocks past the Italian restaurant, Park Heights split into a divided highway. He considered going the wrong way, just to test the resolve of his pursuer, but couldn't quite swallow the concept of certain death. Stopping and assailing

Victor was an option, but the big man had backup, and Sarah might not appreciate Kennedy being in a two-on-one street brawl.

Sarah, still on the phone, said to Kennedy, "Lizia wants to know what to do."

Kennedy saw what he wanted—a major cross-street intersection, the light red. "Tell her to hang tight." He squinted his eyes, trying to see behind him, hoping for a face. "We'll call her back."

Kennedy stopped at the light, second in line, with one car behind him—big and black. "Call 911. Tell them there's a car stalled in the intersection of Park Heights and"—he read the cross street sign—"West Cold Spring Lane. Tell them you're a tourist, just driving by."

The light turned green. Kennedy drove to the center of the intersection—bright lights on his tail—and stopped the car. He turned off his headlights and punched the emergency blinker button while Sarah spoke into the phone. The turn-signal indicators on the dash lighted up and flashed.

Horns honked.

Kennedy locked the doors, wishing to hell he could trade the ice scraper in the back seat for a baseball bat.

"The driver's an old man," Sarah said into the phone. "Really, really old. Probably a stroke, maybe a heart attack."

Kennedy, with cars facing him from the left, right,

and behind, tuned out the honking horns and focused on his rearview mirror. "Perfect," he whispered.

Behind him, the bright headlights backed up a few feet, and then pulled right before passing Kennedy's vehicle on the passenger side.

Kennedy scanned the car, tried to penetrate blackened windows, tried to see who was inside. Not even a shadow.

The car crossed the intersection, pulled forward half a block, and stopped on the right, where it waited.

"We're out of here," Kennedy said. He started the engine, waited for his light to turn green, and then turned hard left, eastbound. He floored the gas pedal and made another left.

Sarah said into the phone, "The driver just turned west on Cold Spring, so I'd guess he's OK," and then hung up. As random turns followed, she watched out the back window.

Kennedy, thankful for her diligence, concentrated on quick turns onto narrow streets with cars parked on both sides. "Get the name of the next cross street." He slowed through a neighborhood intersection, pulled to the right, and parked. Foot off the brake, he turned off the lights and engine.

"Oakley Avenue," Sarah said.

"Call Lizia and tell her we're near the intersection of Lanier and Oakley. Ask her what they want to do."

Sarah threw her palms up. "Them? Lizia and

Racine? Such as what?"

"Such as," he said, "they need to get the hell away from Betty's place because Victor may watch for them in the morning, and he'll damn sure spot us if we go there. So we meet them here or wherever else they want—their call."

"Bullcrap. If Racine's that scared of Victor, she should call the cops."

Kennedy stopped cold. Something didn't fit. "So why hasn't she?" he asked. "Why's she running so scared, afraid for her life, yet no cops?"

"That, we don't know," Sarah said. "And I'm betting she won't tell us."

"That may be the case," Kennedy said, "but I'll bet that whatever's going on between Victor and Racine is something more than a pity party just because her mom died."

Sarah picked up her phone. "If you ever get to talk to her, I suggest you hold that thought."

Kennedy nodded. While Sarah dialed Lizia, he watched the rearview mirror, his mind churning thoughts and memories and concerns into alphabet confetti. Running from bad guys wasn't his forte. He was a writer, for better or worse. He wrote fiction, made up stuff, killed off pricks who deserved to die. But this sonofabitch—Victor—had it backward. His aggression had evolved into something beyond embellished storytelling. Something like brute rage. And Kennedy's only possible weapon against Victor seemed to be Victor's own stepdaughter, Racine.

Racine—not afraid to talk.

Racine—not dead.

48

Sarah: "Lizia, he faked leaving town. We think he found us at dinner and followed us, but it's not *us* he wants. He wants Racine."

The speakerphone carried sounds of crying in the background, and then Lizia said, "You'll never get her to talk."

Kennedy leaned toward the phone. "Lizia, tell Racine we know Victor's threatening her."

Sarah gave Kennedy a news-to-me look.

The white noise from the phone stopped.

Kennedy reached for the phone. "What—"

"She may have muted it," Sarah said. "Just hang on. And where'd the threat stuff come from?"

"I'm just guessing, but since she hasn't gone to the cops about Victor, there might be a threat lurking in the wings."

"You think Victor would hurt her?"

"I wouldn't put it past him."

Two long minutes later, the white noise returned, and Lizia said, "Sarah, as soon as I mentioned you knew about the threats, Racine went into, like, shock. She may not be too good at talking, but she wants to hear what you have to say. What's that all about?"

"Lizia," Sarah said, "we need to meet face-to-face, and it doesn't matter where, just so her stepdad can't find us. Do you have a suggestion?"

"Somewhere on campus?" Kennedy asked. "Somebody else's house? Or we can meet here and follow you to a hotel, get you two your own room, and we can visit in private."

Getting a reluctant agreement to meet, Sarah asked Lizia if she and Racine could get to their own car without being seen.

"Racine's parked in a carport behind the house, off the alley. We'll come to where you are. Give us about five minutes."

"Did you notice she said *threats,* plural?" Kennedy asked.

"Yes, but I didn't mention it since they agreed to meet."

Unable to wait past the seventh minute, Sarah called. As soon as Lizia answered, Sarah asked, "Are you lost?"

"No. I'm watching out the upstairs window. There's a black car parked in the alley, no lights. It was here when we first looked out, and it hasn't moved. We're guessing it's empty."

"Trust me," Kennedy said into the phone. "It's not empty. Victor's in the car. He's probably not expecting you to leave tonight, and he's waiting for morning."

"Stay on the phone, Lizia," Sarah said. "We're coming to your place. If the car stays in the alley, watch out the front door. As soon as we get there—we're in a white sedan—you and Racine come out. We'll have the doors open, but you'll have to hurry."

Sarah's self-made promise to allow no harm to come to either girl seemed hollow as she and Kennedy drove toward the rendezvous, knowing Victor would be only an alley away.

Sarah stared out the passenger-side window.

The front door opened, and Lizia and a second young woman—Racine, Sarah presumed—started toward the car.

"Ray!" a voice bellowed from the side yard. "Goddamn it. Come here."

The girls, startled, ran hard without looking back. A giant of a man loomed after them, a giant of a man named Victor.

Sarah tried to yell to the running girls, but fear had sucked her lungs dry. All she could do was hold the passenger-side doors fully open.

Kennedy had his two doors open and snapped orders: "Keep your bags. Get in. One each side. We'll close your doors."

Lizia and Racine split up and bailed into the back seats.

Sarah slammed the rear door, piled back into her front seat, and yanked her own door shut as Victor charged the car.

Kennedy hit the gas.

The rental car lurched from the starting blocks—Victor screaming and pounding on the passenger-side windows.

Sarah sucked tiny breaths and scrunched deep muscles and pinched her legs together to keep from peeing in her pants. Only as they gained speed was it apparent to her that five people had yelled throughout the escape: Victor had spewed vulgarities; Lizia and Racine had cried and screamed and pounded on the seats; Kennedy had shouted directions about bags, doors, and speed as if his passengers had never seen a car; and Sarah, herself, from deep inside, had squeaked and ejaculated breathless unladylike red-faced curses at the fat bastard who'd better not ever let her catch him alone.

Finally feeling safe, Sarah loosened her seatbelt and turned in her seat, ready to introduce herself, while Lizia gave Kennedy a staccato sequence of right-left-right directions.

Lizia held up her hand to Sarah and shook her head. Her other arm was around Racine, a cowering wisp of a girl who sat with her legs tucked beneath her, her hands fisted together, tight against her mouth.

Sarah thought about the trauma Racine had been

through and the fear that encased her now.

"Turn right and go to the first light," Lizia said, "then right again. You'll be on Reisterstown Road, going north. There's a Hilton in Pikesville, maybe two or three miles up the road."

"Just make sure we're not being followed," Kennedy said.

"We're good so far," Sarah said, alternately looking over her shoulder and into her wing mirror. "Nobody behind us since we left the house."

"Hilton's on the left side," a new voice from the backseat said, "just before the interstate."

Finally, Sarah thought—there's hope. She looked toward the voice and said, "Thanks, Racine. We want to help you get through this."

Minutes later, Kennedy pulled into the rear of the Hilton. "How's this?" he asked, as he backed into a slot between a Ford Excursion from California and a U-Haul truck towing a small Jeep.

"Good, as long as we can find it tomorrow," Sarah said.

"Really good," Racine said, "as long as nobody finds us tonight."

Tonight? Sarah wondered. A potential problem.

But sunrise worried her more.

49

Kennedy straddled a hogback—a truth-stretching pseudo journalist on one side, an investigator passionate to help Racine on the other. And right down the skinny middle stood Sarah, whose suitcase was already packed for Denver. As much as he hated to perpetuate the lie, when it came time for introductions, he and Sarah were once again writers for a documentary on shark-attack deaths.

Neither Racine nor Lizia seemed impressed by Kennedy's writing challenge.

With the foursome checked into adjoining rooms, Kennedy ordered two large pizzas and soft drinks, which arrived just in time for the not-so-happy party in Kennedy and Sarah's room. Kennedy pulled a chair from a small desk and faced the beds—Sarah on one, the girls on the other. To a person, the tiny group seemed reluctant to talk while eating.

"Racine, it's late," Kennedy said, "and it's been a stressful day for all of us. We have all night to talk, but we're concerned you may not be up to it. If you'd rather talk in the morning, we can wait."

The girls looked at each other—one head shook, the other nodded. "It's gotta be tonight," Lizia said, wiping her hands. "We have classes tomorrow."

"And you guys can leave in the morning," Racine said, "because it won't take me long to tell you what I know."

Something grumbled in Kennedy's stomach. Two stories? he wondered. The Mexican version, and perhaps another that might spill secrets? He considered the irony of having to lie with conviction to get her to tell the truth.

Kennedy: "You may think I want to talk about the boat. About what you told the police. About what happened to your mother, for which we truly offer our condolences. Those things are all important to the kind of story we're writing, but I have a different concern."

Racine, lips puckered, looked from Lizia to Sarah, and then back to Kennedy. "I don't know what you're talking about."

"Racine, you told the Mexican police what happened because they asked. And because they had a right to know. Your stepdad and stepbrother told the same story, as did Eloise DeLaney. It seems the police, with four credible witnesses, are satisfied your mother's death was an accident."

"And they let us go. What's the big deal?"

"The big deal," Kennedy said, "is Victor, your

stepfather. He made it that way. It's not that he didn't want us to write an article. It's that he realized, at his house yesterday morning, we had spoken to the Mexican police. And he realized we were getting inside the story, penetrating it. And with that, like a crazy man, he blew up. He kicked us out. No questions about our motives, no second chances, just get the hell out of his house."

Racine shrank in place, even as Lizia moved closer and offered a hugging arm.

Sarah said nothing but watched the girls, her focus intent.

Kennedy had the feeling that at any moment the three women were going to take over, so he kept going. "When Victor found us at your place, and the next day at Rick's, his whole world went crazy. He didn't just get mad, he turned lethal. His actions, everything he's done since that time, are totally disproportionate to whatever he thinks we've done wrong."

"He's always like that," Racine said, as if explaining life to a child. "Mad, and screaming, and cussing, but that doesn't change anything."

"I disagree," Kennedy said. "Change is the magic word. Change is what Victor fears. Specifically, he doesn't want anybody—you, Rick, Eloise—to change your story. The story you told to the Mexican police."

Kennedy looked for a reaction—nothing. "So, two questions," he said. "First, why does Victor care who says what? And second, what makes him think he can keep you from talking to us?"

Racine's face crinkled as she folded her arms. "You're not the police. Why should I even talk to you?"

"Simple reason," Kennedy said. "Victor came to your house this morning and found us. What if we hadn't been there and you'd been home? What if he found out Lizia called us and told us he was in Lexington?"

Racine sat up. "Good God, he's not going to hurt me. Maybe he just doesn't like you in his business."

"Racine," Sarah said, "you mentioned we're not the police. Do you think this whole affair is something the police should be involved in?"

Racine's face froze, as if hit by a Taser. She scooted toward the edge of the bed, folded her hands together, and spoke directly to Sarah. "My mother died," she said, her words cold. "It was an accident. The Mexicans investigated and let us go, which means *you* are making a big deal about nothing."

"Racine," Sarah said, "you know better than anybody that nothing could be worse than your mother dying. But at a time when one might expect the entire family to be devastated, you seem to be the only one who cares."

Lizia, who had said nothing since downing a single slice of pizza, lowered her head and mumbled, "One's bad; two's terminal."

Racine's neck stiffened, and she cast a fast glance

at her roommate.

Kennedy asked, "What do you mean, one or two?"

Lizia looked up, as if surprised she'd been heard. "Sorry," she said. "Nothing. Something personal."

Racine, her hands clasped in her lap, stayed mute.

Deadlock, Kennedy surmised. Same old story. Something wrong. Nobody talking.

Sarah stretched her arms and arched her back. "Ladies, thanks for visiting with us. But please don't forget that our being here has to do with safety—yours and ours—and we can use all the help you can give us. Unfortunately, spending the night in a hotel changes nothing. I say we get some sleep and talk over breakfast before we take you back to campus. We'll see how tomorrow plays out."

The foursome said their goodnights, and Lizia and Racine went to their adjoining room.

Good timing, Kennedy thought, as Sarah went into the bathroom and closed the door. With all the women happy, he looked forward to a good night's sleep, a big breakfast in the morning, and breaking through Racine's defenses.

Unless he woke up to find his own head hanging beside the wildebeest on Victor's trophy wall.

50

To Sarah, the tapping fit into her dream—Denver, a northern flicker pecking on stucco, looking for a new home. Then consciousness sorted the facts. Flickers—woodpeckers—don't rap on doors. Eyes wide, she felt Kennedy beside her. "Somebody's at the door," she whispered. "The hallway door."

He lifted his head from his pillow. "Dial 9, and if anything goes wrong, call 911." He threw back the covers, went to the door and looked through the peephole. "Just a minute," he said, loud enough to be heard in the hall.

He tapped a light switch, blinding Sarah. "It's Lizia." He put on a robe and wrapped his body.

Sarah stayed in bed. "She alone?"

"Yes." He opened the door and let her in.

"Are you OK?" Sarah asked. She pointed to the bed the girls had sat on earlier. "Come in; have a seat."

"Thanks. No." Barefooted, her hair victimized by the night, she stepped into the room and whispered, "I can't stay long. Racine will kill me if she finds out

I'm here."

"What's going on?" Kennedy asked, his early morning voice a low grumble.

Sarah patted the air to shush him.

"Today . . . yesterday," Lizia said, "this entire mess. It has something to do with Racine's father."

"Victor," Kennedy said.

Lizia rolled her eyes. "Not her stepdad; her biological father, Mr. Levine. Racine told me he met the plane when they got back from Mexico. He'd wanted private time with Racine, but Mr. Perry made him leave, threatened him, and told him to stay away. I'm guessing the Levines' divorce might have been messy, but Racine never said."

Sarah: "What makes you think Mr. Levine is still involved?"

"Because Racine, during one of her crying fits, said if she wasn't careful, she'd lose both parents."

"Lose?" Kennedy asked. "Like dead?"

"God, I don't know. That's all she said, but every time she sees her stepdad, or hears his name, she panics and cries. The only reason we came with you tonight is because he's in town, and she's afraid for her father. Now, please, I have to go."

"Do you have an address or phone number for Levine?"

Lizia opened her fist and handed a rolled-up note to Sarah. "Please don't tell Racine I gave it to you."

"She won't ever know," Sarah said. "Thank you for

coming. And get some sleep."

Kennedy opened the door for her. "Goodnight, and thanks for your help. I'll watch until you get inside."

Kennedy watched—closed the door.

Sarah: "I'm confused."

"And I'd like to kick some ass."

Sarah opened the note and pulled the covers up. "Jack Levine and a phone number."

Kennedy shucked his robe and turned out the light. "Credit goes to Lizia because I'm guessing Racine would not have given up her father."

They nestled and slipped into a quiet, brainstorming mode.

Somebody wondered why Victor would threaten Levine.

"Maybe he remembers Madrilène's side of the divorce story."

"Maybe Levine's a wife beater, and Victor doesn't like him."

"Or there's insurance or an inheritance involved with Madrilène's death."

"Maybe Victor threatened Levine to keep Racine from talking."

"So why doesn't Levine go to the police and report the crazy bastard who threatened him?"

"Maybe Levine's protecting his daughter."

"And only Racine knows why."

"We need to talk to Levine."

"And to Racine."
"I'm cold."
"Move closer."
"We need sleep."
"Sleep?"
"Mmmm."
"Hah."

51

Kennedy, buttered toast in hand, said, "Racine, we met Victor and your stepbrother, and even Eloise, but I'm not sure how they all fit together. Like how your mom met your stepfather and where Eloise fits into the picture."

That got him a hard look from Sarah.

Lizia sat in the corner of the booth and said nothing.

Racine cut her pancake with the side of her fork, scraping the plate with enough force to play a tune. "Actually, sir, it's none of your business."

"I know," Kennedy said, "but I'm trying to understand why Victor's so upset. If Sarah and I leave town right now, the problem isn't solved. He's angry, and he seems especially angry at us . . . *and you*. And maybe even at Lizia just for being involved."

"Nobody's in trouble," Racine said. "And I like the idea of you leaving."

"I'm glad you think we're all safe," he lied, ignoring further reference to leaving. "Your mother obviously liked Victor enough to marry him, and Lizia liked him when they first met. What changed?"

Racine sat back in her chair. "Duh. Maybe Mom dying can be considered a change."

Sarah placed her hand on Racine's forearm. "And my guess is that *everything* we've talked about started when your mom died."

"*My* guess," Racine said, "is that since it's Monday morning, we need to go to class." She opened her small purse and took out a wallet.

Kennedy said, "I got it, but thanks for offering."

Sarah folded her napkin. "Ladies, restrooms are by the front door. Care to join me?"

Kennedy watched them go and then removed the bill from his pocket and left cash on the table. He went to the desk and checked out of both rooms. Still alone, he waited by the front door—thirteen minutes— unable to grasp why women elected to piddle in pairs or even small groups. Could there possibly be a wide-screen TV in the ladies' room? Video poker machines? His neck cramped from shaking his head, and he wondered about his future as a detective when he knew so little about fully half of the world's population.

Kennedy—again in his role as chauffeur—followed Lizia's directions back to campus. Along the way, he watched for the black sedan, watched for anything suspicious, watched for eyes that might be watching him.

Racine, who'd been mute on the trip back to campus, said, "Next building. Just pull into the lot."

Kennedy parked, got out, and handed the girls their bags. Again he looked for Victor, his own paranoia rampant.

Sarah hugged the girls as if they were longtime friends.

Then Racine and Lizia hugged Kennedy as if they were longtime friends. "Sorry I was rude," Racine told him. "And please don't worry about me."

While Sarah and Racine talked, Lizia singled out Kennedy. "I'll call you if there's trouble. I don't know what else to do."

"Anytime. You have our numbers, but don't be afraid to call 911. Maybe getting the Baltimore cops involved will influence Victor to stay in Tampa."

Because if he were either Racine or Lizia, Kennedy thought, the first time Victor forced his fat ass through the front door, he'd catch a bullet.

52

Kennedy cranked up the heater, his body still not acclimated to sixty-degree mornings. He let Sarah do the talking.

"And while you were paying the bill," she said, "Racine told me about Victor, Rick, and Eloise."

"I knew I should have gone in with you."

Sarah ignored him. "In short, Racine liked Victor, even with his bad temper. But that all changed when her mother died and he went crazy. She has no use for him now and doesn't care if she ever sees him again."

"How about brother Rick?" Kennedy asked.

"No brotherly love there—try pure rage. Racine couldn't even talk about him."

"She say why?"

"Didn't even try," Sarah said. "She locked up when I asked, so I changed the subject."

"That leaves Eloise, I presume. Any problems?"

"Hah," Sarah said. "There's something to be said about a large woman losing fifty pounds just before a month at sea. Her big boobs, with lots of bikini time in the sun, apparently caused a few problems. Victor played Captain Stud, horny Rick was on the make, Madrilène was on a rampage, and Racine did a lot of reading."

"So maybe it was Victor and Eloise, on the yacht, playing house in the forecastle?"

"Not according to Racine," Sarah said. "Victor strutted, but Eloise avoided him. Wherever he was, she'd be somewhere else."

"So what's next?"

"Jack Levine. And we have his number."

Kennedy nodded and scanned the parking lot while Sarah placed the call on speakerphone.

Two rings. "This is Jack."

Jack Levine's voice came through church-apology quiet. Kennedy identified himself and Sarah as journalists but named no magazine and told Levine they had him on a speakerphone. "We're writing an article about recent shark-attack deaths in Belize and Mexico, and we just finished a quiet breakfast with Racine here at BHU, or BHI."

"Which means," Levine said, "you're writing about her mother, Madrilène. Such a tragic death. I'm surprised Racine, bless her heart, spoke with you. How is she doing?"

"She's the picture of health," Sarah said, "a beautiful young woman. She is, of course, devastated by the loss of her mother, but today's her first day of class, and she's excited, or at least pretending to be."

Kennedy said, "We also met Victor and Rick Perry, though I don't think they like us too much."

The phone went quiet. Then Levine asked, "What's this about, Mr. Bracken?"

Surprising Kennedy, the mere mention of the two Perrys, father and son, had caused Levine's demeanor and voice to change, the previous aura of Brooklyn warmth replaced by a garden-killing frost. "We're worried about Racine," Kennedy said. "We're worried something's going on between her and Victor. Something about Madrilène's death. And it somehow includes you."

Levine groaned. "Mr. Bracken, is Racine safe? Has Victor hurt her, even touched her?"

Sarah waved Kennedy off. "Mr. Levine, I spoke to Racine privately this morning. She's safe on all counts, and there's been nothing physical that we know of."

"Thanks to God," Levine said. "This must be some story you're writing: sharks, Jews, drugs, death. Where do I fit into the melee?"

Sarah, eyes wide, mouthed, "Drugs?"

"We don't know, sir," Kennedy said, "because we don't know how you fit together with Racine, Victor, and of course Madrilène."

"And Rick," Sarah added. "And please trust us that we're beyond writing an article—our concern is for Racine."

"For my daughter, then," Levine said, "I will tell

you what I know—"

Kennedy leaned over and tapped Sarah's notebook to make sure she'd scribe the important parts and then dodged her elbow.

"Madrilène and I married almost twenty years ago, when she was seventeen. I was twice her age. Though we had Racine, Madrilène stayed young while I aged beyond my years. Not because of health, mind you, but because socially and spiritually we matured along different lines. Madrilène went to school, got degrees in finance and international relations, and grew to love the world. She started and ran her own successful business. I studied Judaism—obsessed Judaism, to hear Madrilène tell it—and grew in my orthodox beliefs. When we divorced, we did it entirely for Racine, to get her out of the day-to-day conflict that had defined our lives."

"That had to be a difficult decision," Kennedy said.

"It was. Two years later," Levine said, "Madrilène met Victor Perry, from Boston. A good man, a religious man, he treated Madrilène and Racine as if they were angels. A widower, he had a ten-year-old son, a year older than Racine."

"Twice widowed had to be difficult," Kennedy said. "Do you know how his first wife died?"

"Madrilène told me an accident, which may have been suicide, during an angry divorce. She'd fallen or jumped off a balcony, according to a witness. She left no note. Her son, Rick, seven at the time, was home, but Victor had been with friends—fishing—and didn't find out until that night."

Sarah whispered, "Victor probably drove her to jump."

Levine continued. "Madrilène had always been careful with her money, preparing for the future. So she was happy that Victor—a wealthy man who develops shopping malls along the East Coast—had no need for her savings."

"Mr. Levine," Sarah said, "new subject. I have the impression Victor's anything but Jewish."

"He's not," Levine said. "Madrilène invited me to the wedding, in Florida. I didn't know Victor wasn't Jewish until I shook his hand and saw the cross around his neck. Catholic, Episcopal, definitely Christian—I don't know. I asked, but Madrilène told me to mind my business."

"How did Madrilène take to the mixed-religion marriage?" Sarah asked.

"Good, for several years, as far as I could tell. She and Racine took the Perry family name, but neither considered converting. Nor did Victor. But then the troubles started. Victor, out with his pals, drinking, coming home abusive. And his son, Rick, evil in spirit, worse than his father—pure evil. The little—*punk* is a good word—should be in jail."

"Not so little," Kennedy said, his memory all too clear. "He's almost as big as Victor."

"Yes," Levine said. "I saw him last week at the

airport. His body grew big, to better match his penchant for lust and greed."

"How so?" Kennedy asked.

"According to Racine, drugs. She says he's a pusher, a dealer at his school. He pressured Racine to introduce him to her friends. She refused."

"Mr. Levine," Sarah said, "we don't want to keep you, but can you tell us what happened when you met the plane? Racine was very upset when she mentioned it."

"And she had every right to be," Levine said, his increasingly scornful voice rattling the phone as he vented each word. "Victor was a perfect ass. Yes, he lost his wife, but Racine lost her mother, and I lost somebody I never stopped loving. I was there for my daughter, at the airport, and she needed me there with her, to share her loss. Victor, though, professing to protect Racine, pulled me to one side and threatened to do me in if I ever went near her again."

Sarah said, "You were being kind when you called him an ass."

Levine kept going. "I stood up to him, right there in the airport. I told him he couldn't scare me, that I had no fear, that I was there for my daughter, and he couldn't stop me."

Kennedy felt the heat of anger through the phone. "Mr. Levine, you're a strong man, and I admire your boldness."

"Thank you. We call it *chutzpah*, but Victor wasn't

done. He put his giant arms across my shoulders and said ever so quietly, 'Perhaps it's not *you* who should worry about staying healthy. Stay away from her.'"

Sarah and Kennedy spoke at the same time: "He threatened Racine?"

"Not in so many words," Levine said, "but what can I assume? I must believe that if I try to get back in her life, either I'm in danger, which I care nothing about, or she's in danger. And she's now the one person in the world for whom I would die to keep safe."

"Does Racine know about Victor's threats?" Sarah asked.

"No, and she mustn't," Levine said. "She knew only that I wouldn't be at the next day's memorial services for her mother, which Victor and Racine had arranged in Tampa, or so he said. Racine was devastated when I left. I haven't spoken to her since."

"Call the damn cops," Kennedy said, disbelieving Levine could be so laissez-faire. "At least do something."

Jack Levine skipped a beat before answering. "I fear for her, Mr. Bracken, Ms. McGarrity, and of course I can't let this go on. I have not spoken to the police, but I've hired an attorney, who is working even as we speak. He advises that to keep Victor away from Racine, we will have to press charges in Baltimore and have a court issue a civil restraining order. We hope to make it happen before the end of the week."

"That's good." Kennedy pumped his fist. "That's very good."

"I'm so sorry," Sarah said. "What Victor's done isn't right, and both you and Racine are suffering the consequences."

"Don't worry about me," Levine said. "It's far worse that Victor's threats and his belligerence are against a child who just lost her mother."

Kennedy, pleased about the attorney, had another topic. "Mr. Levine, do you know Eloise DeLaney?"

"Yes, of course. She worked for Madrilène and came with her to New York last spring. The three of us spent hours together over lunch. She's originally from Abilene, Texas, and eventually moved to Florida, where she met Madrilène in grad school. She's a delightful person and learned the business rapidly. She was at the airport, but she looked different. I can only hope she was able to put up with the animals, Victor and Rick, for so long on the boat."

"How do you mean she looked different?" Sarah asked.

"You embarrass me to have to say, Ms. McGarrity. Besides being very tan and her hair being blond, she had lost weight and looked more fit and more glamorous than when I met her in New York."

"But you didn't get to talk to her?" Sarah asked.

"No. And a pity that was. I'd like to know what she'll do with the business."

"She may keep it running," Kennedy said. "When we first met Victor, day before yesterday, she was with him at his home."

"Good," Levine said, apparently missing Kennedy's dangled carrot. "Losing Madrilène is bad enough, but I'd hate to see the business fail too."

While Levine answered, Kennedy handed Sarah a short note: "Ask about hamsa."

Sarah rolled her eyes. "Mr. Levine, you mentioned Victor's necklace. The one with the cross. Did Madrilène wear jewelry?"

"Of course—necklaces, earrings, her wedding band."

Sarah was on a roll. "Anything religious?"

"Oh my, yes. The hand of Fatima. A beautiful piece, to keep evil away. She wore it with a necklace or on her ankle, but most often with a bracelet. She seldom removed it."

"Can you describe it?" Sarah asked.

"Yes," Levine said. "It was her mother's. Gold, filigree, shaped like a hand, open, fingers together."

Sarah nodded at Kennedy, an I'll-be-damned look on her face. "Is it symbolic," she asked, "perhaps called by another name?"

"Yes to both questions. The symbol is ancient and is used by Muslims and Jews alike throughout the Middle East—Egypt, Israel, Tunisia, Algeria. Some call it the hand of Miriam, or *Yad Ha'Chamesh*. Most American Jews call it a hamsa. Why do you ask?"

Sarah's face betrayed her inability to answer.

Kennedy pumped his fist. "You said she wore it to keep evil away. Might she have been wearing it on the trip?"

Levine answered as if reminiscing. "She'd wanted so much to pass it on to Racine when she married, and they'd talked about it often. And now that will never happen."

"Because of the accident, of course."

"No, sir," Levine said. "Not the accident. Racine wore it the summer after high school, when the child and her friends went to the Bahamas for a week. Racine had been reluctant to go—the first time to travel without her mother. Madrilène loaned her the hamsa and told her it would keep her safe. She had a wonderful trip, the hamsa apparently working its charm, but she came back without it. The child was devastated, and it almost killed her, but Madrilène's pain went deeper because the link to her own mother was broken."

"I'm so sorry," Sarah said, looking askance at Kennedy.

Kennedy had heard Levine's words, and he'd caught Sarah's I-told-you-so look, but he'd also seen a car—a black Chrysler—as it pulled into the BHI parking lot. "Trouble," he whispered, watching his outside wing mirror. He slouched into his seat and signaled Sarah to do the same. "Get down."

"Sorry," Levine said. "I missed that."

"Hold on, Mr. Levine," Kennedy said. "We're in a bad parking spot and I may have to move the car." He held his left foot on the brake and slipped the gear shift into "drive."

Sarah peeked at her mirror. "We're not going anywhere," she said. "They've got the exit blocked."

Kennedy pulled forward, made a U-turn, and pulled into another slot, facing the exit.

The black sedan didn't move.

"You're making me nervous," Levine said. "What's going on?"

"Trash truck," Kennedy lied. "And we don't want to get blocked in."

The back door of the sedan opened, and a young man climbed out. Two women got out of the front doors. They shared hugs.

Kennedy relaxed. He shifted into "park," his foot off the brake. "We're good, Mr. Levine. Crisis over," he said, though he didn't believe it.

Sarah sat up. "May we call you again if we have other questions?"

"Of course," Levine said. "Anytime. And please keep me informed if you learn anything I need to know."

"Mr. Levine," Kennedy said, "our goal is to keep Racine safe, and it helps that we've spoken. So now it's your turn."

"Sorry. My turn to what?"

"Call Racine—tonight," Kennedy said. "Be honest

with her. Talk this through. Do what's best for both of you."

"So many times I've picked up my phone to call her," Levine said. "Just to talk. To hear her voice."

Sarah leaned toward the phone. "Don't let Victor stop you, Mr. Levine. It's not *you* who needs the call."

After the goodbyes faded and the phone went silent, Kennedy and Sarah stared out the windshield.

"You thinking about the hamsa?" Sarah asked.

"Touché," he said, "but gloating doesn't become you. And no, I'm thinking about bigger fish. First, Levine should shoot Victor, or at least invite the cops to the meeting with the lawyer. Second, before you go back to Denver, we need to stir a little sex and drugs into the kettle of unknowns and talk to Racine again."

"Or maybe," Sarah said, "a lot of sex and drugs."

Kennedy pondered the difference between a little sex and drugs and a lot of sex and drugs and tried to picture what a typical day on the yacht might have looked like. Well, specifically, what Eloise might have looked like.

Then, with no hint of a segue, Sarah said, "I'm glad I stayed. You couldn't get me off this story now even if you quit and went home to Belize."

Kennedy turned to face her. "Don't tell me we've found something with which we're compatible."

Sarah squinted her eyes and gave him an I'm-thinking-about-it look. "Maybe, but don't press your luck."

"If we do build on this partnership," he said, "I'll need two phones."

"Two. Why?"

"One," he said, "so we can keep calling people like we just did. And a second phone so I can call 911 the next time you elbow me."

Her hands tickled into his ribs so fast and intense his attempted escape drove him half under the steering wheel.

Kennedy loved the laughter and high energy of their sparring, yet he couldn't help but wonder how big a bucket of adrenaline he'd need for his imminent showdown with gorilla Victor.

Or perhaps his ape of a son.

Or both.

53

Sarah hung up the phone—again. "Still no answer."

"After-class activities?" Kennedy asked.

"No. Trouble. With all she's been through, anything beyond going to class would be at the bottom of her list. Let's go by the house. See if Victor's lurking in the shadows."

Kennedy started the car, drove the few blocks and approached the house from the uphill side.

Lizia, seated on the top step, saw them coming and waved.

"Some sleuths we are," Kennedy said.

Sarah joined Kennedy in waving to Lizia, as if they were long-lost relatives arriving for Christmas dinner.

"She's not home," Lizia said as soon as Sarah stepped onto the curb. "We were supposed to meet here at two fifteen, and she's too afraid to do anything but go to class."

Sarah replayed Lizia's words—*too afraid*—and combined them with the facts: no Racine, no Victor.

And she understood. "Lizia, will you call me as soon as you hear from her?"

"Of course. Where will you be?"

"I don't know," Sarah said, "but I'll answer if you call." Sarah nudged Kennedy and went straight to the car.

Kennedy got in behind the wheel.

Sarah buckled up. "Head to the airport," she said. "I have a call to make." And if she was right, the pot had already boiled dry.

Sarah dug out the number, dialed, and got an answer.

"Eloise, Sarah here. How you doing?"

The voice crackled from the speakerphone. "Sarah, good to hear from you. Y'all decided to get some pool time after all? Well, come on down; I can't wait."

"Don't know when I can," Sarah said, "but spending time under the Tampa sun is definitely on my radar."

Kennedy, managing traffic as he drove south, mouthed, "Me too."

Sarah ignored him. "Eloise," she said, "we visited Mr. Perry a couple of times over the weekend, and now he's headed back home. It's important we talk to him. Have you heard when he'll be in?"

"He never calls," Eloise said, "but I keep track of him through a friend at TIJC—the Tampa

International Jet Center. Should I call her?"

"Can you do that for me?" Sarah asked.

"Of course. Now stay on the line—I'm fixin' to put you on hold."

The phone got quiet, and Kennedy whispered, "You amaze me."

Sarah leaned over and kissed his temple. "I have lots of experience tracking down clients."

The phone clicked. "You there?" Eloise asked.

"Ready for news," Sarah said.

"Oh, you're so funny. I wish you could've been on our trip. We had so much fun. Well, except for . . . you know."

"Yes, sorry I wasn't there," Sarah said. "And I missed what you said about Mr. Perry's flight."

"ETA for Charlie-Tango-Tango-three-one-eight is 17:25 with three people on board. So he'll be home about six or seven."

"Thanks. And I'm impressed—two pilots for one passenger."

"No," Eloise said. "The three would include Victor, the pilot, and one passenger, unnamed. Probably one of his frigging golfing buddies."

"Eloise, you're the best," Sarah said. "I'll call him this evening or first thing in the morning. But don't tell him since I don't want him changing his plans waiting for my call."

"Count on it," Eloise said. "I won't say a word."

Goodbyes behind them, Sarah hung up. "I didn't

like being deceptive, and hope she didn't pick up on it."

"Truthfully?" Kennedy asked.

"Truthfully."

He nodded and squinted his eyes almost shut. "She's no dummy, and I reckon she read you like a book."

54

Minutes after landing in Tampa, Kennedy checked his watch. "It's 12:05," he said, his feet yearning for sand, his throat needing a Belikin beer. "Put me on the baggage carousel, and I could sleep for a week."

"Or wait an hour, and you can sleep with me."

"Hah. You don't let me sleep."

Seven hours later, breakfast behind them, Kennedy felt the glow of déjà vu, again—Tampa airport, rental car, nice hotel, wonderful memories of sack time with Sarah plus a little sleep, and now the drive to Victor's place. Except it was Tuesday, not Saturday. And the car was a Chrysler 300 rather than a Chevy Malibu.

"I like the skyline and the water and the beautiful homes," he said, driving slowly along the waterfront, on a road with three lanes in each direction, "but the traffic sucks."

"Faster than a San Pedro golf cart," Sarah said.

He shrugged. "But not too good if you're trying to get away from a lunatic with a gun."

"You think he'd use a gun?" Sarah asked.

"Probably wouldn't need one. He could grab my head one-handed and pop it like a grape. And we're avoiding the mission. You still think it'll work?"

"Show me a better idea that won't get us killed," she said, "and I'm all for it."

"Nope," he said. "Your show. And our target's the next big place on the right." He drove by slowly. Two familiar vehicles in the circular drive. The last time he'd seen the cars, two people had been inside—Victor and Eloise.

"Down the street, on the left," Sarah said. "For-sale sign. Maybe turn the car around and get in the shade of the tree."

Kennedy made the turn and checked the time. "Eight fifteen too early?"

"Just needs to be before he goes to class."

"Then now's good," Kennedy said. He parked with a view of Victor's front door three hundred feet down the street and shut off the engine.

Sarah dialed, waited, and punched the speakerphone button.

"Yeah. Hello." Male voice, morning gruff.

"Rick, Sarah McGarrity. We met a couple of days ago, and I recall you were quite upset when we left, for which I'm sorry." Sarah rolled her eyes for Kennedy's benefit. "I've talked to your dad since then, and I now understand what happened on the boat."

No response.

Kennedy waved his hand and mouthed, "Keep going."

"Kenn and I found a couple of convenient airline tickets that will allow us to stop in Lexington this afternoon on our way to Denver. If we do that, can we visit you for a few minutes? Purely a social call?"

Rick didn't answer.

"If you don't want us to, just say no."

Kennedy willed Sarah to tell him they were coming and to get his lard-ass ready.

"Maybe," Rick finally said, "but it depends on classes. What time?"

"If we make the connection," Sarah said, "a visit between four and five at your place will work for us."

"What's your number?" Rick asked.

Sarah gave him her number, guessing he already had it. "If you let us know in the next hour, we'll be sure to make the Lexington flight."

"Give me a few minutes. I'll call you back."

Sarah's phone connection closed.

Neither spoke while they waited.

Four minutes later, Sarah's phone vibrated and rang. She answered on speakerphone.

Rick, previously grouchy but now effervescent, told Sarah he'd be glad to meet with her. "Call me when you get in, and we'll agree on the time. And please make sure Mr. Bracken's with you."

"Not a problem," she said. "We'll both be there."

Sarah killed her connection.

"Nice job," Kennedy said.

"Thank you, *Mr. Bracken.*"

"What was that for?"

"Rick either has a good memory from our first visit, *Mr. Bracken*, or somebody just reminded him of your surname."

Kennedy watched with increased interest out the front window. "Then we'll know soon."

Kennedy pointed to a white SUV as it turned into Victor's driveway. He checked his watch—*soon* had occurred only fifteen minutes after the call to Rick.

"Must be the pilot," Sarah said.

Two guys got out of the vehicle and lit cigarettes. Though one was tall and muscular and the other short and scrawny, they were clean-cut and wore matching white golf shirts and dark slacks. They chatted with each other but made no move toward the house.

Sarah rubbed her hands together. "One's the pilot; the other's probably a hit man."

"Hit man?" Kennedy asked. "Which one? Hard for me to tell from here who's who."

"The tall one," she said, "with black hair, big arms, and no butt—definitely a hit man."

A second car, a glossy-black Lincoln, pulled up and stopped beside the SUV, but nobody got out. "The plot thickens," Kennedy said.

"Or maybe the driver's also the pilot, and we have two hit men."

The front door to the house opened. Three hundred and fifty pounds of pure Victor, wearing black slacks and a red golf shirt, emerged and bounded down the stairs like a defensive lineman running stadium steps. Somebody inside the house closed the door behind him. Victor lit a cigarette and spoke to the two early arrivals. The big-arm guy nodded. His little-shit clone laughed like the class idiot.

"Big Arms looks like he can handle himself," Kennedy said, "but Little Shit's likely related to somebody important."

Victor climbed into the front passenger seat of the black Lincoln, and Big Arms closed the door behind him. As soon as the goons got into the back seat, the driver maneuvered his way along the circular drive and turned back in the direction from which he'd come.

"Well choreographed," Sarah said. "What's your guess?"

"Victor, a pilot, and two thugs," Kennedy said. "Glad we're not in Lexington."

"How long do you want to wait?"

Kennedy believed his gut, which didn't often lie. "Long enough for them to get to the airport and take off."

With FAA confirmation of departure, he thought.

55

Sarah checked her watch. "It's 9:10; time to go."

"Another half hour won't hurt," Kennedy said.

"True, but the bad guys are gone, and we need to get inside. Let's park in front."

Kennedy started to say something. Instead, he sniffed his nose and flexed his jaw muscles. He started the car, drove the short distance down the street, and pulled into the circular drive. He parked at the bottom of the steps that led to the front door.

Sarah opened the passenger door and looked out. "You're a little far from the steps." She looked back at Kennedy as his mouth seemed to dislocate into a painful open position. "Just kidding, sourpuss The car's fine. Now cheer up, because this is the part of the plan where we really need to work together."

Kennedy reached over and held her arm, his touch gentle. "Sarah, if this part is so critical, I need you to think through what we're doing, and not be cocky about having to hurry so you can get back to work. If these guys come back because Victor forgot something, we've got absolutely no defense, and for damn sure no backup plan."

"And you think," she said, "having the car parked down the street would save us from certain death?"

"No. But having it parked down the street with us in it when they come back might just do the trick."

"Kennedy Bracken, you're paranoid."

"And I'm alive," he said, "to hear you say those words because I've survived every close call I've ever had."

"You've said that before."

"And written about it," he said.

"Fiction. Short stories."

"What I wrote about surviving close calls was the absolute truth. Only the names, circumstances, and outcomes were changed."

Sarah gave him a half smile. "You're not going to win this argument, partner."

"Didn't think I would." He pulled the door handle and pushed the door open a crack. "Just be careful— I've got an awful lot of me invested in you."

Sarah stepped from the car and waited until he was beside her. She liked the concept—him invested in her. They climbed the steps in step. This, she knew, was her time to shine. Time to seal the deal. Time to make full partner. And she was ready.

What wasn't ready was her mouth, which was so dry she was unable to feel her teeth with the tip of her tongue.

56

Sarah rang Victor Perry's doorbell.

Eloise opened the door. Encapsulated throat to ankles in neon yellow, she gasped and threw her hands to her chest. True delight filled her face. "Oh, Sarah, I didn't expect you," she said, as if Kennedy weren't there. "What a nice surprise."

Sarah held out her hand but got a hug instead. "It's good to see you, Eloise. And you remember Kenn Bracken."

"Of course, of course. My beer buddy." Kennedy got and returned the same hug.

"Please, y'all come in," Eloise said, her words rapid-fire. She closed the door behind them. "Make yourself comfortable. What can I get you? The same as before?"

Sarah had expected the nervousness. "None for me. Thanks."

"I'll pass on the beer," Kennedy said, "and have whatever Victor's drinking."

Sarah held her breath.

Eloise was slow to answer. "I'm sorry. He's not here."

Kennedy contorted his face with shock. "Crap, we talked to him yesterday afternoon when he was in Baltimore. He said he was flying home with Racine. We got in late last night so we could meet him here this morning."

Perfect, Sarah thought, unless Racine's in Baltimore.

"He went—" Eloise stopped cold and wrung her hands together, drinks seemingly no longer important. "He left an hour ago," she said, "but I've got no idea where he's going."

"Oh, man," Kennedy said. "We need to ask him and Racine just a few more questions. Then we need to get on the road. Did Racine go with him?"

Eloise looked flustered, as if deciding how to answer. "No. She's here, but she's probably still sleeping. Poor girl. Vic said school was just too much for her, what with her mom . . . the accident."

Sarah: "I hate to wake her, but if we can have just a few minutes of her time, I think we'll have everything we need before we go home and leave you guys alone."

"Oh, I just don't know," Eloise said, on the verge of tears. "Vic's not here, and he gets plumb crazy about people in the house."

"Eloise," Sarah said, "we had dinner with Racine in Baltimore, plus a nice breakfast and hours of conversation, all with Victor's knowledge."

Sarah reckoned she was telling Eloise *facts* that resided halfway between an almost truth and a partial lie.

"If she's awake," Eloise said, "I'll ask her if she wants to visit."

"I'll go with you," Sarah said. "She might feel more comfortable talking girl talk with me rather than having Kenn lurking in the shadows."

Eloise gave a what-else-can-I-do nod. To Kennedy she said, "Make yourself comfortable. Dig through the bar and fetch whatever you'd like."

Sarah followed the yellow pantsuit along a hallway and up an elegant curving staircase. At the top, she stopped Eloise. "One thing, if you would. If Racine wants to talk about her mom, the accident, would you mind if it's just the two of us? And maybe you can keep Kenn busy while we talk."

"Me?" Eloise said. "Keep him busy? That won't be a problem." She tapped lightly on a hallway door—no response—and then entered.

Sarah followed her into the room. Racine lay curled up on the bed, knees to chest, eyes open a crack, comatose, unseeing.

Eloise didn't seem to notice. "Racine, honey, you've got company."

Nothing in the bed stirred.

"May I have some time with her?" Sarah asked.

"Goodness gracious, yes. Take all the time you

want. I'll go pester Mr. Bracken while he rummages through Vic's liquor cabinet.

Sarah nodded her agreement. "He's all yours. Just hang him up to dry when you're done with him."

Eloise laughed and then cupped her hand over her mouth, apparently afraid she'd wake Racine.

Exactly Sarah's goal. She followed Eloise to the door, closed it softly behind her, and then walked to the head of the bed. "She's gone."

Racine looked up. "How'd you know?"

"You looked through the crack in the door while we were on the landing. Then you pushed it shut."

"So much for being sneaky," Racine said. Dressed in a BHI T-shirt and track pants, she swung her bare feet to the floor and sat on the edge of the bed. "I thought you'd still be looking for me in Baltimore, calling the cops, looking in ditches. How'd you get here?"

Sarah sat beside her. "American, late last night. We saw Victor leave the house this morning, and here we are."

Racine shook her head. "You *don't* want to be here when he gets back."

"That won't be for a while. He's on his way to Lexington." Sarah couldn't help but smile. "We think he somehow heard we were on our way to Transy."

Racine scrunched her face. "Why would . . ." She studied Sarah's eyes. "Did you—"

"We called Rick and invited ourselves to his place.

We're supposed to be there about four this afternoon." All the while Sarah spoke and filled in the details, Racine laughed, trying to keep quiet. Then Sarah, too, joined in the laughter, as if they were seventh graders talking about boys.

When they settled, Sarah said, "Time to get serious."

"I'll say. The bastard kidnapped me. And it's going to cost me at least a semester, maybe my scholarship."

"We talked to your father."

Racine tilted her head, as if to weigh the word *father.*

"Jack Levine," Sarah said, "in New York."

Fear wracked Racine's face, filled her eyes with terror. "My God, no. Please keep him out of this."

"We know Victor's threatening you to keep your mouth shut. And because he's also put your father at risk, you've kept quiet." She pulled Racine's hand to her chest. "Racine, this can't go on. You can't let it happen."

"I'll never say a word that will ever cause my father to be hurt. He's all I have, which means I've said all I'll ever say about Mexico."

"When's the last time you spoke to your father?" Sarah asked.

"Victor says I can't. Even if Father calls me, which he hasn't—not since I saw him at the airport." Racine shifted her position to face Sarah. "Keep my father out of this or it's the last we'll ever talk." She waggled her head like a wild woman while she spoke. "And I mean it. Never again."

"I believe you but do you have the slightest clue as to why your father hasn't called you?"

"What do you mean? We always talk. He's just been busy since we got back."

"That, I suppose. But Victor threatened to harm *you*, unless Jack Levine stays away from you, *forever*. And that's the only reason he doesn't call you."

Racine's face, arms, and torso stiffened in a convulsion of sinew and muscle and limbs and tears. Her attempted scream was as quiet as a baby's breath, air falling from her lungs and onto the bed, as she clutched her hands to her face.

Sarah hugged her—a loving, sister hug. "You're not the problem, Racine. Victor is."

They rocked against one another until Racine settled and broke the hug.

"Victor and I know what happened," Racine said. Her words were monotone, a notch above a trance. "We know *exactly* what happened. And why. But I can never tell you because I don't want my father—"

The bedroom door burst open and crashed against the wall.

Victor filled the frame.

Sarah screamed and Racine squeezed harder.

Little Shit, cocky and strutting, followed Victor into the room. Then Big Arms, one arm wrapped around a neck—Kennedy's.

Kennedy's tan face had turned blue.

"Ms. McGarrity," Victor said, "I'd appreciate it if you would follow us downstairs. You can either follow quietly, or I'll make arrangements for your unconscious body to be carried. Your choice."

Sarah gathered resolve, looked up into Victor's face. "Tell Tarzan to back off and give Kenn some air, and I'll be glad to walk."

"And if I say no?"

"Then piss off. You'll have to carry me too."

Little Shit cracked up.

Big Arms smacked him with his free hand.

Victor nodded toward the guy holding Kennedy's slumping body. "Ease off. He ain't goin' nowhere."

Then Victor pointed at Racine. "You! Stay in the goddamn bed. I'll talk to you later."

Sarah, thankful Kennedy was at least gagging for air, whispered to Racine. "You can't protect your father, and he can't protect you. Somehow, you have to—"

"You, missy," Victor bellowed, "shut the hell up and get away from my daughter."

Daughter, my ass, Sarah thought. She added final quiet words to Racine. "Time to make it right." As ladylike as possible, she stood and straightened her clothing. Then she put her hands in her sweater pockets and said to Victor, "I'm ready." As soon as the big man turned toward the door, she pushed a well-memorized set of buttons on her cellphone.

For Sarah, the words, the bravado, the cockiness came easy.

But just the thought of the encore, whatever Victor had planned, wrapped her torso in scraggly, icy fingers.

57

Kennedy reckoned his jaw might be dislocated, but that was secondary to his desire for one more deep breath before he died. Then there'd been a voice from heaven—Sarah's—followed by air, no restraint, and a seat on a couch next to his partner. A perfect life, he thought, except for the trio who wanted Sarah and him dead.

"Imagine my surprise," Victor said, "when I got a call last night from my Baltimore buddy that you two had boarded a flight to Tampa." Fully reclined in a leather La-Z-Boy recliner, feet up, cigarette in hand, he spoke with a soft, arrogant voice. "Tampa, Florida. That's where I live. What a coincidence, I thought."

Little Shit, standing beside Victor's chair, with Big Arms on the other side, said, "They was comin' to see you, boss."

Kennedy hacked his thumb toward the little guy and spoke to Victor. "Good man. Smart too." His words came out raspy, since all that lumpy stuff in his neck had been rearranged.

Victor nestled his head deeper into the cushioned back of his chair. "Too late to be nice, Mr. Bracken, because I'm tired of lookin' at your face."

"Ditto," Kennedy growled.

Sarah gave Kennedy a shut-the-hell-up nudge.

Victor sucked on his cigarette. Eyes on Kennedy, he asked, "Ever been on a Hatteras?"

Kennedy brightened. "Been to Cape Hatteras."

"Different animal. Mine's a fifty-six-footer. A fine motor yacht, she is. Twin thousand-horse Cats, and she can run at almost thirty knots. I was thinkin' you might like to join me when we try out a new Olympic sport, an open-ocean triathlon, so to speak—divin', swimmin', and chummin'."

Sarah's body tensed against Kennedy's side.

"What if I told you I can't swim?" Kennedy asked.

"Wouldn't matter. At thirty knots, you two hitting the water will be one spectacular sight."

"Victor," Kennedy said, straining to talk, "as you know, whether the boat's going thirty knots—or *ten* knots, as Rick described—you're bound to miss all the excitement and never even see a shark."

"Hey, boss," Little Shit said, "this guy knows sharks. We ought to take him fishing next time we go."

Big Arms reached over Victor and backhanded Little Shit upside his skinny little—

A raucous burst of energy accompanied Racine and Eloise—each with a pistol—as they rushed into the room and yelled, "Freeze, everybody." They spread their feet, took a solid stance, and swept their respective weapons back and forth—as if metronomes—at Victor, Big Arms, and Little Shit.

Victor laughed. "Those are my rat guns, ladies. Twenty-two shorts. They won't hardly break the skin, so I suggest you put 'em down before you get hurt."

"I don't think so, *Victor*," Racine said, "because when I aim at the top button on your shirt and pull the trigger, it's not me who's gonna get hurt."

Victor's eyes bulged, and he appeared in shock. "What the hell do you want, girl?"

"Nothing from you, but I'll ask Sarah to call 911."

Sarah, already on the phone, gave the circle-finger OK sign, plugged her ear, and kept talking, even as Victor flexed his legs, snapped the footstool into the recliner, and jumped from the chair.

Racine pointed the pistol toward the center of his chest. "Get back in your chair, *Victor*."

"No. You can't do this. You know what'll happen, and to who." He lowered his voice and shook his head. "And it won't be pretty."

Racine stood her ground, gun in hand. "And neither will this when I pull the trigger."

Kennedy reckoned the standoff was about to turn ugly. He surveyed the room, inventoried the players, and checked on Sarah, who said into the phone, "If I get cut off, get here even faster."

"That the cops?" Kennedy asked, his raspy voice louder than he wanted.

"On the way."

"No!" Victor screamed as he charged Sarah.

Kennedy lowered his shoulder and blasted into the surprised giant. With his arms almost around Victor's behemoth torso, Kennedy drove as if pushing a football sled. Together the duo flattened a mahogany coffee table and sent a cut-glass lamp flying to the floor. Then, as if he were a twin to the lamp, Kennedy, with Victor's help, flew and landed hard.

Victor, already up, roared and again charged Sarah.

Kennedy tackled him from behind. As soon as the duo hit the floor, the big man rolled over, and air erupted from Kennedy's lungs, his ribs threatening to crush his heart. Then hands, giant hands, closed around Kennedy's throat, and—

Racine yelled, "No," simultaneous to the "Boom!"

Victor screamed and rolled off Kennedy.

Kennedy saw stars and sucked air as Big Arms slung Little Shit into Racine, who screamed and crashed to the floor, which prompted Eloise to fire her weapon, which sent a bullet into Big Arms' butt.

Victor, on his knees, held his left man boob with both hands, while blood seeped between his fingers. He thundered like a rutting walrus, a vulgar mix of "bitch," "bullet," and "bleeding," even as Big Arms— his right hand grasping his back crotch— screamed in tongues and danced on tiptoes as if the extra height might take the pressure off whatever it was that got shot.

Kennedy turned his attention to Little Shit, who screamed as if being raped. He reckoned Little Shit must have taken a bullet, too, until he saw that Victor's knee was on the mental-midget's hand.

Racine, back on her feet, pointed her gun and said, "Unless you want another one, *Victor*, and another one after that, get back in the chair."

Victor was slow to rise, but he sat, his massive machismo, from Kennedy's perspective, apparently deflated by runt Racine's bullet into his chest.

With Racine and Eloise manning their respective weapons, and with Big Arms still dancing, Little Shit crying, and Victor slumped in his chair, Kennedy worked his way to Sarah, who remained on the couch with her phone driven into her ear. He got face-to-face with her. "Anybody coming?" he asked.

"Maybe. The 911 operator said something about Apollo Beach Metro, Florida State Troopers, Tampa PD, and paramedics." She waved Kennedy off, her attention back on the phone. "No, ma'am. No change." She listened. "Good. I'll open the door."

Kennedy helped Sarah up from the couch and went with her, leaving the living room under feminine-control lockdown.

He opened the front door to a wall of no-nonsense, fast-moving figures dressed in black jackets labeled POLICE, and was immediately taken to the floor and searched. Unable to see Sarah, he reckoned she was being similarly treated.

Kennedy was directed to a chair in the entry, with a young policeman at his side. He told Kennedy to be patient, that he would have time for a statement later.

Somebody, voice deep, said, "First floor secure," followed by a woman's voice: "Second floor secure."

A gray-haired officer reopened the front door and advised more uniforms and two crews of paramedics that all weapons had been secured and that there were injured persons in the living room.

Kennedy, mentally and physically debilitated, thought about a young woman who'd just shot her stepfather. The same young woman who'd already lost her mother.

Racine's mother, Madrilène, Kennedy surmised, would have been sickened with all the mess, both tangible and human, dealt to her by her marriage to Victor Perry. Madrilène, the woman who, without some good detective work, might yet suffer an eternity in her oceanic grave, having taken with her the secret Victor Perry would never tell, the secret Racine refused to tell.

And with that, Kennedy prepared himself to tell what he needed to tell—the whole truth—to anybody nice enough to listen.

58

For an hour, Kennedy sat almost alone in a small parlor by the front door of Victor Perry's home. A young cop—PLONKK on his name badge—sat with him, both in comfortable chairs. Kennedy's orders were to stay in the room so detectives could talk to him "in a few minutes." Sarah, Racine, and Eloise were elsewhere in the house, he surmised, likely in separate rooms, interrogations in progress.

Kennedy's fingers drummed a tattoo on his knee. He kept watch out the front window and into the hallway. He'd twice told the cop he was thirsty and asked if he could have a glass of water, a cup of coffee, or a Diet Coke in a tall glass with lots of ice. Hah.

A team of uniforms and efficient paramedics escorted Victor Perry and Big Arms—both on gurneys—to the front hallway. Kennedy got a dozen seconds of eye-to-eye time with Victor and detected something that made him wonder. Instead of Victor's massive mug being etched with anger or the frowns of fear that had followed the bullet, the quiet man's sweating face seemed drenched in resolve, soaked in *c'est la vie.*

Even as paramedics and cops pushed Victor and Big Arms out the front door to waiting ambulances, Kennedy asked himself questions and looked for answers, with Victor being the target.

As a writer, Kennedy had created, challenged, and killed characters rich in body language, voice inflections, ass coverings, and the average man's occasional tirade.

But Victor's Saturday-morning outburst had been only the first symptom of an acute, bone-deep anger. An anger that had metastasized as Kennedy continued to dig into the Perry family's private affairs. Which meant Victor was hiding something. Something one or more of the other survivors were privy to. Something about Madrilène's death, Victor's threats, and hidden truths.

Kennedy considered the players. Racine? Victor had threatened to harm her father, Jack Levine, to keep her from talking. And Victor had threatened Levine that Racine was in danger if Levine didn't stay away from her. Yes—Racine knew the truth.

Rick? The bloodline son? The drug peddler? Nobody, Kennedy recalled, including the Mexicans in their police reports, had mentioned drugs. Perhaps a smart-ass college kid—a known dealer according to Racine—whose cruising of Central America for the summer with stops in numerous ports, would produce some temptation to buy. Maybe a lot of temptation to buy. Or maybe it was sex rather than drugs. Hadn't Racine said something to Sarah about Rick being horny? On Victor's yacht, at sea, Kennedy wondered, horny for whom? Racine hadn't said, but Rick's target could have been his stepsister, Racine, or, more likely, bikini-clad Eloise.

Kennedy tried to picture Rick and Eloise together. Not a pretty sight. But if Rick chased Eloise, had drugs as an agenda, was Victor's heir to the throne, and perhaps saw what happened to Madrilène, maybe he was a bigger player in the game—with more to lose by talking—than Kennedy had given him credit for. And hadn't Racine almost puked when Sarah asked her about Rick? Perhaps more important, what father-son relationship, regardless of how good, would ever survive a formal indictment for *murder*? Would Rick talk? Tell the truth? Probably not, unless he was willing to suffer his father's wrath, perhaps be disinherited.

Bored, wishing he had Sarah to talk to, Kennedy got to his feet and looked out the window. Little Shit had been escorted to a patrol car, where he'd apparently been forgotten since the car was still there—with him in the back seat—his forlorn idiot face pressed against the glass. Kennedy wondered if Little Shit was of average intelligence. Probably so, he concluded, which led to a scary thought—that half the people in the world were dumber than Little Shit.

Kennedy sat back down, connecting the dots in his mental spreadsheet. Had Madrilène been *murdered*? Hard to say, but if it'd been an accident, why all the intrigue? The threats? Was Madrilène's money the problem? Maybe, but she ran a small import-export company, likely a pittance compared with Victor's shopping-mall wealth.

So, he wondered. If it wasn't for money, why would Victor, or anyone, kill Madrilène? Was it lust related? Victor hot after voluptuous Eloise? Madrilène in the way? Could be. But killing your wife on a yacht while at sea with three onboard witnesses seemed an imbecile's version of the perfect murder.

What about Eloise? Sarah had been positive there was no passion between Victor and Eloise, and Kennedy had seen firsthand that Eloise was not intimidated by Victor. Nor, according to Racine, had Eloise succumbed to Victor's strutting during the trip. And hadn't Eloise said something about "my fault"? Had she seen a murder? Had *she* been threatened? Was she clueless there'd even been a murder? Or, maybe, she was part of a murder plot and had climbed in bed with devil Victor to keep from being implicated.

Kennedy noticed the young officer's head bobbed and his eyelids drooped. "Officer Plonkk, there's a bar in the other room with an espresso machine. Can I buy you a cup? Maybe one for me, too?"

Plonkk recovered, eyes wide, and casually looked

up. "Not now. Be patient."

Kennedy shrugged. Didn't matter. He'd soon be in Belize, sipping rum and lime. He leaned back in his seat, crossed his ankles, and clasped his hands behind his head. Confident he was asking himself the right questions, he focused on Victor and why he'd kicked Kennedy and Sarah out that first morning. Because Kennedy had lied? Revealed too much? That Madrilène slipped? That Rick got hurt? And what, other than self-preservation, could have driven the big man to make felonious threats and chase Kennedy with malice at both Racine's and Rick's places?

Rick? Dysfunction on the hoof. What had triggered humorous Rick to kick them out, to make his "bitch" comment? That *bitch* Racine had spoken to Sarah? That *bitch* Eloise was at Victor's place? Or that *bitch* Madrilène had—What?

Madrilène? Kennedy could only shake his head. Too bad about her hand-me-down hamsa, loaned to Racine for protection. Too bad Kennedy's life involved a body with a hamsa, a jewel in the middle of its palm, its owner unknown. Too bad Jack Levine had opened a door with his story that the anti-evil amulets were common with Muslims and Jews alike throughout the Middle East. *Common.* Kennedy played with the word. *Common*, as in not unique.

Kennedy leaned forward in his seat, elbows on his knees, fingers steepled. He felt the power, knew he was making progress. He juggled puzzle pieces—

people, what-ifs, words said, threats made—and found several good-versus-evil patterns that worked, some better than others. One pattern, though, worked quite well. He reminded himself to breathe, paced the room, started from scratch, considered the logic, and eliminated alternatives. A slight chill crossed over his shoulders.

"Officer Plonkk, for a simple cup of coffee, you could be a hero, if that's what you want."

The cop leaned forward in his chair, nonplussed.

"I need paper," Kennedy said. "I've got a pen."

"You gonna confess?"

"Nope. We're gonna fry a killer."

"Then forget the coffee." Plonkk stepped into the hallway, asked somebody a question, and returned with a yellow notepad.

Kennedy wrote his draft note. Hating cursive and missing "Delete" and "Backspace," he scribbled, scratched, and edited, and then he drew arrows to change the order of sentences until he got them right. He tore off the top sheet, rewrote the note, and then pulled out his wallet and jotted a phone number onto the note. He signed and folded the yellow paper and gave it to the cop. "Take this to the room where your buddies are interviewing Racine Perry. Give it to the most senior officer in the room."

Officer Plonkk read the note, refolded it, and then triggered his shoulder-mounted walkie-talkie and requested assistance, which came immediately in the form of two big cops ready for action. Standing erect, the young cop said, "Watch this guy for a few minutes. Keep him here." He walked briskly from the room and didn't come back.

Ten minutes later, three officers—two men, one woman—introduced themselves to Kennedy and excused the two big cops.

Kennedy reckoned they were there to congratulate him as the sleuth of the year.

"Mr. Bracken," the female officer said, "I understand you took some pictures. Please tell us about them. Start at the beginning."

My time to shine, he thought, but they want a show and tell.

"In the beginning," he began.

59

For two hours, Kennedy had answered the three officers' questions. Nobody had mentioned his note, his prowess in proving Madrilène's murder.

Released at last, he stepped into the sunshine on Victor Perry's front porch, where Sarah waited for him, and inhaled salt air. They shared a long hug. Exhausted, he could barely talk.

"Yeah, me too," Sarah said. "They wanted every detail starting with Cancún."

"Have you seen Racine or Eloise?"

"Not since the cops split us up."

The vehicles that had filled Victor Perry's circular drive, front yard, and beautiful Cocoa Lane were mostly gone. Kennedy noted that Little Shit, too, was gone, but probably not to a better place.

Sarah slapped the handrail a couple of times. "Victor broke U.S. law with property damage, threats, and kidnapping Racine, but it's the Mexicans who'll want him."

"Why Mexico?" Kennedy asked, unsure if he

should broach his Madrilène-murder theory. "The truth may be something different than faking a death."

"You can suspect whatever you want," she said, "and never find out for sure."

"By the time Racine and Eloise get done inside," he said, "we may all know the truth. But because it's an international problem, it could be months, maybe years, before it's resolved." The look of frustration on Sarah's face made him wish he hadn't said it.

The quiet that followed meant she was thinking. "I'll go home tonight. It's been a hell of a long week and a half."

He had no good reply. It was over. He'd screwed up her vacation. They'd had a good partnership, but her departure was inevitable.

"I thought I'd have to stay," he said. "Maybe for the grand jury and all, but they let me go too."

"Why," Sarah asked, "would they have wanted you, *partner*, and not me?"

"Maybe because you, *partner*, mentioned my Belize pictures before I was ever asked a question. And that led to me having to show them the pictures—using their laptop—and to your cropped pictures, and to Azalee, and to the theft, and to the idiocy of chumming, and how we got interested in the Mexican case. They said you did good work."

"Do I get a medal?" Sarah asked.

"No. But when I went back to the originals, as they

requested, and I showed them the hamsa, they shut down. No more questions. Formal interview to follow."

"Kenn—" She stopped, seemed to deflate, shook her head. "Why make a point about the hamsa you saw in Belize? It's no more relevant than Madrilène's missing hamsa."

The front door opened behind them, and a mix of people filed out: plainclothes detectives, Feds, uniformed cops.

Racine, her eyes swollen, went straight to Sarah and gave her a hug. She cried softly.

Eloise, face droopy, wasn't smiling. Apparently feeling left out, she hugged Kennedy.

By damn, despite a pain in his chest, where he guessed Victor might have broken a rib, Kennedy appreciated Eloise's gentle hug . . . a lot.

Sarah, squinty-eyed, ended the moment.

In minutes, the foursome was alone.

"Anybody besides me hungry?" Eloise asked.

Racine remained mute.

"Sorry," Sarah said. "Kenn's taking me to the airport, and I'm going home to celebrate."

Eloise: "Celebrate?"

"You bet," Sarah said. "We put a murderer behind bars, our good deed for the year."

Racine cocked her head, gave Sarah a puzzled look. "You put who behind bars?"

Kennedy stopped midbreath.

"Victor!" Sarah almost squealed the name. "He killed your mother, and he's in jail."

Racine's mouth dropped open. "Wrong, wrong, wrong." She grabbed the handrail to support herself. "Victor did *not* kill my mother." She tried to say something else, but deep sobbing and wobbly legs collapsed her to her knees.

Kennedy digested Racine's words—that the big sonofabitch who'd almost killed Kennedy three hours before was not Madrilène's killer. Those words made sense to Kennedy, but only if Racine wasn't still cowering under Victor's threat.

"Not Victor," Racine said, as Sarah helped her to her feet. She spoke as if exhausted. "Rick. Rick killed my mother—his stepmother—because of drugs. His drugs." Racine cried, and she struggled for words. "The bastard picked her up like a sack of potatoes and threw her overboard. The FBI, they were—" Racine's body seemed to melt, her legs going first, her sobbing intense.

Kennedy and Sarah grabbed her, got her to sit on the steps, her head on Sarah's shoulder.

Sarah rocked her, and then caught Kennedy's attention. Slack-jawed, eyebrows ramped up, she managed to mouth the word "Rick?" and barely shook her head.

Kennedy shrugged.

Eloise sat by herself, eyes wide, tears flowing, hands over her mouth, hyperventilating. Muted words—"no, no, no"—leaked through her fingers.

Racine sat up, wiped her eyes, and put her hands in her lap. "The FBI—two of the guys who just left—kept me inside until the police in Lexington arrested Rick." She looked at her watch. "Almost an hour ago."

Kennedy pursed his lips, his joy bittersweet. "Racine, so many things made it look like Victor had done it."

"No," she said. "Victor's only goal was to protect Rick, his precious little boy, and he didn't care who got in his way."

"And that's where Victor used Jack Levine," Sarah said. "To keep you quiet."

"Yes," Racine said. "The police had me call Father to make sure he was OK. I told him what was going on. He was so relieved—I've never heard him happier."

Eloise moved next to Racine and spoke to Sarah and Kennedy. "The night it happened, I was down below, reading. Rick pounded on my door and said Victor wanted to see me on deck. I found Racine crying and screaming for her mom so hard I thought she'd die. Vic told me Madi had fallen overboard—an accident, he said—and that Rick got hurt and was down below. I didn't even know Rick was involved."

To Racine she said, "I'm so sorry."

"Don't go there," Racine said. "You made up for it. First, by telling my mom about the drugs, and then by proving you're a dang good shot."

"Yeah, but I almost killed a gorgeous hunk of man."

Nobody laughed.

But all four heads turned toward a patrol car making its way up the circular drive. It stopped at the bottom of the steps and a cop got out.

Kennedy recognized him as the young cop, Officer Plonkk, who had taken off with the yellow note and not returned.

The cop climbed the steps and went straight to Kennedy. "Sorry to interrupt, sir," Officer Plonkk said. "This is for you." He handed Kennedy a Starbucks paper cup. "And just so you know, my boss said to tell you thanks." Plonkk shook his hand and left.

As the car pulled away from the house, Sarah asked, "What the hell was that about?"

Kennedy sipped hot, black coffee. "I told him twice I needed a cup of coffee. He's slow, but apparently follows through." And he has a smart boss, Kennedy mused.

Sarah shook her head. "Men." Then she singled out Racine. "You mentioned drugs."

"That's what started the whole thing," Racine said, her voice barely audible. "Eloise told Mom she'd found a stash of drugs on board."

"Because I felt guilty," Eloise said. "Madi and Victor were serious about no drugs. They talked to all of us, but I knew they were really talking to Rick. Then, two weeks into the trip . . . well, Rick's a tease.

We had a good time. Nothing serious, but he pestered me constantly and was always on the make. One afternoon he wouldn't leave me alone—"

Kennedy dribbled coffee down his chin.

"When Madi noticed us, she went crazy. She was mad at him and wouldn't even talk to me."

"What changed?" Sarah asked.

"The drugs. When I found them, I showed her. We didn't even know what was in the little packages. From the way the packs had been wrapped and hidden, we guessed pills, but they didn't rattle, so maybe cocaine, whatever. Or maybe it was nothing." Tears in her eyes, she looked at Racine. "I'm so sorry, honey. If I'd known—"

Racine hugged her. "Don't go there. You did nothing wrong."

Kennedy: "Can you tell us what happened that night?"

Racine nodded. "Yes, but like I told the police, it's not a fun story." She paused and seemed to gather resolve. "We'd been in Puerto Cortés, Honduras, for a day and then sailed north. We cut the corner across Guatemala and were off the coast of Belize that evening. Victor told us we would need to dodge a bunch of islands and the Belize barrier reef on our way to Mexico. Even though he was drinking, he did OK with GPS, keeping us out of trouble. Mom ignored him and let him play captain."

Belize, Kennedy thought, wishing he had a tape

recorder. He noticed Sarah, too, was barely breathing.

Racine sat taller on the porch. "Mom was so upset with Rick she could barely talk. We stayed up late and she told me about the drugs, which she planned to dump. Later, I was supposed to make sure Rick stayed in his bunk and warn Mom if he got up. Except he must have heard something because the first thing I knew he ran by me." She stopped talking, sobbed, and pounded her hands on her knees. "This makes me so mad to talk about."

"Just go slow," Eloise said.

Racine wiped her eyes. "Rick screamed and cussed at Mom. Victor was drunk on rum, as usual. He stumbled out of the wheelhouse and fell on the steps, but we both saw Rick and yelled at him. Rick was crazy, fighting Mom. She pushed back, screamed at him, and threw something overboard. He slugged her and knocked her down." Racine clamped her eyes shut tight and scrunched her face.

"With Victor yelling and me screaming, Rick picked her up like a wrestler on TV and threw her off the back of the boat. It was *not* an accident." Then she scrunched her face and shook her head, as if to pull herself away from demon memories. "I like to imagine Mom was unconscious when she went in because she never made a sound. No scream. Nothing. I never saw her again."

Kennedy knew the truth. The truth about the Belizean body's ripped hands—Madrilène's ripped hands. The coral cuts on her body. Her obvious will to live. That she didn't just sink and drown. That for no more than ten to twenty seconds she might have hopelessly watched the boat disappear into the night, hundreds of feet away.

"And Victor?" Kennedy asked.

"He slugged Rick and threw him across the deck."

Sarah: "Did you go back for your mother?"

"Of course. Victor was yelling and cussing but he took the wheel, reversed the engines, and turned us around. We went back south, yelling and screaming and using spotlights. There was a little slice of moon, but we never saw or heard a thing except the waves hitting the reef."

Kennedy thought not about the flurry of panic on the boat but about the very real living person—Madrilène—in the water.

"When Rick finally got up, his head was bleeding. He yelled, 'My shit, damn it. My shit.' And then he started collecting the little packets that were scattered on the deck. Victor went crazy. He got in Rick's face and made him dump the stuff overboard. Then he threw Rick again and made him get on one of the spotlights. I was on the stern, yelling for Mom, when Victor put his hand on the back of my neck. I remember because he'd never hugged me before. 'It was an accident,' he said. 'Plain and simple.' Then he squeezed even harder and told me, 'Even your daddy would understand a simple accident.'"

Kennedy seethed.

"As soon as I left my room," Eloise said, "I heard Racine screaming. It was so—" Eloise quit talking, scrunched her face.

"When Victor saw Eloise," Racine said, "he told me, 'Might as well start right now.' Then, while making a big deal about yelling for Mom, he told Eloise what had happened, that it was an accident, that Rick had fallen trying to help her, and that I'd seen it happen."

"And in the meantime," Kennedy said, "your mom's out in the water somewhere. Did Victor call for help? Radio? Mayday? Man overboard? There're a heck of lot of people in Belize who would have helped search, even in the middle of the night."

"Victor wouldn't listen," Racine said. "He said it'd be a waste of time because we were in the best position to look for her. When I kept pushing him to call, he blew up and got Rick and me together. He was so mad he could barely talk. Belizeans throw drunk captains in jail, he told us, especially for losing somebody overboard. And drug runners, he told Rick, go away for life."

"So you kept looking," Sarah said.

Racine rocked on the porch step and gazed toward the street. "Yeah," she said. "While we used the spotlights and yelled, Victor used GPS and made U-turns to stay alongside the reef—but we never saw Mom. Then, in the early dawn, even before sunrise, we were able to see big swells breaking over miles of reef with open ocean in every direction."

Kennedy understood more than he could say.

"Victor got me one-on-one," Racine whispered, "and told me he was truly sorry about my mom—the last nice thing he ever said to me. Then—without even mentioning what Rick had done—he pointed to a fishing boat and said we couldn't afford to have company . . . so we were done looking." She took a deep breath. "And with that—we motored north and left Belize and my mom behind."

His guts rumbling, Kennedy knew more of the truth. Rick had thrown Madrilène overboard, but Victor had abandoned her, the culpability shared, father and son. "And that was Tuesday," Kennedy said, the day forever engrained in the deepest of his black memories.

Racine nodded. "Rick murdered my mom about three in the morning, the first Tuesday in August." She folded her arms tight across her chest. "After Victor made us quit looking, and with me on the wheel, he made Rick dump the rest of his stash. Then he and Rick spent hours washing all the hold areas and lockers to ensure nothing got left behind."

Tuesday—Kennedy's memories of the body and the sharks were all too vivid.

Racine sat up. "When the boat was totally clean, Victor told us a fairy tale—a fun family shark chumming story, about my mom, Madi, having an accident in Mexico. He made us repeat the story, to get us all on the same page, he said. I was so mad I almost puked. That evening, Victor again mentioned my father . . . just to make sure I understood the details of the shark story."

Racine blew her nose. "I thought Mexican Customs—a whole boatload of guys with guns— would board us that Tuesday night when we got to Cozumel, but they ignored us, probably because we were a family. We spent that night and all the next day anchored in Cozumel, though Victor made us all stay onboard. We left Wednesday evening for Cancún, where Mom had her official 'accident' on the way."

Wednesday—Kennedy pictured Gutierrez first seeing the photos.

"Victor told me," Eloise said, "the kids would lose Madi's accidental-death insurance if we didn't all agree on the Mexican version, the one about feeding the sharks. Criminy! To me, at the time, all Victor had done was change locations—an accident in Belize for an accident in Mexico."

Eloise said to Sarah, "I'm sorry I hassled you when you called about Victor coming home with Racine. He told me that if I heard from you, I was to play dumb, that you were probably from the insurance company."

"You did a good job," Kennedy said, expecting but not getting Sarah's elbow. Then, he couldn't help himself: "Eloise, I've been meaning to ask since we met you on Saturday. How do you and Victor fit in the grand scheme of things? You know, personally?"

Eloise got up and faced Kennedy, stance akimbo, feet apart. "We?" she said. "Me and Victor? Never! Madi and I met in school. She was a grad student with her own company, and I was a junior in business finance. I interned with her on one of her summer trips, and she hired me when I graduated. My only reservation was that she was married to asshole Victor." She stole a quick glance toward Racine. "Sorry, honey. Y'all know how I feel."

Kennedy avoided the look he knew Sarah was giving him.

"It's OK," Racine said to Eloise. "They need to hear your story."

Eloise folded her arms across her chest. "I can't stand him," she said. "He's abusive and chauvinistic, and his frigging breath smells like a week-old ashtray in a country bar. The only thing he thinks about from morning 'til night is getting in my pants." She grabbed one of the foot-long ends of her black satin belt and twirled it. "And let me tell y'all this—Racine knows there's no way in tarnation that hand's gonna play."

As if to answer Kennedy's unasked question, Eloise continued. "The only reason I'm still here is because my brother and I are buying half of Madi's business, as provided for in the letter of incorporation. We'll be fifty-fifty with Racine. I've been catching up on customer profiles, profit-and-loss reports, and cash-flow ledgers. I can't wait to finish, get the hell away from this house, and get back to work, as in gallivanting my way through Central America."

Racine said, "She'll run the company until I graduate, and then we'll work together."

Kennedy, knowing he'd been wrong about Eloise, spoke around the chunk of crow stuck in his throat. "Eloise and Racine, I'm impressed, and I wish you and your company all the best."

He added, "Racine, another question for you. Did Victor take a day off when you guys were in Cancún? Maybe he was gone all day? Or even overnight?"

Racine nodded. "He spent most of his time in Cancún at a computer in the hotel lobby. He's an internet freak. But the morning before we flew home, he and Rick took off. I don't know where to. They didn't get back to the hotel until that night. I remember, because just after lunch the police had told Eloise and me that we could leave, but we had to wait until the next day."

Kennedy sorted facts and looked for something that fit. Something like: Victor and Rick—following a Belize article in a Mexican newspaper—take a trip south to Belize, to Ambergris Caye, to a resort named Bacalar Vista, looking for a diver who had photographed a shark attack. They break in and find what they're looking for—the diver's pictures. Kennedy's pictures. His body shots. His body shots not of Azalee Castillo, but of Madrilène Perry—the only evidence. And Rick—had to be Rick—takes the time to send *bitch* Sarah an illiterate-looking, threatening note that mentions *chum*. Kennedy chuckled silently, realizing that without the note he might never have sensed a potential link between what appeared to be unrelated cases. Coincidences.

Racine continued to lean back, her face in the sun, eyes closed. Nobody bothered her until she leaned forward. "Rick drowned my mother in Belize, murdered her, and Victor made sure I wouldn't talk. The Mexican police bought it."

Kennedy stared at the girl. Brave. Mature. And if there were anything he could wish away, it was the batch of pictures on the internet. Pictures, with or without faces, he'd never want Racine to see. Pictures that, in addition to the gore, showed Madrilène Perry wearing—

He spoke quietly. "Racine, when we talked to your father, he told us a story about a family heirloom, a hamsa. Perhaps I misunderstood. I thought—"

"It was my mom's, a gift from my grandmother." For a brief moment, her face collapsed into harsh, crying anguish. She wiped her eyes with the heels of her hands. "Father probably told you I lost it. With it gone, I'll always wonder if things might have been different. New versus old."

"I don't follow," Kennedy said. "New and old."

"I lost the old one, so I bought Mom a new one,

right before the trip. She loved it and wore it on her ankle, but apparently it didn't work as well as Grandmother's might have."

Oh, but it had, Kennedy thought. He knew the truth. The hamsa, the *new hamsa*, a gift from Racine, had led them to this day of reckoning. And in the end, it would do its anti-evil work through jurors, who would send young Rick Perry away for a long time. Victor too. He caught Sarah's glance, a private arc of understanding between them.

Kennedy broke from the small crowd on the porch and again recovered a phone number from his wallet. As soon as he got Jack Levine on the line, he told him to wait, and then put in a conference call to American Airlines. Within minutes, Levine had an open-ended round-trip ticket to Tampa, and Kennedy had one more line item on his American Express card.

"Thank you, Kenn, for everything," Levine said.

"Just keep me informed," Kennedy said. "Racine's a very special young woman, like her mother must have been."

"Yes, Madrilène was exactly that. Your lady, Sarah, also seems special. Perhaps under different circumstances, they would have been friends."

"You're very kind, Jack. I'll tell her that."

"No, don't. My words are for you, as you're a lucky man. Don't ever let her get away. Not now. Not ever. Nothing is more important than what you have for each other."

Kennedy hung up as Sarah called to him, waving her wrist to show her watch. "Come on, Kenn. I've got to go. It's either now or never."

Kennedy looked at the phone, at Sarah, and then at Racine and Eloise.

Yes. Time for Sarah and him to go. But to where?

A cellphone rang.

Racine answered.

Then she screamed.

60

What now? Kennedy wondered.

Racine dropped her phone and ran from the porch, crying.

Sarah and Eloise caught her in the circular drive and formed a group hug.

Kennedy picked up the phone and identified himself.

The caller was Will.

And Will had a very big problem.

A very big problem named Rick, who was no longer in custody.

"The city cops got here," Will said, breathing hard, "the same time as campus security. The cops asked Rick a bunch of questions, but it's like they didn't know why they were here. By the time Rick told them about his mom and the sharks and the Mexican police, Rick and the woman cop were all teary. Campus security called a counselor, and she confirmed Rick's story. And that was it—the cops told Rick he wasn't to leave the apartment, and they left."

"Where's Rick now?" Kennedy asked.

"You kidding?" Will said. "He was in a rage about the cops, and then he called somebody—I think one of his dad's buddies. I don't know what the guy said, but Rick grabbed a few things and boogied. Wasn't a half hour later, the cops were back—they're looking for Rick now. I'm supposed to stay here in case they have questions."

"Good," Kennedy said, "I've got a few. For starters, does Rick have a gun?"

"No way," Will said. "Not on campus. At least not that I know of. Besides, if he did, he would've shot the cops, especially the woman. He was really nice to them when they were here, but for him, being an asshole is like a light switch—either on or off. As soon as the cops left, he got really ugly. He called her the b-word, and then the c-word, then most of the rest of the alphabet. He wanted to cut her up, drink her blood. Bad stuff, Mr. Bracken."

Not good, Kennedy thought. "I've been flying too much lately," he said. "Remind me how long it takes to get to the airport."

"Blue Grass is due west," Will said, excitement in his voice, "maybe ten minutes. Why? Want me to fly somewhere?"

"Thanks, no," Kennedy said. "That's not necessary. I recommend you stay away from Rick and call the cops if you hear from him. Please keep me updated if you get any news." He gave Will his number and hung up.

Kennedy checked his watch. He then put himself in psychopath Rick's shoes—no clue. So he tried on Victor's shoes—they fit better. And he had no doubt what daddy Vic would do. Which meant—

Kennedy motioned for Eloise to join him on the porch.

She wiped her eyes, but they remained puffy and red. "Racine's crushed," she said. "She says the effing police let her down, and now Rick will go after her and her father. You think we should call him?"

"No," Kennedy said. "I think Rick's on his way to Tampa, so her father's safe."

Eloise: "Tampa? Here? What should we do? Should I tell Racine? Call the police?"

"Hold tight, Eloise. If I remember right, don't you have a good friend at the Tampa Jet Center?"

"The best. What do you need?"

Kennedy told her.

Then he called the Tampa Police Department and asked for Officer Plonkk. "No, sorry," he told the dispatcher. "I don't know his given name, but how many Plonkks can you have? P-L-O-N-K-K."

To answer the dispatcher's next question, he said, "Yes, ma'am. Officer Plonkk was part of a major investigative team that resulted in the arrest of Mr. Victor Perry. P-E-R-R-Y. I was one of the witnesses. I have additional information for Officer Plonkk that's vital to the case."

The dispatcher put Kennedy on hold.

No music.

Like the phone was dead.

Maybe it was.

Then, "This is Officer James Plonkk. How can I help you?"

"Officer Plonkk, I asked you earlier today if you wanted to be a hero. You didn't answer me."

A beat. "You're the coffee guy. Bracken. What's this about?"

Kennedy told him.

Sarah, Racine, and Eloise yielded to Kennedy's suggestion, and the foursome ordered gourmet dinners at an Outback Steakhouse in downtown Tampa, as far from Victor's home as possible. While Sarah and Eloise mothered Racine and all three women picked at their food, Kennedy—knowing Belize was in his immediate future—worked on his rib eye. And a large salad. And the accompanying loaded baked potato. And steamed broccoli. And sourdough bread.

Racine asked what-if questions. What if he runs? Disappears? Kills somebody else?

Sarah and Eloise answered the best they could.

Kennedy ordered dessert.

At 9:35, as Sarah and Eloise drank wine and Kennedy and Racine drank coffee in the almost-empty restaurant, Kennedy's phone rang.

It was Officer James Plonkk.

"The FBI made a big deal out of it," Officer Plonkk told Kennedy. "My boss and I stayed next to his patrol car, near the runway exit, while the Feds met the plane. Though the kid was bigger than any of the agents and had a handgun, he about shit his pants with all the firepower in his face."

"Too bad he didn't fight," Kennedy said. "Sounds like he missed what could have been a well-earned lesson. Anything else?"

"The last I saw of the perp," Plonkk said, "he was wearing a bracelet and being shoved into the back seat of a shiny black SUV. As soon as they left, my boss and I met with airport management and thanked them for identifying the plane and clearing everybody else out of the way."

"Good job, Officer Plonkk. I'll drink a cold beer for you when I get to my hotel."

"Thanks for what you did," Plonkk told Kennedy.

"Amazing," Kennedy said, "the power of a simple cup of coffee, served at the right time."

A beat. Then Officer James Plonkk said, "I consider that a well-learned lesson, sir."

Hilton Hotel. Adjoining rooms. Eloise and Racine in a double joined Kennedy and Sarah next door. Two bottles of cold chardonnay. One room-temperature merlot. One bottle of not-too-damn-bad Brazilian rum. Two limes. A bucket of ice.

Racine so happy she glowed.

Eloise yakking like a deejay.

Sarah sitting close to Kennedy.

"Ladies," Kennedy said, "I propose a toast."

They all looked at him.

"To Madrilène, a good mother with a good daughter—may our memories of her last forever."

Sarah sipped.

Eloise sipped.

Racine looked at Kennedy, her eyes moist. She mouthed the words "Thank you." As her lips touched the rim of her glass, not drinking, she closed her eyes and smiled, her thoughts, Kennedy reckoned, known only to herself.

But it was enough for Kennedy.

He called it closure.

Finally.

61

Not yet ready for security screening, Sarah was reluctant to leave, as if something important had ended, a hope had died, her dream had faded.

Never had she been so close to Kennedy. She'd seen him in action and watched him handle people, situations, conflicts, emotions. Even his own emotions, emotions that at one time drove him to quit his job, take up writing, move to Belize.

They sat at a food-court table in the Tampa International Airport and drank coffee, the late-afternoon sun spilling across their table. She returned his copy of James O. Born's *Field of Fire*.

He took it and grinned like he'd won the lottery.

"You were right about the coincidence," Sarah said.

"Wrong. If there'd been two separate events, two bodies, then there could have been coincidences, but only as statistical rarities. But there was only one truth, one event, one body, so everything matched exactly, which is the opposite of coincidental."

"You say that now, but you've felt something was wrong from the beginning. I'm just giving you credit."

Kennedy, seemingly oblivious to her need to talk, said, "Thanks, but I need to find a men's room."

Sarah held out her hand. "I'll take my boarding pass." She smiled. "In case you don't come back."

He dug in his back pocket and gave her more than she bargained for. "I'll be back," he said, his fake accent mimicking a voice she'd heard before.

She found rental car receipts, a folded piece of yellow paper, and her boarding pass. She put her boarding pass in her purse and opened the yellow paper, which was filled with handwriting, Kennedy's, most everything edited, crossed out, arrows everywhere. Some writer, she thought. As if it were a game, she followed the cryptic edits and arrows:

"Racine Perry likely witnessed her stepbrother, Rick, murder her mother, Madrilène. If the mom wore a piece of jewelry, a hamsa, she may have died in Belize (I have photo evidence). Otherwise, she died in Mexico (and my photos are unrelated). Regardless of location, stepfather Victor threatened to harm both Racine and her biological father, Jack Levine, to keep her quiet about Rick being a murderer. Have Racine call Jack Levine (number listed below) to tell him Victor's been arrested and Racine is safe (with police protection). As soon as Racine knows her father is safe, and Victor and Rick have been arrested, she'll tell you the whole story.

Or I could be wrong. Victor might have done it. Or Eloise. Or maybe it was suicide. Please send me a cup of coffee."

Sarah's face flushed as she refolded the note and replaced it in the stack. Holy wow, she thought. He solved the mystery. Never said a word. Yet, she wondered if he'd given the unfinished cryptic note— lacking Levine's number—to the police. She could ask him, but if he'd wanted her to know, he would've told her. She thought about the last line of the scribbled note and recalled the coffee incident on the porch. Perhaps the cop with the cup of Starbucks had delivered more than just coffee.

But none of that mattered, she thought, as Kennedy returned to the table. The bad guys were in jail, and she was going home.

And her mind was on something she'd wanted to do for several days—had her vacation in paradise not been continually interrupted by Kennedy's newest unpredictable plan. She opened her purse. "You might want this," she told him, handing him a clear sandwich bag containing a single item.

He examined the contents, looked baffled.

"It's your flash drive. You left it on my chest of drawers in February. I figured it must have been part of my Valentine's present."

"Not at all, but thanks. I gave up trying to find it months ago."

"Then think about it some more. Like what it has

on it."

"My stuff, unless you deleted it."

"Kenn, let it sink in. It probably has everything on it that was stolen. Your files. Records. Stories."

The more she talked, the bigger his eyes got. "Damn." He opened the bag and held the tiny device in cupped hands, as if it were a precious jewel. "My manuscript. *Blood Ruin*. It's got my manuscript."

"At least the February version."

"February's good enough—it's the complete draft." Where only moments before he'd kept his voice coffee-shop quiet, the pace and volume of his words picked up, his awareness of his surroundings nonexistent. "With the break-in, I thought my book was gone forever. I kind of started over when we flew to Miami, but, Christ, even if I could type, it would have taken me months to rewrite it from scratch. With this, we're talking days."

"Then I'm glad I brought it. I could have given it to you sooner, but death threats took precedence."

As if it weighed a pound, Kennedy hefted and stared at the tiny device, his eyes seeing, his ears deaf.

"And this way," Sarah said, wishing she could speak Swahili just to test him, "you'll have something to keep you busy when I leave."

"I bet I can have it done by the weekend." He moved his hands close to his face and stared at the tiny object of his affection, as if to read its entrapped binary code by telepathy. "Maybe not the weekend, but surely by the end of next week."

Sarah shook her head. The Kenn she loved—and would never understand—was back. She looked at her watch and then reached over and covered his hand with hers. "I need to go."

He did a classic double take, as if confused by the identity of his tablemate. He looked at his own watch. "We've been here a half hour?"

"I have," she said. "I don't know where you've been."

Kennedy did a bobble-head scan of the room, as if trying to spot a buzzing fly. "Have I missed something?" He laughed. "Maybe something subliminal?"

Yeah, she thought, you have. "No," she said, "you haven't. I just hate to go and leave you behind."

"Not to worry. I'll be OK."

At a time when she really needed the perfect cuss word, she could manage only a groan. She looked at her watch again, not really interested. "That's not what I meant."

Kennedy's face stayed aimed at hers, but his eyes wandered as if filled with rum. "Is this some sort of quiz? I've got no clue what you're talking about."

Sarah had a retort but picked the easy way out. "I hate to leave you behind because I'd rather we be together."

He grabbed her hands. "That's a relief. That subject I can handle. Cancer? No. Pregnancy? No way. Well, getting married and having a baby would be all right, but I don't think it's anything either of us really wants. At least not now. I could handle it, but of course it might seriously interfere with your career. At least—"

Sarah yanked her hands from his and slapped the table, rattling dishes, making other diners jump.

Kennedy froze, lips puckered, head sucked back like a turtle. "What was that for?"

"Because," she said, "I thought it would get your attention just as well as me slugging you, and this way I don't have to go to jail."

Frozen in his seat, he spoke quietly, eyes wide. "You've got my attention. What?"

"You haven't heard a word I've said in the time we've sat here."

"That's not right. You found my flash drive, my manuscript, all my files. I can't be more thankful." Shoulders hunched, he added, "What else can I say?"

"I don't think you get it that I'm leaving, that my vacation's over. Somehow you have it in your head that everything about my stay was wonderful. That we got the bad guys, that I'm finally headed home, and that you're on your way back to Belize. Perfect ending."

"Miami tonight," he said. "Direct flight to Belize City early tomorrow."

"Yeah, sorry. Wouldn't want to mix up your flights." She rested her chin on laced fingers, not to look pretty, but because her head felt heavy.

"Whatever happened to those late-night texts and face-to-face calls—where you had some deep-down wish that I'd move to Belize and I hoped you'd move back to Denver? Have you given thought to either possibility since the day I arrived?"

Kennedy exhaled through puffed cheeks. "Sarah, I'd love for you to live with me in Belize. But from what I've seen, there're too many things about Ambergris Caye—boats, water, bugs, raw jungle, small planes—that don't fit your style."

"Fair assessment," she said. "But put me in San Pedro, in a condo, and I could like it. And what about you? What about Denver?"

"Denver has a nice ring to it, especially with you. I love the place. But I have the feeling if I move there, it'd be forever. Forever planted in some condo, maybe a house, writing all day, sunrise to sunset, while you're at work. I don't ski. I don't hunt. I hate ice fishing for those puny little trout, elusive bastards that they are, and being a thousand miles from saltwater—"

Sarah held up her hands, palms facing Kennedy. "You don't have to convince me, but I do have to ask. Now that you have your manuscript back and it'll be complete in the next few days, what's next?"

"Hah. That's when it'll get really busy. I'll need to get an agent, an editor, a publisher, and then—"

"No," she interrupted. "Jump to the end. Your book gets published. You make a bundle. What're you going to do with the rest of your life? More of the same?"

Kennedy stalled just long enough that Sarah reckoned he was actually thinking, the subject perhaps virgin to his never-plan-ahead persona.

"No. Not more of the same," he said. "*Blood Ruins* is about hundred-year-old vampires haunting tourists in Belize, in and around the Maya ruins. Its premise—"

"Sorry I didn't read it," Sarah lied.

"I'll send you an autographed copy," he said, "as soon as it's done. It's a good story, but I've got something else in mind. Been thinking about it this past week."

"I'm impressed you had time to think about writing while Victor was trying to kill us."

"The action did interfere a bit," he said. "My next book will be a mystery. Set in Belize, of course."

"You mean like *mysterious* hundred-year-old vampires? Maybe solving crimes with magnifying glasses?"

"Nope," he said. "A real mystery. Like a dead body in the palapa. Ceviche spilled on the floor. Missing darts. A half-empty bottle of Belikin beer on the bar."

"Sounds exciting. But couldn't it be a dead body on the fifty-yard line? Mustard spilled on the escalator? A half-empty can of Coors in the men's room?"

Kennedy's face wrinkled as if he'd stepped in

something brown. "Why write about Denver when I live in Belize?"

Sarah watched his face. He was serious. She scooted her chair back. "I love you, Kenn Bracken. I love the ten percent you gave me today. And I love the different ten you gave me yesterday. Gosh, I wonder what it'd be like to get twenty percent of you all in the same day."

He grinned. "Out-damn-standing, I'd guess. And thirty percent blows even my mind."

They laughed and hugged and kissed. He apologized about her vacation from hell, thanked her for her partnership, and wished her a safe trip.

She did the same.

Sarah's eyes blinked dry when she went through security.

She didn't look back.

Epilogue

Kennedy paced and wrung his hands. He'd thought about Sarah for days, for weeks. He missed her, missed the bantering, missed the dead-body-closure action. He considered recent headlines that appeared to suggest a need for outside help: a property manager shot for stealing metered water from his tenants; a Cuban refugee's body washed up on a pristine beach; the previous day's Blue Hole body shocker.

Just before dinner, he saw the icon he wanted. Sarah, online. He opened his—

Then he yanked his hands from the keyboard. No, he thought. Not yet. He opened a new bottle of Travellers 5 Barrel rum and made himself a rum and lime, heavy on the rum, added ice, and then a bit more lime and another double shot of rum. He leaned over and sipped from the brim-full lip of the cut-glass tumbler, perched on the kitchen counter, so as not to lose a drop.

Then he settled at his desk. Leaning back, legs

crossed, he heard the soft click of nails on tile.

Intuitive, Krash put her head in his lap and looked up with sad eyes, as if to say don't forget about me.

Kennedy softly dug his hands into her ears, rubbed with his knuckles, and got her eyes to roll back in her head. "You miss her too, don't you?"

No response.

"You miss Sarah?"

Krash yanked her head from his hands, eyes wide, as if to say: Sarah? Where? Here? She then went to the entry and collapsed on the floor, her nose nuzzled to the crack in the door, where Kennedy knew she could stay for hours.

Kennedy asked himself the same question: Sarah? He hoisted his glass, sipped, and wondered what the hell had happened to her, to them, to Sarah and him. Yes, they'd agreed to part ways, to quell the forever-yours dialog, but they were still friends, close friends. He smiled, remembering just how close they'd been, how close she could get, how close, in body and spirit, was never close enough. Yet, they hadn't talked in more than a month, whether by phone or online chat. She'd gone home to Denver, invisible to Kennedy, no doubt buried in work. No mushy letters to him about lovely Belize. Nothing about how exciting their escapades had been. No mention about how much she missed him. If she did.

He slurped up a small piece of ice bathed in priceless nectar, crunched loudly, and allowed the frozen slurry to slip down his gullet, fuel for his aching brain.

Got what I deserved, he thought, knowing he'd sent her the same zero count of cards and letters. Zero, for fear of being presumptuous. Zero, for fear of saying something mushy he wasn't willing to follow through on. He had, though, called a Denver florist a number of times.

So maybe he'd been an asshole, pushing the two cases too hard, his obsession for closure rampant. He'd dragged her away from the pool and away from sunsets, breezy decks, and memorable meals. He'd taken her to places she'd never wanted to visit and exposed her to risks no sane person ever needed.

He pushed his drink forward on his desk and lowered his chin to rest on his crossed arms, his nose hanging over the lip of the tumbler, the aroma close, succulent, enticing.

Friends and lovers, they'd talked for hours, no subject off limits. Even with her hellish vacation, she'd been a good sport, a major contributor, a perfect partner. And she'd stayed with him during his jaunt through the States, forgoing her own precious job when she could have ignored his plight from her mile-high vantage point.

Her actions and inactions made sense, he convinced himself. She was back at work, digging in, making up time, building her own career—a career like the one he'd had, the one he'd retired from, the one he wanted no more of.

He looked inward. Had he done any better with his time since leaving Florida? Well, in addition to several respectable bonefish and a tarpon—all caught and released—he'd purchased a beachfront lot on the west side of the island at Secret Beach, signed a letter of intent for a two-bedroom ultra-luxury residence at La Sirene—a golf-cart ride south of San Pedro (no boat needed, he would tell Sarah)—and finished once again his edited-edited-edited Maya vampire book. And by damn, it'd turned out pretty good. He hefted the 300-page manuscript, placed it back on his desk beside a list of prospective literary agents, and enjoyed the last sip of his mighty-fine rum and lime.

He rang Sarah on Skype, hoping for face-to-face. No response.

Fingers to keyboard, he sent her a text: "It's been five weeks since Florida, and I've been chasing lots of trouble down here. Good news: Sergeant Gutierrez found Azalee, pregnant, living with Christopher in Punta Gorda. Both sets of parents are ecstatic, and the moms are planning a big wedding. If your Skype's working, please call me."

He waited—no response. "I also called Racine, got an update. First, to confirm, her mom died wearing the replacement hamsa that Racine had given her just before their trip (and without which you might have had a better vacation and Rick might never have been charged). Second, Racine confirmed *again* that Victor and Rick disappeared the last day the family was in Cancún—the same day my condo was trashed (by El Torro). Third, Rick's roommate Will (recall Kentucky MSN address knowillpower) told me he posted the shark-attack pictures on behalf of demented Rick, though I'm sure he has no clue that Rick's *Mexican-black-market photos* were of Rick's own stepmother."

Kennedy waited a minute, and then typed: "Rick's out on bail, confined at home with Victor, wearing— get this—an ankle bracelet. His murder case may drag on for years with jurisdictional disputes in the US, Belize, and Mexico. Like I care, as long as he does time."

No response.

"Also, I sent the copied pages we stole back to Captain Lobos with a note about our involvement in the Belize, Mexico, Madrilène Perry murder mystery, and to let him know how much we appreciate his help in solving the case, and that he might be deposed. I also sent him an anonymous-donor subscription to Sports Illustrated."

Besides the news update, Kennedy got to the guts of his message: "Unrelated to all the above, there have been a few Belize deaths lately. Got time to help me investigate? Details on request".

Nothing—no response for a full minute. Then the message "Sarah typing" appeared. He pictured her thinking, listing all the reasons she never wanted anything to do with Belize ever again, or perhaps with Kennedy himself.

Then, Sarah: "I'm at the airport, Chicago, twenty minutes until I board, headed home for a few days. Too crowded here for Skype. Thanks for note. Now—important: I'm thrilled for Azalee and her parents, and that Racine's hamsa worked. Rick deserves two life sentences, one for Madrilène, the other for kicking Krash. I recommend you stay away from Mexico And last, will I help investigate? Yes, but with caveats:"

Kennedy waited a quiet beat, then got a new paragraph:

"Cash the check I sent that reconciles our costs. I keep my current job. We divide our time, Denver and Belize. You do small boats and planes. And you get to cook breakfast."

Kennedy danced a jig that got Krash excited. He had to take a break for hugs and baby talk to settle her down.

Then he thought about Sarah's response, how much he missed her, how much of a jerk he'd been, what he needed to do, what he *wanted* to do. She'd listed provisos, her caveats, but—What the hell?—she hadn't even mentioned what was important to him. His writing. His manuscript. His *complete* manuscript.

Sarah: "Clock ticking. Departure imminent."

He paced. He planned. Scribbled a decision tree. Considered possible responses. He modified the plan and then did it all again. Finally. Yes. Perfect plan.

Kennedy: "Handshake agreement accepted. I'll send more details as soon as I can. In the meantime, you'll receive a Priority Mail package. Guaranteed arrival, your home address, day after tomorrow, Wednesday evening. Please accept. Signature required.

Sarah: Great. Sure. I'll cancel my dinner plans and stand by my door, pen in hand."

Kennedy: "Tut, tut. Safe trip. Gotta go. Later."

After a long day at the office, Sarah fought traffic from the Denver Tech Center across town to the Belleview exit off C-470. Thirty minutes later, in her Willow Springs hillside home, she stood at her kitchen window and looked over the hogback, across the Denver basin, to the city skyline in the distance. She trimmed the stalks from a bouquet of fresh flowers— delivered weekly to her front door, the donor anonymous.

Anonymous? she thought. Not likely. She missed him desperately.

She'd thought about her response back to Kennedy. More investigating? New subject? Maybe somebody dead? Really dead? Her stomach tightened.

She liked the excitement, the rush, of tracking down people, asking them questions, figuring out who did what to whom. But it dismayed her that Kennedy shot from the hip, did things as if by random choice. He got results, but only because he acted fast, used good brains, ignored emotions, and charged ahead with brute force when necessary.

She liked his writing, the act of his writing—just not *what* he wrote. Vampires? No way. To her, the only thing worse than an up-front vampire book was learning, on page two hundred of an otherwise-good mystery, that vampires, or werewolves, or some other morphed yuk had inserted its way into the story.

She watched the news and ate quietly—a big wedge of iceberg lettuce with chunky blue cheese dressing. She ate alone, more alone than usual.

And a writer could write anywhere, she reckoned, continuing her muse. She looked out the window to the lights in the distance. Even in Denver. With Krash at his side.

Or she could pack it in and move to Belize, loving Kennedy every day, and Krash, and the best food in the world. And for sure, they'd do well financially— two retirements, one place to live. English-speaking country. Just two hours from Houston, five from Denver.

But not logical. Tourists may love it, but she didn't. Too far away from the rest of the world, and too close to water, the jungle, small planes, and boats.

The doorbell rang, chiming *Frère Jacques*.

And it hit her. Kennedy's book. The book he was so damn proud of. The autographed manuscript she'd now have to read.

Holy wow. Vampires.

Priority Mail, signature required—she picked up her favorite pen and went to the door.

And in the open doorway, there he stood— Kennedy—with a suitcase at his feet and Krash on a short leash. On his head was a catawampus Priority Mail envelope, torn and shaped into a hat, from which protruded his sun-bleached hair.

Krash went spastic, and a big dumb-ass smile cracked across Kennedy's suntanned face. "Divers found a body wearing a tux at the bottom of the Blue Hole last week. You in or out?"

She grabbed his shirt and yanked hard, buttons flying. "In."

Addendum 1
Previously published:

THE ~~W~~HOLE TRUTH
A work of fiction (Pub 2018)
Colorado Authors' League
Winner—Mystery/Suspense—2019

Prologue

Francine Elizabeth Rach, PhD, outdrove the arrogant bastard and his high-beam headlights as he chased her in and out of traffic southbound on Houston's Beltway 8. Looking ahead, she blasted her well-tuned Mazda RX-8 up the elevated US 59 overpass and backed off the gas only slightly as she approached the curve at the top, where he caught up, pulled alongside, and shot her in the face.

Had the brilliant geophysicist not been dead when her bright-red coffin spun out of control, flipped end to end, jumped the retaining wall, and fell to the roadway below in a ball of flame, she might have screamed his name.

Accident investigators took pictures, measured skid marks, interviewed shocked witnesses, and eventually added one more tragic, random, road-rage death to Houston vehicular statistics.

They were right only about it being tragic.

Addendum 2
Previously published:

DEEPWATER HORIZON 2020
Remembering BP's 2010 Disastrous Blowout—
Ten Years Later
(Pub 2020)

This combined work includes:

THE SIMPLE TRUTH—
BP'S Macondo Blowout
(Pub 2012)

and

FROM THE PODIUM—
The Cause of the Macondo Blowout
(Pub 2018)
Nonfiction—based on the author's
2015-2016 presentations as a
Society of Petroleum Engineers
Distinguished Lecturer

Author Bio

John Turley (California) and Janet Decker (Nebraska) married in 1964. They traveled the world in career-related moves, including eight years in the UK, before retiring in Colorado.

The Turleys reside in a community of seniors who share similar backgrounds, bridge conventions, good food, and feeble golf swings.

But most important, John insists, are his six decades side-by-side with his still-best-friend, Jan.

Made in United States
Orlando, FL
18 October 2024

52858878R00202

Kennedy Bracken, scuba diving the Belize Barrier Reef, witnesses and photographs sharks in a feeding frenzy—their target a young woman's body. Minutes later, alone at sea, Bracken is left with little more than bad memories, morbid photos, and questions about the woman who will never again be seen.

As a retired accident investigator obsessed with death resolution, Bracken is compelled to learn who she was and how she died. It's good news that local police use the best of Bracken's partial-face photos to identify the accidental-death victim, but details in other photos force Bracken to discount the who, where, and how of the official story.

Bracken recruits Sarah McGarrity, his vacationing, Denver-based, almost fiancée, and the self-appointed detectives dig deep, follow evidence, and look for answers . . . only to exhume a truth more brutal than the sharks.

BODY
SHOTS

Belize Justice—
A Caribbean Myste

$17.00
ISBN 978-0-9858772-8-6
5 1700

9 780985 877286